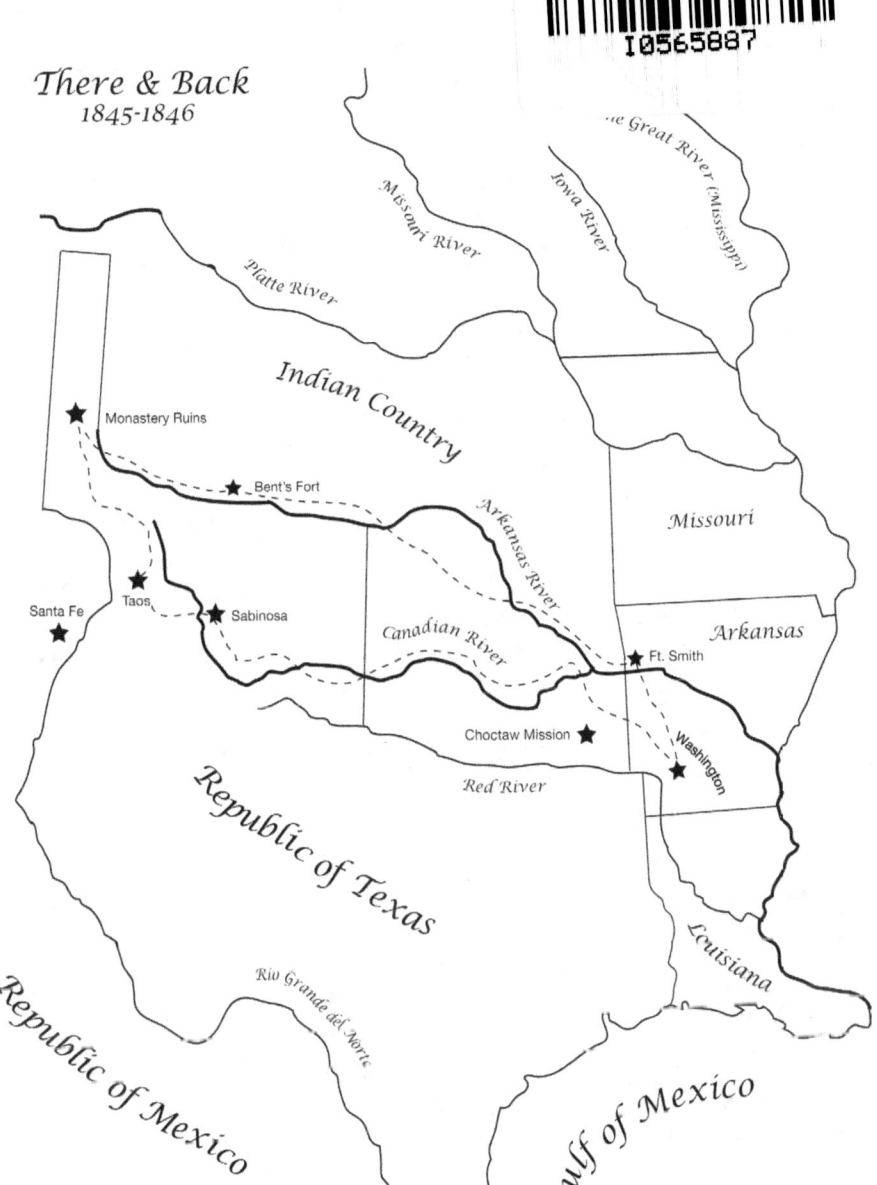

There & Back
1845-1846

I0565887

...he Great River (Mississippi)

Iowa River

Missouri River

Platte River

Indian Country

Monastery Ruins

Bent's Fort

Arkansas River

Missouri

Santa Fe

Taos

Sabinosa

Canadian River

Arkansas

Ft. Smith

Choctaw Mission

Washington

Red River

Republic of Texas

Rio Grande del Norte

Louisiana

Republic of Mexico

Gulf of Mexico

Other Titles from White Turtle Books

The Jazz Phillips Mystery Series

Murder in the Choir

Murder by the Board

Murder in the Kirk

Murder was a Blast

The Clan McKee Intrigue Series

Angels Fight Dirty

Black Seraph

Children of Dust

Adventure & Quest

Lakota Spring

Raven Wolf

Paul Radford's Private War

Spirituality

Agnostic's Guide to Prayer

Abbot's Gold

A Western Odyssey

by

Joe Pete Blackwolf

White Turtle Books

North Mankato, Minnesota

This is a work of fiction. This means that while none of this ever happened exactly this way except in the mind of the author, it might have in a parallel universe. So any resemblance between one of the characters of this novel and any person, historical or hysterical, is purely coincidental. So far as I know there was no missionary activity among the Ute, Arapaho, or Cheyenne in southeastern Colorado and no monastery there in the eighteenth or early nineteenth century.

The exceptions are Sam Watrous, for whom the town in northern New Mexico is named, Kit Carson, who resided in Taos, New Mexico during this period, Cyrus Byington, missionary to the Choctaw, and Lieutenants James W. Abert and Wiliam Peck, whose survey of the Canadian River took place later in the summer of 1845 than implied here. I have also reduced the number of the survey company from thirty-five men to about a dozen. I admire all these historical figures for their positive contributions to American history and have tried to treat them with all due respect. Any statements attributed to them here is pure fiction.

On the other hand, geographical places, historical towns, and the Rocky Mountains have been left pretty much where they still were the last time I looked. JPB

ISBN 978-1-933482-01-9
Library of Congress Control Number: 2008931709

Cover design by Joel B. Reed

Dedication & Acknowledgment

This story is dedicated to all those who believe they were born in the wrong century. You are not alone. Our numbers are many.

You will make many changes before you find satisfaction.
Chinese fortune cookie

CHAPTER ONE

Spring 1845

The whiplash crack of the rifle jerked me awake. I come up fast, my Colt's .44 Army at full cock, dead on target. I found myself staring into the cool, level eyes of the saltiest character I ever seen. Only blue eyes under the wide brim of a plainsman's hat and the bushy salt and pepper beard told me it was a white man. The rest was buckskin and beads, and the knife handle sticking out of a broad French sash was carved out of antler.

"Go easy, young 'un," he murmured. "Don't be a drillin' me just yet." Very gently he raised the still smoking barrel of the ancient Hawken and leaned the weapon against a tree. Then he chuckled. "Old bar studied he'd found an easy breakfast, I'm thinkin'." His eyes flickered at my Colt's and he grinned and I was surprised to see he had a full set of the whitest teeth you ever seen. "Yet I'm thinkin' he might 'ave found yourself a bit 'ard to swallow."

Below the acrid smell of burnt gun powder I become aware of a pungent smell surrounding me. It was a deep musk that filled the small holler where I camped the night afore. I glanced over my shoulder. Not fifteen foot from where I stood lay a huge mound of fur crumpled on the ground, deep brown frosted with silver. One huge paw lay pointing in my direction, six inch claws extended like razor sharp scythes.

I raised the muzzle of the Colt's, eased the hammer down to half cocked. A reflexive shiver ran down my spine. I glanced back to the old man. "Much obliged," I said, replacing the weapon in its holster.

The old timer grinned, waved it off as he picked up his rifle. I noticed he reloaded right away. It was a habit I am sure kept him alive long enough for his hair to turn the iron grey streaking his beard and showing under his broad hat. "Think nothin' of it, lad," he chuckled. "More than one's saved me bacon when I wa'n't lookin'." Though he spoke with the melodious chant of a man from Eire, I had trouble placing his accent. "Scots," he said, reading my mind, and laughed. "Keenan McAdams, late of 'is Majesty's Royal Marines, now retired these many years." Then a worried look crossed his face. "Say, you wouldn't be havin' some coffee, would ye, now? I've been run out a week ago."

The switch in mood was so much I couldn't help but laugh. "You're in luck, McAdams," I said reaching for the chuck sack next to my bed roll. I pulled out a five pound sack of coffee beans and the small mill. "And you're just in time for a morning cup."

"No wonder the beggar was coming at you," he said. "Probably he was smellin' your food bag." He shook his head and frowned. The level blue eyes looked me over gravely. "Not to be minding your business." he said politely, as if telling me I was about to step on a pile of horse apples, "but hasn't anyone been tellin' ya it's a mite safer to be hangin' your food in a tree in bear country?"

While I can still hear his voice in my hear these many years later, I think you know by now how the man talked. So I won't be trying to get it exactly right every time I tell you he said something. I come to find out much later, McAdams' father was a Highlander sent to the emerald isle to fight as a mercenary for the King. Yet he was soon overcome by a buxom maid of County Cork, and departed the King's service on French leave for the wilds of the far north, there to live out his days in peace among the gentle folk he was sent to conquer. Which explains why my salty companion, Keenan McAdams, spoke with a Scottish burr in the lilting manner of the gentle folk of Eire.

Not waiting my answer, he shrugged. "Well, never mind now. It's got us breakfast, didn't it?" Rising, he crossed to the dead grizzly and drew a wicked looking knife from his belt. "Why don't you be making us a pot of coffee while I cut us a couple of steaks fresh for breakfast?" Then he chuckled again. It was like the sound of dry leaves blowing across a rocky ledge. "Plumb nice of old bar to drop in so convenient." I stared in him in disbelief. Hadn't I been looking right at him I'd thought someone else snuck up. Seeing my look he laughed aloud. "A member of the profession I might add, too, lad," he said in his regular voice.

"The profession?" I asked him, not knowing what the hell he was talking about. He didn't look like no doctor or lawyer to me. "You an undertaker or something?"

"An actor, sir," he said in a perfect imitation of an English gentleman's man. "Don't you know?" Somehow it seemed to me that was like hitching a mule with an ox, hearing his voice that way and seeing as how he was dressed the way he was and cleaving a hunk of meat off a bear he'd just killed with a knife that looked like it come from Arkansas. Glancing my way he laughed at my consternation. "Don't try to be studying me out, lad. I've yet to do it and I've been at it over a half century now." Standing up with the two fresh steaks he just cut he nodded. "It's kept me out of jail a few times.."

I nodded and stirred up the coals, blowing on them as I broke up a few small dry branches and lay them crosshatch on the glowing coals. The branches began to smoke and I fanned them gently with my hat to break up the smoke so it didn't signal where I'd camped. "Don't believe I caught your name," McAdams said casually. "Not that a name matters. I've used a number meself, but I'd like something to be calling you."

"Bear," I told him. "The name's Jack Bear."

"Bear? Would that be Indian, lad?" he asked. "Not that it matters, but I am curious, you know."

"German," I told him. "We spell it B-a-e-r. My granddaddy changed it when he came over." That wasn't strictly true but I've told it that way so long I've started to believe it myself. I stirred up the coals and added more wood, larger sticks this time. The fresh wood began to catch, but it was dry and didn't give off enough smoke for me to fan.

McAdams nodded his approval. "You're wiser to the ways of the woods than I thought, Jack," he observed. "You been on the run long?"

I glanced up sharp like, but McAdams laughed. "No, lad, I ain't a bounty hunter, just a curious old fool. Your horse looks hard ridden." Cutting two limbs he made paddles by bending forked branches and twisting them around to hold the steaks. After he stripped off the bark he charred them in the fire so the sap wouldn't spoil the meat. "I've had to leave places in a hurry myself."

Thing is, the man had the facts right and somehow I trusted him right off. Normally wouldn't no man nor any bear sneak up on me so easy, and I known much better than leave salt pork unhung in bear country. I was raised in the woods the first nine years of my life and known the ways of the wilderness, taught by my daddy and my mama's older brother, a battle tested warrior and our band's best hunter, better, maybe, than Pa.

Yet, I'd come in second best in the only kind of play a man loves losing, and that happened more miles than I cared to remember east of where I collapsed after a week of riding damn near day and night getting away. I was plumb give out.

The thing started in a saloon, and I should have knowed better, too. All women are spoken for in a small town except the girls at a funhouse, and there weren't one of those nowhere around. I'd been a long time without a woman and when the lady smiled I couldn't help nodding back. One thing led to another and the next thing I known, we was drinking like old friends and dancing up a storm. That should tell you something 'cause I don't dance. At least not until I've had a few, and then you cain't get me off the table.

That night I tried to swallow the Creature whole, as McAdams would say. It was a good thing, too, or I might not have survived what come next. Her and me slipped out the back door of the cantina and up the back stairs to her rooming house, where the lady, and I use the term loosely, understand, give me the ride of my life. I mean I've forked some stormy broncs in my time, but I never rode nothing so wild as that woman when she got her clothes off.

Not that you'd ever know it looking at her. At least, not dressed. Fully rigged she looked like a school marm, and no bigger than half a minute. Outside her petticoats it was a different story and when I saw her rising beauties shake free of the harness I just like to split my jeans. They was about the size of mush melons, and proud rising, too, and her waist was so small it seemed like I could circle it with both hands. When she let down her bloomers her sweet thing was so bright and curly with red hair it looked like somebody struck it with a match. And you better believe it felt like it, too, when she grabbed me by the ears and pulled me down.

When I hit leather she started bucking and crow hopping like a stud just saddled the first time, and I thought sure she was going to bounce my sweet butt off the ceiling. As I say, it had been a long time and even though it only taken me about four seconds to loose the first load, we never stopped for a breath. When she hit her peak she screeched like a mountain lion and throwed me off, flipping me on my back like a yearling steer and riding me like the devil was on her trail. Then after we done that a while, she turned around in mid stroke and began to work on me with the other end. Her mouth was as greedy as her tunnel of love

and after she taken me to the gates of heaven and showed me the stars
one way, she taken me around the world the other. And the only time
I said "no" was when she stopped a moment to ask if I was ready to cry
"uncle".

That must have been a signal or something, because the next thing
I known the door flies open and there's this rude bastid waving a gun
around threatening to shoot everybody in sight. "Oh, my God, it's my
husband," the lady hollers, and I'm thinking she never mentioned no
husband afore this. So I begin wondering right away if this is a setup.
Sheriff I known one time called it the badger game and he told me about
it being worked down in St. Louis.

"Shut up, you whore!" he shouts, slapping her, but I could see it
weren't too hard, and getting a good look at him, I know for sure
something's sour. There ain't too many men look like a cross between a
polecat and a wharf rat, which is exactly how the sheriff described the
man play-acting a mad husband. Fact is, describing the man just that way
is downright slander to polecats and wharf rats both. He was thin and
greasy, just plain dirty, and he was squinting at me out of thin set black
eyes like two lumps of coals, the eyes of a killer natural born. The clothes
he was wearing looked brand new, but on him they must of got filthy the
minute he put them on, like a fresh rag soaking up hot grease.

Anyways, he slaps the lady aside and starts to pull down on me. The
very instant he slaps her I'm grabbing for something to defend myself
with and what comes to hand is the glass oil lamp on the table by the
bed. Just as he turns back to shoot me between the legs, I fling it right at
his chest. Somehow he does manage to swing his gun and get off a shot
at the lamp, but that is exactly the wrong thing to do. His shot busts the
glass chimney and breaks loose the whole top brass, spilling him with
oil, which catches fire when the burning wick hits the floor. I hear him
and the woman both screaming behind me as I grab my boots and my
gun and clothes, and go out the window headfirst.

Turns out I must be one of the luckiest men alive. Matter of fact, wasn't
for bad luck I sometimes think I wouldn't have no luck at all. When I lit
on the top of a wood shed behind the rooming house, good luck kept
me from breaking a leg, but the shed collapsed under me, dumping me
buck naked into a mud puddle in the alley. I's sort of stunned and by
the time I clear my head I heard people hollering and looked up to see

the fire brigade coming my way up the alley. Just then someone taken a shot at me and I seen the weasel standing at the window his greasy hair all singed off and dropping his pistol to take another shot. "Stop!" he hollered. "Thief!" And damned if the fire brigade didn't drop their buckets and take off after me.

I ain't had time to worry about running over broken glass in the alley in my bare feet, and when I felt it cut my foot I just kept running. Someone taken a shot I heard whiz by my right ear, and I turned the corner to the next alley a shittin' and a flying. Somewhere behind me I heard someone shouting, "There's blood! I must of got him." Several more shots was fired, and I ain't known what at, but I weren't about to hang around to ask. I turned the next corner as soon as I could and run for the edge of town. Somehow I had to get to my horse in front of the cantina to leave this berg behind, but that could wait. Right then I still heard them behind me and I thought it prudent to put as much distance between them and me as I could. I'd study how to get my horse later.

One thing my uncle taught me was to run like the fury and ignore the pain if I stepped on something. That night it come in handy. I was damn near the end of town and to a creek I crossed coming in when I heard someone shout, "Get the horses. He's headed for the creek."

Looking back over my shoulder I ain't seen no one but I turned down the next alley heading back into town, anyways. There weren't no use heading for the creek if that's where they'd be looking, and while I may be fast on my feet, I cain't outrun no horse. I can run one down, but I cain't outrun it. I know cause that's how me and my uncle used to catch wild horses when we first come west, and when I get to running low on money, I still do it.

I decided it was about time to put on some clothes, so I stopped in the gateway of a high stone wall. 'Tain't much more obvious than a man running buck naked in the street, and I thought won't nobody see me getting dressed. Didn't nobody but the woman and her man know what I look like, and I figured I could join the crowd looking for me and get back to my horse. It were risky, but I decided if the weasel spotted me I'd drill him and tell the crowd he's me. After all, he looks like a thief and I don't, and ain't no one cain't see that. I ain't quite known what I'd do with the woman, but with weasel dead I figured she'd know she'd best keep her damn mouth shut.

Yet just as I leaned up against a heavy wood gate to pull on my jeans, the gate flys open behind me. I tumbled back into an open courtyard, landing my bare butt on flagstone as hot as ice. This knocked the breath out of me and afore I got my wits back, my clothes and my boots hit me in the face, too. I grabbed my Colt's and come up cranking back the hammer, but then a woman's voice stopped me cold. "Now don't you look silly," the voice hisses. "Standing there naked as the day your mother brought you into the world and pointing at me with a gun, now!"

By this time my head's cleared a bit and I seen a light face high above me framed by what looks like something even whiter. Damned if I ain't thunk it's a halo and I was looking at the face of an angel. Only angels ain't supposed to be this plain. Then I seen the dark outline of the huge figure below and I realized I was looking at a Catholic nun.

"Sorry, sister," I said, trying to cover myself with my boots. "I didn't know but you wasn't somebody after me."

"So why are they chasing you, now, man?" she demanded. "And put on your clothes while you're at it. One of the novices might look out and you look silly standing there in your altogether. Not that you'd tempt anyone but a foolish girl," she added, setting me straight.

As I pulled on my pants I tried to explain what's happened without being too specific or talking too loud. This was harder than it might sound because I was whispering over my shoulder. You might think a nun would turn her back until a man was done in such a situation, but not Sister Carmelita. I found out that was her name later on. Right then, she looked me up and down like she was inspecting a side of beef just hung to season, and there was no mistaking her lack of interest in me as a man. After the grand time the weasel's woman shown me, you could say it was more than a little deflating.

Finally, I pulled on my shirt, tucked it in and turned around. My feet wasn't bleeding any more but they was way too swollen to go back into my boots and I was limping. "I cut my feet while I was running, sister," I told her, trying to explain, not realizing just what I was saying. "Don't cut your foot!" was something my Momma used to say when I was about to step in something I shouldn't.

"Well if you stepped in some dung, then wash it off!" Sister Carmelita hissed. "Heavens, man, don't you have a lick of sense?"

"Not much, sister," I admitted, grinning at her mistake. "Or I wouldn't be here now. But it weren't no horse apples. I stepped on some glass when I was running."

She was instantly concerned. "Oh, you poor man! Well let's get you into the kitchen, then. We'll need to be cleaning the cut."

That was the beginning of a life-long friendship, but didn't neither of us know it then. Carmelita died here a couple of years back, and you know, I felt as bad as when I lost Momma. She always seemed to be real fond of me, too, even when it sounded like she was thrashing me with her tongue. When they taken me to her bedside as she lay dying she told me something I'll never forget. "Ah, me sweet Jackie," she said gently, stroking my face with her hand. "And you never knew, now did you, man?"

"I never known what, Sis?" I asked, using what I called her in later years, at least when we was by ourselves.

"You never knew how close you came to spoiling me vows tumbling into me garden naked like that." She smiled the way a woman smiles about such things. "You looked like the wrath of God himself, Jackie, but it was all I could do to keep me hands to myself. You're a fine looking man and you always were."

Right then that was a long way ahead of us. After she cleaned up my foot and I washed up, we set and talked a spell. Carmelita woken up her gardener and sent him for my horse. It was getting close to light about then and she told me to keep out of sight in the barn. "And you better wear this, Jack," she said with a grin, handing me a long black habit. "We'll be calling you Sister Jackie."

I shook my head and started to say no, but Sister Carmelita give me a look she must of used to keep her nuns in line. "It's wearing that or your burial shroud, Jackie," she said severely. "We depend on the good will of the town and if you don't wear that, one of the children is like to talk. Jesus is the only man around here and you're far too young to be mistaken for him."

"You have children?" I ask her.

"Ah, yes, lots of children, Jackie," she tells me, smiling. "I have more tiny ones than the good wives of Dublin."

Well, I thought she was joshing me. Come to find out she weren't. The sisters was running an orphanage, as well as a school for kids from town. I needed to be out of sight soon because they'd be getting up, and she was right that the kids from town would talk when they get home. So I put on the habit and she giggled like a young girl. "Well, Sister Jacqueline, I trust you'll be tending your prayers today in the barn." Then she frowned and taken a string of rosary beads off her belt and tucked it into mine. "There, that's better. And you might want to be using it, too. You're needing all the help you can get."

Right about then I was craving a smoke and reached for the makings, but the sister stoped me cold. "Ah, Jackie, none of that now. Wouldn't do for a novice to be seen smoking, now would it?" Right then and there I realizes it was going to be a real long day.

When I left that evening I offered Carmelita some money. As it happens, I was carrying a bundle, having met up with a gent who didn't believe in odds, and I peeled off half of it and held it out to her. "I know you didn't help me for money," I tell her, "but I'd like you to have it. I got more than I need."

Sister Carmelita's eyes misted up as she reached out and taken it. "Only for the children, Jackie," she said softly. "Only for the children. It's so hard making the ends meet, you know." Then she done something that just about floored me. She reached up and kissed me on the cheek. "You're a good man, Jack Bear," she said. "Neither God nor myself will be forgetting your gift." Then she turned around and was gone.

"*Vaya con dios, senor,*" said Jesus, the gardener, telling me to go with God. It was with that blessing, better to my mind than any padre could ever give, I rode off into the night. It was only when the old timer and I was breaking camp four days later I found the rosary Carmelita give me, right where she tucked it deep into my saddle bag. I guess it worked, too. McAdams and the bear both come to my camp at exactly the same time. Some might call that luck or coincidence, but I sure as shootin' don't.

CHAPTER TWO

Moving On

Well, it weren't an hour after I stirred up the fire and started coffee that I was so full I could hardly move. The old man lay stretched out across the fire from me, his back to a rock and the Hawken not far from hand. "My, my," he groaned, rubbing his belly. "Who taught you to make biscuits like that, Jack? Your ma?"

"No, my pa." McAdams looked at me, a little surprised, but said nothing. After a moment I answered his unspoken questions. "He was a chef down New Orleans way. They taught him how to cook in Paris."

The old man nodded. "Well, he sure taught you well. I know a heap of women would be proud to be cooking biscuits like that." He looked at the fire and was quiet a long time. Yet I known he was watching me closely, missing not a whit and weighing things carefully in his mind. I was watching him, too, trying to look as relaxed as him. Yet I known his languor was like that of a big cat, ready to explode into swift and deadly action. As was mine, and I seen him come to a decision. Don't ask me how, but I known he had.

Very casually he picked up a long thin stick and stirred the coals. Then he raised his eyes and caught me weighing him out and chuckled. "You and me minds me of two old boar coons eyeing each other," he said, speaking the plain patios of the western mountains and plains. Reaching out he poured himself a cup of coffee and offered to pour mine. I shook my head. "You headed west?"

I nodded. "That's what I was thinking."

"Any particular place in mind?"

"No," I told him. "I've just a mind to see the country. I heard it was kind of pretty around Santa Fe."

"Yeah, it is," he said, almost reverently. "It goes beyond pretty. It's the most lovely country these eyes have seen since I left the Highlands. Yet, for all its grace, it won't come close to holding a candle to Montana and parts north." As he spoke there was a reverence in his voice, almost an awe, mixed with a sadness so deep I couldn't begin to guess its source. Then he shut it away, locked in the dungeon of memory of another time, another place, and most likely a woman he loved with all his soul. He nodded and sighed, then went on. "Yes, I was of a mind to head west from here to the mountains, meself, then north a way. Maybe up to the Wind River country. I hear of magnificent hot springs up there I've yet to see." He looked at me. "Would you care to come along, Jack?"

There it was, just simple as that. I nodded and nothing more was said. No contracts was written, no blood oaths signed. Yet in that simple exchange we was partners in an unspoken covenant more binding than any contract could ever be on the likes of us. Nor was it his saving my life. It went deeper than that and if any debt was owed on my part for his act of compassion for a fellow man, it weren't never mentioned. As if coffee and good talk was pay enough for the shot and powder it taken to drop the bear. That was the way things was with a lot of men who traveled in the West then. As things turned out, over the years him and me traveled together we swapped the favor many times.

To be honest, I was glad for the man's company. While I tend to be a loner by nature, like so many others who wander the western wilderness, I was clearly out of my element here. There was little I ain't known about the cities along the Great River, or of the customs and manners of life on the river boats and amongst the folk of the gaming houses. Nor was I no stranger to the way of the woodlands to the east.

Yet the West was different, not just the Plains but the mountains of Mexican land west of the Pecos River. They spoken a different language there and enjoyed different customs from folk along the Mississippi. I was a newcomer to the dangers and pitfalls of this country. Only a fool cain't admit his ignorance and take an honest offer of help with thanks to the giver. That manner of foolishness was drummed out of me at my daddy's knee. "You can only run alone so long, son," he told me the last week afore he was killed. "Sooner or later you're going to get sick or hurt and you're going to need friends to see you through. Make them early, Jack. Make them good and make them last." So that's what I've always done. I've had few friends, though many amiable acquaintances, but the friends I taken was for life.

After deciding to ride together, we broken camp quickly and headed west. McAdams said he known of a better place to camp about seven or eight miles further along where we could let my pony rest up for a couple of days afore we pushed on. "Unless there's riders headed this way," he said, looking at me for a straight answer.

I laughed and told him what happened back in town. I was surprised to hear he'd heard of the orphanage there. "I used to know one of their sisters a long time ago," he said, looking I thought a little sad but I ain't asked. A man speaks his heart when he's ready and not afore. "I doubt anyone's after you. The only thing you did was maybe burn down the rooming house, and if I remember that flea trap you did them a favor. Nobody is likely to get too upset about that, not even the folks who lived there." He nodded to himself and added, "The place we're headed is hard to sneak up on, anyway."

Turns out the old man had two horses. One was a tough little paint he used for his pack animal and the other was what I thought he called an Apple-loser. It was a big roan colored gelding with sort of a white and spotted rump he said was favored by the Indians up Montana way. Me, I would have chosen the paint, never seeing an Apple-loser afore, but I soon come to find out why the Indians liked them so much, and it weren't just looks. Maybe it was just that one animal, but Pete, as McAdams called the beast, was all heart and one of the best mounts a man could hope to find. I asked him one time why they are called Apple-losers and the old man grinned like a coon and told me it's because they make so many horse apples. Turns out later I find out Apple-loser is some kind of foreign word that stands for a white rumped horse. But that was Keenan McAdams. He told me about something in Ireland one time called the Blarney Stone. Maybe he was telling me a yarn and maybe not, but if he wasn't I think he didn't lean down just to kiss the damn stone. Surely he must have swallowed it whole.

Anyways, we broke camp and headed west across the plains. When we could, we followed coulees and dry stream beds, scouting out our trail real careful. What we was crossing was northern Comanche country back then, and while we was not looking for trouble in any way, the Comanche had a reputation of being very generous in giving it out to whoever happened by. The only people I understand they never did bother was folks they thought was crazy, and one time old Keenan saved our lives acting that way. On the other hand, I wonder what I'm saying. Never was there a man treated me better than Keenan McAdams, and I think he must of been crazy from the day he was born. Crazy in a good sort of way.

As I was saying, it saved our life not three days after we partnered up. We was easing across the plains late in the day, making our way carefully because we'd come across lots of tracks McAdams said was Indian ponies. Coming out of a stand of brush real quiet, Keenan suddenly started singing something in a tongue I didn't understand and clapped me on the back like a daddy patting his proud son. "Back my play, Jackie," he suddenly sang, switching to American. "No matter how strange it be, back my play. Don't be looking back, but the bastids picked up our sign and are following along behind."

Well, my daddy taught me to be a quick study. Not looking back I began to laugh like a fool, like he's just told me the best joke in the world. Truth is, I'm just about to wet my pants because in laughing I sneak a look back and see six or seven mounted warriors coming out of the coulee we just left. This gives me an idea and I open my britches and begin watering the prairie, turning round and around like a little kid making a tinkle ring. Seeing the warriors, only about fifty yards away by now, I point to them and let out a whoop, throwing myself down on the ground and kicking my feet like it's the funniest thing I ever seen.

"Don't be laying it on too thick, lad," Keenan sings, pointing at me and just about doubling in half laughing. Then all of a sudden he stops laughing, looks right up into the sky like somebody is talking to him, and walks off to the west, singing and holding his arms up as he leads his horses. One of the younger warriors started to go after him, but the older man said something sharp and he stopped.

Sitting there like a fool I acted like I seen something on the ground and pick up an ant, holding it up to my nose close and suddenly dropping it like it stung me. I jump up and stomp the ground, looking up suddenly and putting a wild look on my face when the younger men laugh. Then I begin to sing, too, and get my horse. One of the braves grabs my halter rope and I start dancing around him singing wild stuff and looking up in the sky like I'm calling down lightning. I make a crackling sound with my mouth and my horse goes wild, rearing and pitching and braking away from the brave. I don't pay no attention to the horse running off. I just keep dancing around the brave making crackling noises and getting all the horses restless. The leader said something and the warrior who grabbed my horse jumps on his own and the whole band rides after my horse. I hate losing the horse, but I stop dancing and walk after the old man, staring up into the sky like I see something and crooning like I'm drunk. Not thirty minutes later the brave who grabbed my horse rides back with him and leaves him in my path afore riding off.

A good while later McAdams looks at me and said, "I think that's enough, lad. They're long gone by now." He gives me a strange look and asks, "Jackie, have you ever considered studying the profession?"

"You mean play acting?" I ask back. "No, I never did. Why?"

"A great talent is going to waste here on the plains," he told me. "You had me wondering if you'd gone crazy, meself."

I laugh. "No, I was just scared and done what you told me. I didn't figure we had nothing to lose, and after the first couple of minutes I started enjoying myself."

"Then I suppose I better be watching what it is I'm telling you," the old man murmured, looking around. "Be keeping your eyes out for a water hole, and I'm not meaning the ruddy sea."

It was the next day we reached the spot the old man had in mind, and he was right in all respects. There was plenty of water, fed by a spring, the grass was tall and set on high ground as it was, it would be hard to approach without being seen. As a matter of fact, was a man of a mind to settle to ranch, he could do much worse than the camping grounds McAdams called the spring grove.

That evening we set snares for rabbits or prairie chickens, but the old man was loath to use our rifles unless we was bad in need. Even then he cautioned me to only fire once. "One shot startles anyone who might be hearing," he said, "but as long as it's only one it's hard to be telling exactly where it came from. With two any child will know exactly where you are, but maybe you know that already."

I nodded since my Pa told me exactly the same, but I wasn't really a believer until later on in the high plains when some enterprising souls tried to lighten our pockets. Had the first shooter held his fire for a sure shot, the second shot would have come out of nowhere. As it was, the beggar missed me, barely, since I heard the bullet buzzing by my ear. He hurried off another round at Mac, who was clear by the time it came. By the time the second shooter finally opened up, I was behind cover.

Knowing where the shooter was, it didn't take us long to send the bastid and his partner back to their maker, and we come out of it with another Hawken, a Hall breech loader, and a sweet Arkansas knife, that McAdams insisted I take. We also gained a second riding pony and a pack horse. I felt a little bad about doing the rogues in until I seen their pack horse. No beast, not even the worst tempered bronc, should be treated the way that poor was. A few weeks of decent care and she was fat and sassy with a glossy coat, but the scars they cut with a whip would always show. But that was weeks later. I'm getting way ahead of my story.

We ended staying a week in the spring grove, mostly resting up and letting our ponies graze. The time was passed swapping tales and tending our snares, and keeping a careful eye out for hostiles. It was during this time McAdams told me of his own history, that which he cared to speak of, and I told him much of mine. One thing we unearthed we had in common was a love of learning, and much of our time was spent talking of the books we'd read. When McAdams discovered I carried an old Bible my Pa gave me years ago, you'd thought I'd shown him a map to a lost gold mine, and, in a way, I guess I done so. Wasn't either of us a religious man, but the Good Book give us a powerful lot to jaw on. Many an evening we'd read a story by the light of our campfire and talk 'til the moon went down and the stars was fading away in the eastern sky.

They say it's not good living in the past, but those days and the times like it since, was the best. Nothing beats the company of men around a fire chewing the fat when the stories come out, and these days when things get too crowded or hurried up to suit my taste, I light out for the far places where other people ain't, in the company of a good friend or two. That's when I lie down in the green pastures, as the Good Book says, and let the still waters of peaceful talk restore my soul.

Anyways, after a week in the spring grove we both was feeling a need to move on, so we saddled up and headed west. We broke camp and headed out early on the seventh morning after we arrived, setting off about a half hour afore sunrise to get a good start afore the heat set in after noon. McAdams said to save the horses, he figured to travel early and late and lay up under a tree during the middle of the day, and this made sense to me. Even though it was still middle May and the weather stayed good, except for rain showers now and then, it still got hot after the sun hit its height. A wise traveler in what may be hostile country keeps his horses rested in case he's got to make a run for it.

Like so many things out West, a simple precaution like that often makes the difference between living and dying, and I was too fresh in this world to be eager to leave it. Strange how things is, but McAdams felt the same way. I figured a man who's been around as long and as much as him might not be so anxious to live out the year as a younger man, but in that I was dead wrong.

I like that, dead wrong. And so I was. When I got to know him better I asked McAdams about it and he laughed. "You might think that, lad, but you'd be mistaken. Dying at three score and ten seems younger every day, and I aim to live to be old as the hills." Then he grinned. "Some folks say life gets harder all the time, but that doesn't square with my way of thinking. Me, I'm thinking living is like poking the ladies. The best is always to come."

Well, I like play on words as good as the next man and that one just about undone me. Just thinking about it now after all these years I still have to grin. And it was true. With Keenan McAdams life didn't get tougher, he did.

Well, we covered a lot of ground that morning afore the sun stood high and the old man stopped us at a nice spot by a creek for a mid day rest. This spot wasn't near as good as the spring grove, but like that one, it would be easy to defend if hostiles dropped in on us unexpected. Once we'd loosened our saddle girths and made the ponies as comfortable as we could, we stretched out to eat a bite. When he'd finished his, McAdams sighed and said, "Damn, I wish we had us a cur, lad."

"You mean to eat?" I asked, not quite believing what I was hearing. Like anybody, I'd heard Indians ate dog meat and some of the mountain men developed a taste for it themselves, but I'd never met anybody admitted to trying it personally.

I thought McAdams would split a gut he laughed so hard. "Damn, Jack," he said, wiping the laugh water from his eyes. "If I didn't know better, I'd thought you were pulling my leg."

"Well, what the hell you mean then?" I ask him, getting a little warm.

While he got serious in a flash, the smile never completely disappeared from the corners of his mouth. "Now, Jack, no need to be taking offence, for I wasn't laughing at you at all. What tickled me funny bone was the look on your face when you said it." Then he made a face himself to show me and I couldn't help laughing. "Put me in mind of the first time I tried it."

"You actually have eat dog?" I asked, trying to keep my face straight but failing miserable. He doubled over again.

"It's even worse when you try to hide it," he laughed. "But, yes, Jack, I must confess. Not only have I eaten dog but I've liked it, too. Not that I thought I would, but I did. Course now, I was so hungry about then I was about ready to chew down the next dry buffalo chip I spied." He chuckled at the memory. "Then an Indian found me and took me to his camp. He was right honored to have me there so he fixed a delicacy, fresh roasted dog. I didn't dare make a face."

"You didn't get sick or nothing? I heard eating dog could make a man right sick in the head."

Keenan chuckled. "Well, who am I to say, then? A Scotsman sitting in the middle of the great American wilderness talking to a fugitive from domestic justice? Lad, a good case could be made that neither of us would be here if we weren't both crazy as loons."

"Yeah. I heard about them," I told him. "Some kind of duck, right?"

"Ah, yes, they are. Waterfowl not unlike ducks, but much different in their own way, too. They're divers, Jack, fish eaters, and when one goes under water it's hard to tell just where he'll be popping up." His eyes got a far away look as they often did when he talked about other times and other places. "The strangest thing about them, though, is their cry. It's haunting, Jack, haunting like the cry of the mourning dove, but even more so, if you take my meaning. It's as if every loon is some sad, sad soul mourning a dreadful loss. And to hear them singing at night while the northern lights play across the sky, well, there's nothing like it. So call me crazy as a loon, Jack, and you won't be insulting me. To me it makes far more sense than all the craziness men call civilization, living like ants in a heap in their towns and cities."

"I'm thinking you can call me crazy the same way," I answered, talking mostly to myself. "When you been away from them a while, cities just plain stink. Towns ain't much better."

"Spoken like a true wilderness ranger," McAdams said, stretching and letting out a little air. "As I said, I'm wishing we had us a good dog to keep watch so we could both nap. Would you be wanting to draw straws for the first watch?"

I told him to go ahead and take his nap while he was sleepy. I wasn't feeling drowsy myself and had some things on my mind to puzzle over. McAdams didn't give me a chance to change my mind and was snoring in what must have been five seconds flat. I never seen a man could sleep the way he could, sitting, standing, or laying down. One second he was here and the next he'd shut his eyes and be gone, but I never seen him come out of it groggy, neither. Asleep he was like a cat, totally gone and instantly awake, and the most I ever saw him do when waking was yawn real big. I never asked him about it, and it taken me a while to puzzle out, but I think the way he did this was to make sure he never got short on sleep. We might be starving in the middle of a thunderstorm with it raining cats and dogs, and there he'd be, sound asleep as a baby in a crib. Yet when trouble was near, he never so much as winked until it was passed.

About the time that thinking and the heat from the day was making me sleepy, and I was studying how to wake him up without startling him, Mac come out of it just as quickly as he'd gone under, laying there a second looking around without moving nothing but his eyes. Then seeing me watching him he grinned and sat himself up, absent mindedly patting his pockets for his pipe. Then changing his mind he sort of murmured to himself, "No, best not. Spirit weed can be smelled a long ways off and a long time after."

"Beg pardon?" I asked, not quite catching all he said.

"Old age, Jack," he sighed. "Or maybe living too much alone. I got the habit of talking to myself."

I shrugged. "One way to get an intelligent answer," and he laughed. "I didn't catch what it was you said about some weed," I told him.

"Ah, tobacco, lad. Some of the natives call it spirit weed or spirit plant. Me, I call it good." He sighed. "Except now. I don't want to be leaving a marker of our passing or signal our presence."

I nodded. "I was wondering," I said. "We want to be going west and then north, but we seem to be pushing a little south. You trying to stay away from the river for some reason?"

"No, Jack," he replied, surprised. "Quite the contrary. I'm heading us for it. That's the best way to get us where we want to go."

"Which river you headed for, the Red?"

"That would take us there, too, but that's a long way south. No, I'm headed for the Canadian. Why?"

"The Canadian's north of us," I told him.

He shook his head. "No, Jack, believe me. The only big river north of us is the Arkansas and that will take us too far north. I traveled through that country with Zeb Pike a few years back and we ran into some trouble with the Spanish. I want to hit the mountains to the north of Santa Fe and travel the eastern slope north to Taos. Feelings are still high among the Mexicans over the Texas war and I want to stay away from Santa Fe. We may even want to go further north and bypass Taos, although the Indian village there is well worth seeing."

I shook my head. "Well, I guess you know the country better than me, but what I was told was to head west from Washington and go north to the Canadian."

"Washington?" he asked. "Arkansas?" I nodded and he laughed. "I hate to tell you, Jack, but I think you're lost."

"No, I ain't lost," I told him. "I know right where I am."

"Then you know better than I do," he said. "I only know roughly where we are. Give or take thirty miles."

"Hell, Keenan," I said. "We're both right here."

I didn't know how he'd react but he laughed. "Ah, Jack, you're a sly one now, aren't you? You lead me right up the primrose path."

I started to apologize, but he waved me off. "No, siree. No way am I going to be letting you take that one back. Your turn's a coming, me lad. Your turn is a coming." As it turns out, he was right, and over the years I figure we come out just about even. Turns out he was right about where we was, too. Leaving town as quick as I did I missed some landmarks and ended up way further north than I thought. What I thought was a hundred miles I rode afore he shot the bear looking me over for breakfast turned out more like two hundred and fifty. I guess the old feller was right when he said the wicked flee when no man pursueth. Don't know exactly who said that first, but my Pa used to say it ever once in a while, himself.

CHAPTER THREE

Upriver West

Turns out the old man was right. Next day we hit what he said was the Canadian and it led us damn near all the way to Taos. Only it taken us a while to get there. Though the river was running strong, the country round about it got drier the more we drifted west, and as the river led north the land changed from mountains like where we started to rolling prairie that went on forever. There was plenty of landmarks along the way and no two stretches was quite alike, but I had to learn my eyes to see different.

One thing bothered me a while was telling distance. A mountain might look ten mile away but turned out most often to be forty or fifty, especially out on the plains, and it taken a while to learn to shoot. "Go by the size of the beast, Jack," McAdams told me the second time I tried to drop a deer and shot short. "Not by how well you can see it. That will tell you how far away it is."

Sure enough, when I set up a buffalo chip on edge and paced off the distance, he was right. I could still see ripple lines in the chip a hundred paces away, but the whole thing got smaller.

When the old man taught me to shoot a bow, I caught on real fast. Thing about a bow, you can shoot all day and make no noise to speak of, so I was able to get pretty good in a couple of weeks. Using it also saved us powder and shot which was hard to come by, and like always, McAdams had a pearl of wisdom to cast on the whole thing, too.

"You see, Jack," he said in a way that told me a pearl was about to drop. "I never knew a man who shot himself, or anyone else, with an empty bow."

By then, of course, I was used to his way of making fun, and I always laughed, even though I didn't always get what he was saying. On the other hand, this didn't fool him none, I think. I don't know how he known it but he'd always come up with a round about way of explaining when I didn't understand. Like the way he explained shooting yourself with an unloaded guns that evening in camp.

"Yes," he said, stretching back and scratching his full belly. "I knew a man that did that once. Shot himself with his own rifle not meaning to. You know, Jack, he was the most careful man around guns I ever knew. Always treated them like they were loaded, even when he knew they weren't."

"Then how'd he shoot his self?" I wanted to know. I known I was rising to his bait like a trout to a fly, but by then I didn't mind. McAdams went out of his way to respect a man. Ignorance weren't no sin to him. Only stupidity was.

"Ah, it was a terrible accident, it was," McAdams sighed. "He was cleaning his weapon one night in the house and pulled a candle close to check his flash pan. Being a careful man, of course, he was making sure the muzzle was not pointing at anyone. He thought the rifle was unloaded but come to find out one of his sons tried to load it without telling his dad. When he put the candle too close to the flash hole it caught the power and fired the charge."

The old man stopped talking like he always done when he wanted me to lead him on. Just to wart him a little I nodded and strung him out a bit. "Yeah, that will do her every time," I said, nodding. "Don't matter if it's a flint spark or a candle flame. Powder burns."

Course, the old man known what I was up to. So he nods and makes like he's about to drop off to sleep to prod me on. Sometimes I keep quiet and let it ride for a couple of days afore priming his pump, but I was curious that night, so I waited until just afore he dropped off. "What I don't understand is how."

Now I could see him twitch when I asked and I known he was deciding if to play possum on me or to give me my answer. I guess his itch had to be scratched because he played like I woke him up. "Oh, that," he said, looking at me over his shoulder. "He was the unfortunate victim of a very methodical wife. It turns out she had just washed her iron kettle and hung it on the wall to dry not an hour before. The ball hit the kettle, ricocheted off the hearth and struck him in the leg." Keenan shook his head. "Lucky it didn't kill him or her or one of the children. It was a small cabin." Then he went to sleep.

That got me to thinking and I puzzled out his remarks about the empty bow right quick after that. Just to get his goat I set my mind to it and picked up how to use a bow again even quicker. My daddy taught me the basics when I was six, but it was still a long time since I tried to use one. It taken me a while to get the hang of it again but once I did, I had it good.

Of course, the old man was surprised how quick I learnt. "You're a quick study, Jackie," he said, giving me a sidelong look after I nailed a running rabbit at the end of the second week.

"Lucky shot," I said, throwing it away. "I probably miss the next one." Then not ten minutes later it all happened again and I didn't miss then, neither. "Real lucky today," I said, but he give me one of his looks and I known he wasn't buying, not for a minute. Still, he didn't say nothing, not even around the fire that evening and I known he'd studied it out.

Three days later I known it for sure when we was camped in a nice place for a while and I made him some more biscuits. "You had a good man for a father, Jack," he said, sipping his coffee. "Taught you a lot more than how to make good biscuits and stew. He still alive?"

"No," I tell him. "He died about five years back."

"I'm sorry to hear that," McAdams said. "He must have been a good man judging by his son. Do you mind my asking how he died?"

"No," I said. "White militia attacked our village one night. He died defending me and my mother, but I got his killer. Tracked the son-of-a-bitch down and kilt him."

McAdams sat a long time saying nothing after that. He got a sad look on his face, one I'd never seen afore, and we was quiet a long spell. When he started talking again, it was almost like he was talking to his self. I could hardly hear him.

"Bitterness is plain poison," he said. "I've seen it destroy a man. It ate away at his soul until nothing was left but spite. At that point, the man wasn't worth shooting."

I give this some thought but couldn't make no sense of it. So I didn't say nothing. After a while the old man continued, like he was talking to the fire.

"Bill Chandler was one of the best men I ever knew. He was honest and dependable, and if he gave you his word, it was better than a contract."

Keenan stopped talking again, but I knew there was a bunch more and I kept my peace. Sure enough, he went on after a while.

"We must have rode together five years, the two of us and an old Indian we picked up along the way. The first couple of years, Bill was good to ride with. He could tell a yarn like nobody else and keep you laughing all night. When work was needful, he'd pitch in and do his part, and more, and nobody was better at your back in a tight place."

The old man nodded. "Yeah, he could tell a yarn, but he never talked much about himself. I don't even know where he was from, but I'd guess it was Georgia from the way he talked. He was that close about himself, all locked away inside."

Keenan stopped again and shook his head. "I knew pretty quick something was eating at Bill. There was times he would go days without saying more than a handful of words, and times he didn't talk at all. He just rode for hours, brooding about whatever was in his mind, and when he was like that, I just let him be."

The old man got up and poked the fire. It was just coals by then. When he sat back down, it was directly across from me and he looked me in the eye. "Sometime in the third year we came on a trader with a couple of extra jars of white lightning. Bill was in one of his moody spells and I thought it might do us all good to get drunk." He nodded. "And it worked at first. We were laughing and dancing and carrying on until the moon set, and Bill was at his best."

"Then about dawn, his mood shifted. He began talking about his past and why he was out wandering the hills with the likes of me and old Big-Ass." The ghost of a smile teased the corners of Keenan's mouth. "That's what we called the Indian. I forget his real Indian name. It was something like Walking Bull but me and Bill called him Big Gas Bull the first time we ate beans. I never seen a man could clear a campfire circle so quick."

The old man chuckled. "I think that's why his tribe run him off. On the other hand, I suppose it could have had something to do with his predilection for other men's wives, too."

Then he give me a look I'd seen afore and I known a yarn was on the way. "That was what finally killed him, you know," Keenan nodded. His face was solemn as a hanging judge. "His favorite trick on me and Bill was to save it up until we was eating supper and then sneak a big one out when we was half done. He'd always do it when we least expected."

He chuckled again and nodded. "Me and Bill chewed it over a while about calling him Thunder Butt. We found out later that was what people in his tribe called him, but by then we'd got used to calling him Big Gas. That kind of degenerated into Big Ass and nobody understood why we called him that because Big Ass had a skinny little old butt like a buffalo. But man, could he thunder."

The old man felt absently for his pipe and taken it out. He began to suck on it dry, looking kind of sad. We'd run out of tobacco the week afore and he missed his spirit weed. "Yes sir, that's what killed old Big Ass and it damned near killed Bill, too. One night we camped up on the Little Big Horn and Bill was a cooking. I was coming back from the river bringing some boiling water when I saw Big Ass bend over to pick up a piece of firewood. His back was to the fire and I heard him rip one of the biggest farts I ever heard. Looked like the whole valley lit up when it hit the fire and I saw old Big Ass sailing across the prairie like a shooting star. His pants was on fire all streaming out behind him and old Bill got scorched so bad he looked like a burnt stump!"

Keenan stopped talking and I known he was waiting for me to say something to keep the story going. "What happened?" I asked. "Did Big Ass hit a tree?"

"Didn't come near one!" the old man declared. "When that gas hit the fire and blew up it throwed old Big Ass straight up in the air like a cannon ball."

"So he was killed in the fall?"

"No, sir. That blast blew him all the way over the mountains to the Pacific Ocean. Yes, sir. All the way past San Francisco."

"Ah, he drowned, then."

"Not even that!" Keenan chortled. "He bounced off the bottom and was swimming for shore when a damn shark ate him!"

That was the end of his talk about Bill that night, and I think Mac meant it that way. He was always careful not to grease the goose too much when he was making a point. So we got off on another track swapping lies and then the moon was high and it was time to call it a day. Yet I known Mac would get back to his story sooner or later. We didn't know one another that good yet and he was being careful. Or maybe right then the memory was still too raw and he needed to chew it over in his mind a while afore he spit it out. You never could tell with him. Yet I known that when it was time he'd get back to it.

Sure enough, three days later we was sitting around after supper and he told me, "I need to finish what I was telling you about my partner, Jack. All joking aside, it was his own bitterness that killed him, you know."

"I sort of wondered about that," I admitted. "I couldn't figure what you meant. How did Bill die?"

"I mean it as simple as it is," he told me. "Holding a grudge is as stupid as taking a dose of arsenic and hoping the other man will die from it. The biggest difference is it's not as fast as arsenic, but it's just as deadly." He shook his head. "What killed Bill was a bullet that parted his eyebrows, but it was all his grudges that put him in the bullet's way."

I guess it was obvious I didn't get what Keenan was driving at. He taken out his pipe and settled back against his saddle with his cup of camp coffee close at hand. "Let me tell it my way, young 'un and I think you'll see what I mean."

I poured myself another cup and when I set down Mac began to talk. "Seems Bill was all set to marry his childhood sweetheart, but his step-brother had the same idea. Bill thought he'd won out and the step-brother seemed to accept the idea. What he was doing, of course, was courting at the back door after Bill left by the front, and he taken advantage of the girl. She was barely sixteen and the boys were in their twenties. When she got in a family way, Bill stepped forward to make an honest woman of her, even though he knew it wasn't his child. Six weeks later, she and the step-brother ran off to New Orleans."

Keenan looked me in the eye. "Bill told me all that after we got drunk that night. Trouble was, I had to listen to the story of Bill's life for the next two years. It was like lancing a boil. All this rotten stuff just came pouring out and there wasn't any stopping it. It was like cleaning a barn that hadn't been cleaned in thirty years. Only difference was, manure stops stinking after a while. With old Bill hanging onto it like that, his hurt festered like a bad sore and got worse."

Mac taken a long draw on his coffee cup. "I tell you, lad, there were times I couldn't take listening to it any more and told Bill to leave me be. To give the man credit, he did. Then a few days later we'd be riding along talking about something else, and he'd be off and running all over. After a while I mostly just let him rattle while I looked up the trail and kept us going. The strange thing is, he never repeated himself. For two years he told me every mean thing people ever did to him, and he never once repeated himself! That's what I call the poison eating his soul!"

The old man stopped talking and glared at the fire. "That's what got Bill killed and the only good I can see that come out of that was it gave him some peace. Yet, I wish I had been with Bill when it happened. I might have stopped it. We were at some little place that wasn't more than six buildings. One of them was a saloon with a sporting palace on the second floor and I was upstairs galloping one of the ladies. Tell you the truth, old Bill had been surly all day and I was glad to be shut of him for a spell."

Mac was silent a moment. "The thing is, I would have seen it coming if I wasn't so tired to listening to Bill bellyache. When we hit the saloon he started drinking, but instead of getting happy like he usually did, Bill turned mean and surly. Wouldn't nothing suit him. First, he didn't like the place and then he said the whiskey was bad. When one of the ladies come over to be friendly, he snarled at her and told her she was ugly."

Keenan shook his head. "Well, that was the last straw for me. The lady wasn't no beauty, but she was sweet as she could be and I could see she was hurt by what he said. I told Bill he had no call to talk like that and I left him alone at the table. It taken me an hour and a full quart of whiskey to sooth the poor darling's feelings. By then, of course, we were upstairs and Bill was on his own."

"The lady and I was taking a breather when all hell broke loose in the saloon. By the time I got my pants on and hit the stairs, it was all over, but I damn near got shot, too. Barkeep had his double barrel shotgun pointed right at my middle and all I could do was drop my pistol. When they told me what happened, I could see the man who shot him had no other way out. Bill had pushed him in a corner and was threatening to scalp him alive. As it was, Bill was who started the fuss in the first place."

I thought about all this for a while. I still didn't see a connection and I told McAdams so. "That's my fault, young 'un," he said. "I didn't tell it all. Seems the man who shot Bill reminded him of his step-brother. He was even calling the man by his step-brother's name. What I'm saying is that it was Bill's grudge that put him in the way of that bullet."

I could see what he was saying, but it bothered me. "What was Bill supposed to do?" I asked. "Just forget it?"

"There's no forgetting, Jack, no matter how we may want it. Them as say 'forgive and forget' are talking nonsense. The damned fool who forgets keeps on making the same old mistakes over and over. I know, because I've done it!" The old man gave me a wry grin. "I think the best anybody can do is to just let it go. There's nothing I ever saw written anywhere that says we have a right to revenge."

"What about an eye for an eye?" I asked. "That's what it says in the Good Book."

"That's what it says in one place in the Good Book," McAdams corrected me gently. "Get it out and I'll show you something else."

I handed over the Bible and McAdams found what he was looking for right away. He pointed to a passage and told me to read it aloud. When I had, he looked up another passage and asked me to read that, too. The third time this happened I began to see what he was driving at.

Just to be sure, the old man nailed it down. "There is no place you will find the Boss saying we have a right to revenge. What he teaches is forgiveness, and that's the hardest thing in this world to do. I sure have no mastery of it, but what I do know is that forgiving and forgetting are two different things. Forgiving means letting go, and letting go again every time you remember. Had Bill spent those years doing that instead of bellyaching to me, I believe he would still be alive." He grinned. "Then you'd have two old farts to put up with."

"I don't think I can ever forgive the militia that killed my folks," I said. "I don't think I want to."

"I hear you, but tell me this. Did getting revenge ease your load from losing your folks? Did it make you feel better?"

I thought about that. "No, it didn't make me feel much different at all. It felt like killing a snake that tried to bite me. It was just something that had to be done."

"I want you to chew on this one a couple of days before you answer," Mac told me. "Suppose it was something like lightning or a tree falling over that killed your folks. Would you hold a grudge against the clouds or the forest? Or even the Boss?"

I started to say that was completely different, but the old man held up his hand. "Study it out a while first," he told me. "One thing we have out here is plenty of time for thinking." Then he pointed at a small bush just ahead. "Now are you going to nail that sage hen? If you ain't, then hand me the bow."

"That's sage brush," I protested throwing him a glance. About that moment a grouse flew up from behind the bush.

"Well, you could have fooled me," Keenan chuckled. "My eyes must be giving out."

Massacre

It was two days later we come on the massacre. I never seen anything like it afore or since and I never want to. Just remembering it now is enough to put me off my feed, and there's times I wake up in a cold sweat dreaming about it.

We headed out early that morning, hoping to get to a water hole Mac known about by dark. Long about noon was when we spotted the birds and we headed that way to see what it was. There was too many of them for it to be something small, and Mac told me to keep my eyes open. There was no telling what we might find and if we could see the birds, so could anyone else.

When we got a half mile off, Mac turned us to the left and we started circling, looking for sign. It weren't long afore we come across wagon tracks a couple of days old, and when he saw them Mac's face turned grim. I think he known right then what we might find.

"Two wagons," he said. "Four oxen and three horses. Looks like a milk cow track there, too. Two men walking, and a woman or one older boy."

I looked where he pointed but all I could see was wagon tracks and a bunch of tracks made by big animals. Then the old man pointed to one side and I spotted a man's boot print with one made by a smaller foot not far from it. If he hadn't pointed them out, I'd never of spotted them.

I started to follow the wagon tracks, but Mac turned back to circling and waved me to follow. We wasn't half way around the circle from the wagon tracks when we come across a wide swath of other tracks, and Mac stopped to study them. "Four oxen and seven horses, traveling fast. Looks like the milk cow and calf, too."

"Indians?" I asked, but McAdams shook his head. When I looked closer I could see why. All the horse tracks had the imprint of iron shoes. I had no idea what this might mean but I felt a cold hand grip my belly. What I remembered was the militia that kilt my family.

After studying this a while, Mac taken to circling again. We ain't gone far afore the smell hit us. Wasn't no question what it was, neither. We was still a good quarter to half a mile from where the buzzards was circling but it made me want to heave my guts. Mac's face looked grim as a slab of alabaster stone. At that point, there wasn't no question in his mind of what we'd find. Wasn't in mine, neither. The only question was how bad it was.

Mac continued circling and not far from our starting point he spotted a set of tracks leading away from where we was headed. I would of missed them, but when Mac pointed them out, I seen they was the same tracks made by the smaller man or boy. "We'll track him later," Mac whispered and when we come across our earlier tracks, he turned us toward whatever was there. "Keep your eyes open!" he told me again. "Could be somebody still there." He taken out his Hawken and laid it across his saddle. I checked my Colt's.

Well, I'd never seen nothing like what we found. Even when my folks was shot, it weren't like that. Mac told me later it minded him of a battleground, only not so bad. He also told me it weren't no shame to puke your guts out like I did. He was looking a little green his self.

The two wagons was still there, right where they stopped. There weren't no water hole there but it looked to me like the folks in the wagons stopped to make camp for the night. It was a good place for that, low and protected from the winds and out of sight from the plains. I could see a burnt place where they made them a buffalo chip fire to cook over and the ox yokes was still laying by the side of the wagon. My guess was that they was hit just before dawn, and the old man agreed. "Looks like they were murdered in their beds," he said. "Either that or somebody stripped them." The men had no boots on and only had on their long johns, and they was laying next to the wagons where they must of slept. One of them was shot with an arrow right through his blanket.

It was the sight of the two women that really got me. They was bare assed naked and looked like they was dragged to where they was killed. The way their bodies was laying with their legs splayed wide open told the story. Someone made sport with them and there was nothing gentle about it. "I hope they killed the women afore they raped them," I said, fighting back a sour taste in my mouth.

"I'm afraid not, lad," McAdams said, pointing to the face of one of the women. His voice was soft and gentle and so sad it would break your heart. The woman's face was froze with a look of pure terror.

"How does a man forgive something like this?" I said. My voice sounded like a wounded cougar.

"I don't know," the old man assured me. Though his voice was still gentle, I could tell he was just as grieved as me. "I don't see how the Boss can, either, though I'm told he does."

"Is this how Indians are out here?" I asked.

"Wasn't Indians that did this, Jack," the old man told me. "He pointed to the arrow sticking out of the man in the blanket. "That arrow is Comanche but we're a fair way out of their territory. No way would an Indian ride off and leave a perfectly good blanket like that one, either. There weren't any Indian tracks. All the horses were shod."

I rode over and looked in the back of each of the wagons. "Looks like all they taken was food and maybe some grain. Water barrel's still half full."

"You see a shovel in there?" McAdams asked. I told him I did and he told me to bring it. Once we had the bodies wrapped in blankets, we buried them four foot down, all together in one big grave. Wasn't no telling who belonged with who, so we put them in the same hole. Wherever they went, they can sort it out there. When we was done, Keenan taken off his hat and asked me to do the same. Then he asked for the Bible and read off some stuff I never heard afore, but it fit real good. When he offered up the Lord's prayer, I stumbled along with him.

I asked him about a burial board, but he shook his head. "We don't know their names, lad," he told me and we've got other things to be about. We need to follow that other set of tracks. If the lad's still alive, we need to find him."

We watered the horses from the barrel on the wagon and filled our canteens afore we set off. The sun was getting half way between noon and setting, and McAdams was anxious to follow the tracks while we still had light. Our horses was rested and grazed and we covered a lot of ground afore the sun touched the hills to the west.

Just afore the sun went down, Keenan slipped off his horse and snuck to the top of the closest rise for a quick look around. When he come down, he told me he could see a patch of green trees about a mile ahead, but he didn't want to head in just yet. He figured it was a water hole or a creek and they was no telling who might be camped there. "If the lad made it there, at least he has water," he said. "We'll camp here and go in at first light."

I didn't sleep too good that night, even though I was beat from the day afore. Grave digging is hard work and not just on the body. Every shovel full of dirt I threw minded me of the day I buried my own family, and when I was done I felt like I was whipped. Then riding on the tracks I was all keyed up, waiting for killers to ride out of the next coulee. It was good no fool hen jumped up from under my horse. I think I'd of drawed and blowed it out of midair with my Colt's. That would of been the worst thing I could of done if hostiles was around.

I could tell McAdams was all keyed up, too. He didn't say much but wasn't much his eyes missed and he looked downright nasty. Anybody looking for trouble would have got their money's worth from him. I don't know if he slept that night, but ever time I dozed off and woke up, he was sitting there with his Hawken across his lap. Me, I slept off and on with my Colt's in my hand.

Not long afore dawn I woke up. McAdams was looking at me and when he seen I was awake, he nodded toward the grove he spotted. We saddled up without a word or a bite to eat and led our horses on foot. We was careful to stay off the horizon, though it made our way longer and I'd sacked up the horses feet the night afore to keep them quiet. I could hear the breeze moving over the prairie and I think it was making more sound than us.

We was gone less than half way to the grove when McAdams suddenly stopped and held up his hand. When I looked where he was pointing, I could see a dark patch against the prairie not far up the coulee we was traveling. I couldn't tell what it was, but I couldn't see it move, and I wondered if it was another body for us to bury. Then I heard something, like a real low moan, and Keenan waved us forward.

What we found was the lad we was trailing. I guessed him at fourteen, or maybe sixteen, and he wasn't full growed. Even in the dawn light he looked pale as a ghost when we turned him over, but when his eyes opened, he tried to fight us. Keenan clamped a hand over his mouth and it was all we could do to hold him down at first.

"Easy, lad!" Keenan hissed. "We're friends. Don't yell or talk loud. There may be bad men close by. Understand." The boy stopped struggling and nodded. "We're going to let you go. You can run off if you want to. Just don't make any noise. Understand me?"

The boy nodded again. "Let him go, Jackie," the old man told me and I did. Soon as we did, the kid jumped to his feet and tried to run. He didn't make it two steps afore falling down. I started to get up and help him, but Keenan held up his hand and I squatted myself right back down. The kid watched us without getting up. He minded me of a cornered rat.

"We have water if you want some," the old man told him. After a minute I seen the kid nod and went to my horse for the canteen. "Jackie's going to help you so you don't spill any," Mac told him and I moved closer. "Just take a sip or two at first."

I had to pull the canteen away from the kid after the first gulp. "You'll get some more in just a minute," I whispered. "Drink too fast and you'll puke it up. Understand?" The kid nodded again and I handed him the canteen. He taken several short pulls.

It was getting on toward light by then and I could see the kid looked like one of the men we buried the day afore. I felt sorry for him because I known what he was going through. "Don't worry, son," I said. "We'll get the sons-a-bitches that done this." The old man give me a strange look when I said this but he didn't say nothing.

"You have a name, young 'un?" Mac asked.

"Yes, sir," the boy whispered back. "They call me Charlie."

"Good to meet you, Charlie," the old man said. "My name's Keenan McAdams and this rough oak sapling is Jack Bear." He offered a hand and the kid shook it. When Mac looked at me, it taken me a minute to catch on afore I offered my hand, too. When I did, I was surprised how soft and small the kid's hand was. I decided his folks must have been city folks and I wondered why they was out here in the wilds. Even so, I kept my peace.

"Charlie," McAdams whispered. "After a while Jack and me need to go check out that grove up ahead. We need you to watch the horses for us. Can we trust you to do that and not ride off with them?" After a bit the kid nodded. "You promise?" This time the kid nodded right away. "All right, then," the old man said. "We'll get you to civilization and you can ride behind Jack here until we get you your own horse. Fair enough?"

The kid looked at me and I could have swore the kid almost smiled. "Yeah," he murmured. "I promise. You got anything to eat?"

"Let the water settle your stomach first," the old man whispered. "We'll all eat when we're done with the grove."

McAdams and I left a canteen for the kid and handed him the horses reins. "If we're not back here by sundown, take the horses and head due west. Keep to the low ground and off the horizon and keep as quiet as you can. When you get to the mountains, there'll be a town there somewhere. The people speak Spanish but you'll make out all right. Ask for the Catholic padre. You're on your own from there."

That was the first time I realized the two of us might be dead by sundown. It was unsettling on top of what come our way the day afore, but riding the plains with the old man over the next few weeks, I come to terms with it. That's the way every day is. None of us may see the next sunrise, and sure as shooting, none of us is going to get out of this world alive. When a man accepts that, everything else falls into place. What matters is today.

Even so, it was a lot later on I come to think that. At the moment, I looked the kid square in the eye and pointed my finger at his chest. "I meant it, Charlie. I aim to get the bastids or die trying!"

The old man just looked at me and shaken his head. "We'll be back by sundown or not all all, lad," he told Charlie. "If you hear shooting, lay low until full dark. Don't run unless you have to. Jack's horse is the fastest."

McAdams nodded to me and taken up his Hawken. I taken out my Colt's and checked it was loaded full. Normally I carry it with five shots with the chamber under the hammer empty. It's safer that way but I might need that sixth shot in a hurry afore the morning was over.

We made our way following the lay of the land. Even though it was still dark, we was careful not to outline ourselves against the horizon. Turns out the grove wasn't that big and after a while we found us a place we could watch most of it without being seen.

We wasn't there too long afore I seen something moving. I nudged

McAdams and he nodded, holding up five fingers. I looked again and sure enough, they was five riders. None of them was wearing hats and I guessed they was Indians. "Cheyenne," the old man whispered in my ear.

Wasn't long after that we seen other horses moving out of the grove, and it was light enough I could see women and kids and a few dogs. When McAdams nudged me again and put a finger to his lips, I known what he meant. We had to be extra quiet count of the dogs. It was a small band but we sure didn't need any trouble. Five warriors, not counting the older kids, could give us all we cared to chew on.

We stayed where we was for at least an hour afore moving out of where we was hid. Even then, McAdams circled the grove completely afore we moved in. They wasn't nothing for us to find but Indian tracks and the old man sent me back for Charley. "Whistle before you go in," he told me and puckered his lips. If I wasn't watching him I would have swore it was a meadow lark.

"I cain't do that one," I told him. "How about this?" I made one I known.

"Redwing blackbird is fine," he told me. "Charley just needs to know you're coming. Don't do it more than twice."

He was right. After I whistled, Charlie was waiting for me, but not next to the horses. When I turned around to look for him he was standing behind me, my bow in his hand and an arrow on the string. "You catch on quick, kid," I told him. "Mac's waiting for us at the grove."

"That's why I'm still alive," he said. I noticed he didn't offer me back the bow.

"You know how to use that thing?" I asked. Without a word, Charlie turned around and nailed a dry buffalo chip on the next rise. It must have been thirty yards away and he hit it dead center. "I guess I need to make me a new bow," I said and Charlie smiled. When he did, there was something about it that wasn't quite right. Then I realized at that moment he looked like one of the women we buried and it must of been his mother. "We better get going," I said, rougher than I meant.

I gathered the horse's reins and Charlie trotted over to fetch the arrow. We taken it easy getting to the grove and afore we left cover, I give my bird call again. We heard a meadow lark answer and I was surprised when Charlie answered with the same call.

When we got to the water hole in the middle of the grove, the old man was waiting for us. He raised his eyebrows when he seen Charlie with the bow, and when I nodded, he known Charlie knew how to use it. "There's a stand of willows over there," Mac said, pointing. "Might be a good idea to gather some arrow shafts while we're here. The best ones are already gone, but there may be some good ones left."

"Kid's almost as good as I am with a bow," I told him and I had to laugh when Charlie blushed. Keenan give Charlie a long look but didn't say nothing.

I unsaddled the horses and was about to take the wrapping off their feet when Mac stopped me. "We better leave those on until we're clear of here," he said. "We don't want whoever comes here next to know white men traveled through."

"Then we better get Charlie out of them boots," I told him. McAdams and I both wore moccasins.

"I did, already," Mac told me. "I had a pair in my kit that fit." I turned around to look, and sure enough, Charlie was wearing a pair of the prettiest beaded moccasins you ever saw. I tried not to smile and I didn't have the heart to say nothing, but what Charlie had on was a pair of women's moccasins. He seemed right proud of them, too.

"We'll make Charlie another pair for everyday use," Keenan said, giving me a warning look. "No need to wear the nice ones out."

We made our camp at the edge of the grove, as far away from the water as we could get. We made our fire in a hole already there and we slept next to the horses, with our weapons close to hand. That grove was probably the best waterhole for miles and there was no telling who, or what, might show.

I woke up late that night with my gun in my hand. Something was moving in the brush, so quiet I could scarcely hear it. I started to get up but the old man touched my arm. I saw him shake his head and looked around for Charlie. The kid was gone and I relaxed. He was probably taking a leak.

Next thing I know, I hear something whimpering. I look at the old man and he's grinning. "Sounds like you found us a cur, Charlie," he said. His voice was so quiet I could barely hear him.

Charlie slipped out of the bushes and sat down next to us. There was a half grown pup in his arms. "It's my dog. He ran off when we were attacked and I thought he was dead. He must have trailed me here." The beast looked at me and McAdams, then back at Charlie, just like he understood ever word we said. He looked like he was grinning.

McAdams chuckled. "A man's got to be careful what he wishes for," he told Charlie. "Here I was wishing for a dog not two weeks back and now we have a dog and a new partner."

Charlie looked like he was about to cry and I looked away. It seemed a little unmanly, even with all that happened to him the last couple of days. Yes, I cried for my folks, but not when nobody else was around.

Then I caught McAdams eye and he chuckled. Damned if I didn't think he was laughing at me! "Yes, there's a lot to be thankful for," he murmured gently. "Damn near makes this man cry." I saw his eyes was soft a way I'd never seen them, and tried to figure what he was getting at. I couldn't so I decided to give it a few days.

We stayed in the grove three more days afore McAdams decided we needed to move on. "We've been very lucky nobody else has come along before this," he told me and Charlie the night afore we left. "That bunch who attacked you is probably out of the area by now."

"We ain't going after them?" I asked.

McAdams looked from me to Charlie. "How do you feel about it, young 'un?" he asked Charlie. "It was your folks who were killed."

"I don't want to see them again," Charlie said. "Not now. "There were five of them. All of them had rifles and pistols both. We've only got one rifle, one pistol and two bows." We'd found an ash sapling and made me a new one just the day afore. It still wasn't cured out.

"That's my thinking," McAdams said, nodding. "If I was going after them, and that's a big if, I'd even the odds and take them out one at a time."

I nodded. "That's how I done the militia, but we need to know who they are."

"Oh, I know who they are," Keenan assured me. "I don't know their names but I'm not likely to forget their boot prints."

"I'm not likely to forget their faces, ever!" Charlie declared. One thing I noticed about Charlie right early was how he talked. It was educated, like McAdams, not plain style like me. His folks must have learnt him right, particularly his ma.

"I'm surprised you got away," I said. "You never told us that." When

I said this I regretted it right away. Charlie's face looked like he'd been kicked in the belly. "I ain't rushing you," I added real quick. "Just sometime when you feel like it I'd like to know."

"Charlie doesn't have to," McAdams said. His voice was soft, like he was soothing a scared horse. "The way I read the signs, Charlie was off behind a bush taking care of some personal business, like tonight. You got away because it was still dark when they attacked. Am I right?"

Charlie nodded and this time I saw tears in his eyes. "Sorry," I said. "I didn't mean to pry." The old man looked at me and smiled and I wondered why he was handling Charlie so delicate. How was the boy supposed to toughen up with McAdams mothering him like that?

Keenan looked at me and chuckled again, just like he was reading my thoughts. "Sooner or later we get the answers we need, lad," he said softly. "It doesn't do to push the river. Puzzle it out."

I started to say something, but I seen the look Charlie give him. It was pure gratitude and I taken a notion I best back off. "So that way we headed in the morning?" I asked.

McAdams give me a smile. I knowed he was thanking me for something, but damned if I known what. "I'm thinking we need to head on west to Taos and rest up there a while. That way Charlie can get back in touch with family."

"My family's all gone," Charlie said. "Every one but me and my parents died of small pox. I guess there must relatives in Canada and England, but I don't know who they are. I'm not sure they'd want me and I'm not sure I want to go back east, either."

McAdams looked at me and raised an eyebrow. I nodded and he said, "Well, you're welcome to travel with us as long as you want. You're almost as good a cook as Jack."

"I'm better," Charlie declared, looking me right in the eye.

"Hoot! It looks like we're going to have us a cook-off!" the old man crowed. "We best wait until we have someone from outside the camp to judge, though. I don't want to get caught between two dueling chefs."

"You said 'almost,'" I reminded him.

"Why, lad, I was just being polite," McAdams murmured. It weren't until halfway through our ride the next day I wondered who he was being polite to. I was damned if I was going to ask, neither!

CHAPTER FIVE

High Plains Storm

e started out just afore first light the next morning. To confuse anyone who might be along after us, we rode out on horseback and followed the track the Indians afore us laid down. I give Charlie a hand up behind me and I was surprised how light the young 'un was. I wondered if he wasn't tall for his age and thought maybe he was younger than we thought.

When he bumped into me getting on the horse I thought his chest felt flabby. "What do you got in there?" I asked, turning around for a look. When I did I come nose to nose with the pup and he give my face a lick. I was so surprised I almost fell off my horse.

It didn't help the old man laughed. "That's the only good morning kiss you're like to get around here," he said and Charlie give me kind of a strange look.

"Dog needs to walk," I said, glaring at Charlie.

"I'm training him to growl, not bark," Charlie told me, and the critter growled at me. The old man nodded smiled. I could see the sense of that so I growled back at the dog. He ducked into Charlie's shirt and I had to laugh. "We're ready," I told McAdams and we headed out.

We followed the Indian tracks for a couple of miles until we come to a stony ridge. The old man picked his spot good and when we turned off, we didn't leave no tracks I could see looking back. When we was a good mile down the ridge, the old man pulled up and we began to walk from there. I seen Charlie tie the pup on a long tether and wondered why. Charlie seen my look and read what I was thinking. "I'm teaching him not to run out too far. When he does, I step on the tether."

That made a lot of sense, too, and over the weeks ahead I come to see what a good hand Charlie was with animals. He seemed to know what was going on in their heads afore they did and he had even better eyes than Keenan. Not long afore we reached the ridge where we turned off, I felt his weight shift behind me and was surprised by the twang of Charlie's bow. Next thing I seen was a prairie hen flopping around on the ground. I had no idea how I missed seeing her, but I did and so did McAdams. At least, I thought he did. You just cain't tell when he smiles and winks like that.

We was traveling a good way north of the Canadian River by then, and the old man turned us west and a little south. He was thinking of running into the river in a day or two and we was traveling on foot most of the time. We had plenty of water and the grass was good and every once in a while we run into a feeder stream flowing south. So they wasn't no point in staying too close to the Canadian. It was a major water source and we wasn't anxious to run into nobody. With Indians it was always a question if they was friendly and maybe even more so with white folk. I know McAdams didn't want to come across the bunch that attacked Charlie's train, though I wouldn't have minded a fight. Don't know why I was so proddy, but I was.

Once we got to know each other a bit, it seemed like Charlie was always poking at me. It weren't really picking a fight but more like a younger brother picking at the older one. Most of the time I didn't mind and it kind of taken Charlie's mind away from the massacre. Not that he was soft headed. When it come time to get down to the nut cutting, Charlie got downright serious until it was done. Then he'd do something like throw guts in my face if we was cleaning a couple of fool hens, trying to get me to chase after him.

Trouble was, Charlie could run faster than me, which few can. His wind was better, too. So after a couple of times not catching him I quit chasing. I'd just bide my time waiting for a chance of getting back at him. Sooner or later Charlie would let his guard down and I'd get him down and rub his face in the sod. Ever once in a while one of us would push it too far and the old man would have to step in and cool things down, mostly with a word or two. Other than that, he seemed to like watching two young roosters playing peck-ass.

One thing I noticed right away was that Charlie was pretty shy when it come to taking a leak. Like anybody else, I like my privacy when it comes to laying my burden down and I'd been around the wilds enough to know to bury it when I did. Nothing like a stinky calling card lets the world know you been passing through.

Now I have to admit his wanting privacy was Charlie's business. The only time I tried to make a joke about it with Kennan, he give me a look that told me I was being rude, which I guess I was, and he was not amused. Since then, I puzzled out why he taken offence, but it taken me a good while. As usual with McAdams, it turns out the joke was on me all along.

About a week after we left the grove, we come to the Canadian again. The country was getting a lot drier and more broken about then and it was a welcome sight when we saw the river. Yet, just like that first day at the grove, we didn't head right for it. We hung back until we come to a place McAdams thought was good, and then we scouted it out on both sides of the river. Naturally, we bound up our ponies' feet afore we did. No need letting someone know white folks was around, even though we didn't find nothing but a few tracks laid down a weeks or two afore, maybe even earlier. I could tell it hadn't rained in a good spell.

Where we set up camp was in a coulee about a hundred yards from the riverbank. This meant we had to lead our horses down to the water, but the site McAdams picked was as safe as we could get. Our campsite was on high ground but out of sight from the river, and there weren't no easy way to slip up on it. There was a couple of trees for shade, and a small spring we could of used if we had to. There was a constant breeze off the prairie that never let up while we was there, which kept the flies away from the horses, and there was plenty of good grazing. What seemed strange to me at the time was that it looked like nobody else ever camped there.

There was a stand of willows along the Canadian, so Charlie and I cut some fresh arrow shafts the first day we camped there and laid them out to dry. We made a good team, the two of us working at the same thing, and I noticed McAdams seemed to be smiling a lot that day. Night afore we'd had a light rain and the air was clear. The days was still growing with summer on the way, but it was real nice. Prairie flowers was blooming and the sky was blue like it never was back home in Arkansas. They was so much of it, sky from one horizon to the other and no trees to break it up.

We was sitting there making arrows, Charlie and me, and Keenan was watching us. I heard him a humming but I didn't think he known he was. He was sitting there like a big cat purring and working his paws in the sun and I'd heard him do this afore. This time what I heard was something I thought I heard afore, something I liked. So after a while I asked him what it was.

Keenan blinked when I asked him this, just like I'd shook him awake. "I don't know, lad," he told me, looking a little foolish. "I wasn't really listening? How did it go?"

"Hell, Keenan, I cain't carry a tune in a bucket, but it was something like this." I give it a try and in about ten seconds him and Charlie was about rolling on the ground laughing. "I told you I cain't carry a tune!" I declared. "Ain't no call to make fun of me for it!"

"You're right, lad," the old man said, almost busting a gut trying not to laugh. He done all right until he looked at Charlie, who was having the same trouble. Then he snorted and they started all over again, and damned if it didn't get me laughing, too. By the time it was done, we was all wiping tears from our eyes. Even thinking about it again after all these years, I can see it clear as day and it's still enough to make me smile. I got no idea why.

That evening about dusk we was sitting watching a full moon come up. Way off to the southwest we could see a line of clouds with thunderheads building, and there wasn't nothing prettier I ever seen. The moonlight made the prairie look like a silver ocean and the wind rippling the grass looked like waves. Charlie is sitting close to me and says, "It's called Simple Gifts."

"What's that?" I asked. I had no idea what Charlie was talking about.

"Yes!" McAdams nods. "That's what I was humming this afternoon, Jackie. It's a hymn the old Shakers sing." He chuckled. "Or used to sing. Seems like they didn't believe in procreation and so they all died out." He hummed a few bars and Charlie joined in, singing the words, soft and true.

I was flat amazed and decided Charlie must be younger than I thought. His voice was clear and pure and hadn't begun to change yet. Yet it was the most beautiful singing I ever heard and I was glad it was dark. It was a hymn my Ma used to sing and it brung tears to my eyes. When Charlie was done singing, we sat quiet for a long spell. Then we said goodnight and turned in. Wasn't nothing to be said after something as pretty as that.

A thunderstorm come up that night just like I known it would. I had my slicker out over my bedroll and I settled in behind a crude shelter I throwed up the day afore. It wouldn't keep the rain off but it would break its fall and maybe I'd be a little less wet come morning.

There wasn't a whole lot of rain where we was that night, but on the other side of the river it was like all hell broke loose. Lightening was flashing so bright it was almost like daylight and it woke me up. So I got up to check the river and seen hail coming down the size of pine cones and making the water dance. What was even stranger is I could see a funnel spout four or five miles south of us and moving to the east, a tearing up the prairie like a badger digging roots.

Keenan come up and stood besides me for a while. The river wasn't up that much and was not too likely to get all the way where we was, so he turned back in. I watched the twister for a while more but saw it weren't headed our way, so I went back to my shelter.

I was just getting settled in when Charlie come over to me. He was shaking so hard I could hear his teeth rattle. "You taking sick?" I asked.

Charlie shook his head. "Feels like I'm about to freeze," he told me. "It happens with weather like this. Mind if I lay close a spell?"

I was feeling a little cold myself. "Come on, kid," I told him. "We'll huddle up like sheep."

With both slickers and two blankets over the top of us, it didn't take long to get downright cozy and I dozed off right away. When I woke up a bit later, Charlie was snuggled up with his back up against me like two spoons in a drawer. Somehow my arm was over him and I could feel the pup snuggled in front of Charlie under his shirt.

When I started petting the pup I felt Charlie tense up for a bit but then he relaxed. His breathing got deeper and after a minute it seemed like he fell off to sleep. I heard him moan and guessed he was having a bad dream, so I patted him on the shoulder started to drift off myself.

It was nice and warm under there and I was struck by how soft the kid felt. His butt was up next to my lap and if I hadn't knowed it was Charlie, I'd of sworn there was a woman in my sack. That got me to thinking about that last wild night in Arkansas afore the polecat tried to shoot me, and I felt my pants getting snug. I started to pull back so Charlie wouldn't notice it but when I did, he moved over, wiggling in even closer. This made my pants so snug it almost hurt and I figured if Charlie was beginning to look good, I was getting in a bad way.

I decided it was time to water the prairie and cool off a while, so I climbed out of the bedroll and taken a walk up the hill. The old boy was stiff as a board when I let him out and it taken me a while to calm us both down. I hoped there was a sporting palace wherever we was headed because the need was pretty heavy on me if I was getting stirred up over a youngster like Charlie. I never had feelings like that for another man, and it bothered me considerable.

I was still sitting there just afore dawn when Keenan come up to join me. We did that a lot, just sitting and watching the morning being born. There is something about it that touches me deep down inside, and when I'm troubled, it brings me peace.

This morning Keenan seemed to know I was troubled, but he didn't ask about it. He never did too much unless he thought he had to. Sometimes he'd just start whispering like he was talking to his self like the time he told me about Bill, and I couldn't help listening. Wasn't many times what he had to say was off the mark, neither. Fact is, I cain't think of once.

"Things are never the way we think," he said to himself. "No matter how they look, there's always a deeper meaning. Finding that deeper payload is what always helps me, and it works better when I don't pass judgment on what I see too soon. Things are never what they seem."

He paused and taken out his old corn cob pipe. "Damn, I wish we could find some spirit weed," he said, looking at it a while afore putting it back. "Ever see a jack-in-the-box?" he asked.

"Cain't say I have." I told him, wondering where he was going with this.

"Looks like a plain wooden box, usually a cube about four to six inches across. It may even say something like 'Matches' or 'Candy' on top, but when you go to open it, there's a spring under a clown doll that pops up and makes a loud noise. It can startle the hell out of you!"

"I never seen one," I answered. "What put you in mind of that?"

"You and Charlie, lad. Both of you survived the massacre of your families. Both of you saw it happen and that marks people when they do. They may go along and pull their lives back together and even do well, as you have. They do it by taking all those bad things and shutting them away in a tight box in their mind and burying it away deep inside. Then one day something small happens that releases the catch on that box, and all that bad stuff comes back to mind."

I studied this awhile, then nodded. "All right," I told him. "That sums it up pretty well, but what does it have to do with me and Charlie now?"

"Well, for one thing, you trip the catches on each other's strong-box," Keenan chuckled. "Aside from the fact you're naturally like flint and steel. Rub you together and there's sparks."

"What are you telling me?" I said. "Speak straight out."

The old man thought about this a while and then nodded. "I don't like ruining good surprises," he told me. "Let's just say I think you and Charlie are in for a lot of surprises from one another." After he said this, he chuckled and nodded. "Yes, sir, I'd say you hold a lot of surprises for each other."

Well, he had my attention but he wouldn't say no more, no matter how I pried. And if last night was the kind of surprises he was talking about, I didn't want none. Where other folks find comfort is their own business, and it don't bother me at all. On the other hand, me getting lathered over Charlie seemed unnatural. I know for a fact the Good Book calls it an abomination. I read it there, and even though I ain't a believer, it makes sense to me.

Naturally, things was a little unsettled between me and Charlie the next couple of days. Neither of us made any mention of what happened but I got the feeling Charlie was as bothered by it as me. At first I thought Charlie was asleep and I was the only one who known, but then I caught Charlie giving me a real strange look a couple of days later. When I did they wasn't much question in my mind that Charlie was awake or woke up when he felt what was happening. I started to say something once or twice while we was by ourselves, but I couldn't get words around it. Rest of the time it seemed like the old man was always around.

Charlie wasn't no help, neither. He was cranky as a spring bear for a couple of days and stayed clear of me. It was a blessing we was traveling afoot and wasn't riding the same horse, and when the three of us was together, seemed like Charlie always put Keenan between us. That was fine with me but I don't like walking on eggshells, neither.

I was sure McAdams known what was going on but he didn't pay it no mind. He was cheerful as ever until the morning of the third day when he give us both a hard look. "You two are about as fit company as a skunk at a garden party," he told us. "Today it's my turn to be cross, so I'm going to ride on ahead and cuss for a spell. You can follow my tracks." He taken the reins of the pack horse from Charlie and started off. "Or not," he said back over his shoulder. "I'm in no mood for any more of your silly highjinks. So kill each other or work it out! I don't care which."

Charlie and me looked at each other. The old man sounded like he meant business, and I expect he did. Our camp was too small to carry on like we done the last couple of days. I know it wore on me and I expect it did on Charlie, too. "Look," I said. "You and me, it was an accident. Can we just forget about it?"

Charlie looked me in the eye for the first time in two days. "No, but we can leave it lie. That good enough for you?"

"All right," I said, wondering why Charlie was so bent on remembering something unpleasant. "I guess that will have to do. It won't happen again."

"You damned right about that!" Charlie said, looking me straight in the eye. I couldn't figure why he was still so mad.

"Damn it, it weren't you!" I declared. "I ain't that way. I was dreaming about a sporting woman I run across back in Arkansas."

When I said this, Charlie's eyes got hotter than ever, but he didn't say a thing. He turned and sort of stalked away over the prairie like a pissed off tomcat. "Look," I yelled after him. "I cain't help it I was born this way. I just ain't like that. I don't care if you are, but I ain't. You can like boys all you want. I like girls!"

Charlie stopped and looked me square in the eye. He was so mad he was shaking and I started trying to figure how to take him down without neither of us getting hurt. Then seemed like he give a jerk or two and fell down on the grass, holding his belly.

Well, I thought he was so mad he threwed his self into a fit. "Charlie, stop! You got to get a grip on yourself, boy!" I hollered, but when I said this, he started jerking harder than ever. So I grabbed my canteen off the horse and was about to dump it in his face when I heard him laughing.

"What the hell you laughing about?" I hollered. "I thought you was having a fit!"

"I am!" Charlie gasped. I could see he was trying to control his self, but he wasn't having much luck. "Let's just forget it," he said, and then he set off laughing again.

Wasn't much I could do so I walked up to the top of the coulee and taken off my hat. I eased my head over the top for a look around. When I did I froze. Not a half mile away I seen a band of what looked like eight or ten Indians crossing the horizon. I could see the old man, too, ahead of us about a quarter mile, and the way he was headed, he was sure to run into the Indians.

I run down to Charlie and when he saw the look on my face, he stopped laughing. "Indians!" I hissed. "I got to warn McAdams! You lead the horse!"

"I'm faster than you!" Charlie said back, grabbing his bow and taking off afore I could auger. I slipped my own bow out and followed after him.

We was real lucky that time. Or maybe it weren't luck. I don't know. What I do know is Charlie caught up with the old man in time and they was waiting for me in a side coulee when I caught up. I told the old man what I saw and which way they was headed and he thought about it for a minute. "We'll backtrack and head over to cut their trail," he told us. "Then we'll ride in their tracks a while to break our trail." He looked at me real close. "I'm surprised you saw them. Are you sure they were Indians?"

"They wasn't riding saddles and none of them was wearing hats. They didn't seem to be in no hurry, neither." I shrugged. "Could have been white traders, I guess, but I didn't see no pack mules."

I could see McAdams was puzzled and a little worried, but we backtracked like he said. Yet afore we come to the Indian's tracks, we come across what looked to me like tracks from a cattle drive. What I couldn't figure out was the shallow furrows about a yard apart and running more or less along the same line.

When we seen this, Keenan relaxed a bit. "It's a hunting party," he told us. "They're following this bunch of buffalo." I looked at the tracks again, and sure enough, they was different from cow tracks.

"What's that?" I asked, pointing toward the lines. "They don't look like wagon tracks.

"Travois," the old man answered. Seeing my dumb look, he went on.

"It's a drag for their camp gear. They tie a couple of teepee poles on a horse and load their heavy stuff on it."

Mac pointed at the fresh dung piles along the trail. I could see they was different from cow chips, smaller and not as flat. "The buffalo aren't spooked yet," the old man told us. "They're still grazing and traveling easy through here." He looked around a bit. "We'll follow along for a while but I think we better head back toward the river. We sure don't want to be in the way when then the herd stampedes."

The old man looked at the two of us. "Nothing brings peace like a common threat," he observed. "You settle your differences?"

When he said this, Charlie and me looked at one another. Then Charlie snorted and startled to snicker again and I shook my head. "I don't know what it was, but something tickled his funny bone," I told him, shrugging. "Just ignore him. We decided to put it aside."

McAdams nodded. "Well, I'm glad you did. Life's too short to waste fussing. Did I ever tell you about the time I got caught in the middle of a buffalo stampede?" I told him I hadn't. "Well, ask me about it tonight. It was really something."

"I bet," I answered. "You're lucky to be alive. I hear tell that a lot of people who get caught in a stampede like that don't survive."

"Oh, that's quite true," he assured me shaking his head like he was sad. I known I was about to be taken for a ride. "But my luck ran out that day, too, you know. I didn't survive, either."

I heard Charlie start snickering behind us again. Some days a man just cain't win.

Bushwhack

At some point along the Canadian River we passed out of Indian territory and into the Republic of Texas. Or maybe it was the state of Texas by then. I cain't recall the exact date all that happened, but that don't make no difference except to the lawyers. Nothing really changed but lines on a piece of paper and they wasn't much telling just when we crossed the boundary. The country was the same, though I could tell we was gradually headed uphill. We had to be since the water in the river was flowing back along the way we come.

I know it sounds kind of stupid putting it that way, but I have run into folks over the years that seem to expect water to flow uphill. I learnt real quick it's a bad mistake to try and convince them of the contrary facts of life. Some people seem to be hell bent on chasing a life of disappointment. Then they get mad at other people and blame them for allowing them to shoot themselves in the foot! To my mind, that ain't just stupid. It's downright crazy.

Anyways, we followed them Indians for a half day and then cut to the river along a rocky coulee. This was harder on the horses' feet, of course, and we had to watch out for flash floods. There wasn't no grass growing along the bottom of the coulee and the way the gravel was washed clean and round testified to a lot of water flow coming through.

We turned west out of the coulee a good ways afore we got to the river. The sides was getting pretty steep by then and they was no telling what we might ride into at the outlet. We might find a need to get going pretty quick and there weren't no way we could ride straight up the slopes forming ahead of us.

When we topped over the high bank of the coulee, what we seen ahead like to taken my breath away. The old man reined in and we just sat and looked a spell. "It's simply grand, isn't it?" he whispered, reverent, like he was saying a prayer. "There just aren't words, are there?"

It was all I could do to just nod. Stretched out afore my eyes was a wide deep canyon cut into the red earth. Colored bands ran along some of the walls of the canyon, parallel to the floor, and jagged red rocks cut out by wind and sand sat like statues on the top of steep slopes of red dirt and smaller rock. A deep green belt of grass and tall cottonwoods lay along the wide bottom of the canyon valley, marking the path of the river, and I could see dark clumps of cactus and desert shrub climbing the slopes.

"There's a place south of here like this, only more so," Mac told us. "The Spaniards named it Palo Duro. I have no idea why. The name means hard wood."

"Maybe it's because of these mesquites," Charlie suggested, pointing toward a low green bush with long thorns. "It's sure not because of the cottonwoods."

"Could be," McAdams answered, but I barely heard them. The view of the canyon from the cap rock had me. It was way too much to take in at once and I could of set there looking all day long, or maybe for a week or two. Even seeing the Teton mountains later on in all their glory was not quite like that first sight of the wide canyon floor. The empty land seemed big as the sky, and from where I stood I could see thirty miles, or maybe fifty.

"Riders!" Charlie hissed, bringing us back to earth. We ducked low and looked where he was pointing. Sure enough, there was a band of fifteen or twenty riders maybe a mile away headed east along the other side of the river.

We watched while the riders passed, Charlie and me moving our horses down the slope where they couldn't be seen. Then the old man whispered for his spy glass and I grabbed it out of his saddle bag by feel. "Here," I whispered, handing it to him without taking my eyes off the horsemen.

"What tune shall I play them, lad?" McAdams asked me gravely. He was holding a tin penny whistle. I heard Charlie snicker behind me. "I was more in mind of looking at them," he added, grinning. "It's a good thing I didn't keep a pet snake in there."

This time I paid attention to what I was grabbing and I handed him the spy glass. He pulled it out to full length and glanced through it. "Just as I thought," he said, handing me the glass.

I looked through the glass and was surprised to see that most of the riders was soldiers in uniform. As I watched, they stopped and dismounted. "Looks like they're making camp for the night," the old man muttered. "That's not a place I'd choose."

I looked through the glass again and saw what he meant. From where they was setting up, it looked like a defensible place. Yet I could see a coulee leading up to them, hidden through the trees, and as I looked through the glass, I could also see movement in the tall grass at our side of the coulee. I handed the old man the glass and told him what I'd spotted.

"It's another white man," Mac told us, lowering the glass and handing it to me. "Nor do I think he's one of their number. He seems to be spying on them."

"Let me see," Charlie said. I glanced back at the horses and saw they was tied to a low clump of brush. "I can't see nothing but his back," Charlie told us. "There's another moving up the draw, too."

McAdams taken the glass and looked again. He nodded. "They're together," he hold us. "They seem to be talking."

"Think we should warn the soldiers?" I asked.

The old man thought a minute. "I think one of us should," he said, looking at me. "You're not wanted by the Army, are you?" The way he said this, I figured he might be, but it turned out I was wrong about why he wanted me to go.

"No," I answered. I looked at Charlie and then back at the old man. It was pretty clear I was the one elected. "All right," I said. "I'll warn them and circle back to meet you."

"No need of that, lad," McAdams assured me. "We'll watch you from here and if everything appears all right, we'll follow you in. If not, we'll come to your rescue." He paused a minute and then added, "It might be best to ride in boldly and hail them from this side of the river by that big cottonwood." He pointed. "That gives you a good line of retreat to the east if they aren't what they seem."

I wondered why the old man was being so cagy, but then I looked at Charlie and remembered the massacre of his folks. Even if they wasn't driving stock, this might be the same bunch. There was twice as many men as Charlie told us, but maybe him and his folks met up with only half the gang.

I crossed the coulee behind us and circled to the east afore I turned back toward the river. It taken longer than I figured with the breaks in the land and the sun was a lot lower toward the horizon when I hollered across the river.

Someone must of seen me coming because they was all down by the river watching as I rode up. One of the officers stepped forward and we jawed a bit afore they invited me into camp.

There looked like there was more to the river at that point than there was. The water flowed wide but it weren't too deep and I went over on foot, leading my pony and probing for quicksand. When I got there the lieutenant in charge offered me a hand and asked if I was traveling alone.

I told him there was some others following me in and about the men I seen watching his camp. Quick as a wink he told four of his troopers to take their rifles and check the coulee behind their camp. Then he thanked me for the warning and asked about conditions to the east.

Where we hunkered down I known the old man could see us, and I told the lieutenant about the hunting party after buffalo and coming across the massacre of Charlie's people. I also told him about meeting up with the Comanche and he was surprised I still had my hair. By the time I was done telling that one, most of the troop was gathered around laughing, and no one spotted Charlie and McAdams until they was already in camp.

"It's a good thing you're not hostiles," the lieutenant told the old man when he introduced himself. He glared at his men. "The two of you could have captured us all." Two of the troopers beat a hasty path to their pickets.

"The lad tells a powerful good story," McAdams replied. He was talking with a burr that would strip bark off a tree. "A pity that the truth is not in him. He tends to play things down." Then he give a rendition of my performance that had the rest of the troops holding their bellies. Charlie was laughing so hard he cried.

Turns out there was a dozen soldiers in all, and two of them lieutenants. They told us they was part of the Freemont expedition that was mapping out the Arkansas river, and was on the way back to join the main party. As I recollect, the officer in charge was named Peck and the other was Albert, or something like that. All I heard the soldiers call them was Lieutenant.

The other strange thing was that the lieutenants wasn't what I'd call regular officers. They was engineers, not fighters, and I wondered why in the world the Army put them in charge of what could turn into a hostile situation. As usual, the old man had a good answer.

"Didn't you notice that sergeant and corporal they had, lad?" I allowed as I had. "Well, neither of them is a stranger to battle. Nor are their troops. So when it comes to fighting, I'd bet that's who runs the show."

"Don't the officers give the orders?" I asked.

"Yes, but smart officers always seek the advice of their top sergeants," he told me. "At least, the ones who survive do. The other kind get themselves killed along with their men."

"Don't reckon I'd make a very good soldier," I told him. "I don't like people telling me what to do."

"Ah, it wasn't so bad, Jackie," he said. "There's a lot to be said for regular meals and not having to worry about more than staying alive. Mostly what bothered me was the boredom of post duty between patrols or fights." Then he chuckled. "Can't say as I really miss it but it was a living."

"You ain't there any more, neither," I reminded him.

"There is that," he admitted. There was a far away look in his eyes. Then he laughed. "She was sweet as a honey tree, the captain's wife. Not that her husband ever appreciated what he had. You could say she was the reason for my sudden separation from the marines."

The soldiers sent to check out the coulee behind camp come back and reported they saw tracks of two men but nothing else. It was too late to shift camp, so the lieutenant in charge detailed a couple of men to watch it over night.

We was invited to join the troops for supper that night around the camp fire, but no way was it as good as our own cooking. What was good was the coffee and the biscuits the cook whipped up, and they even had some molasses for the biscuits. By the time we was done, I was right stuffed, and the old man was happy to find there was plenty of tobacco, too.

The old man was curious what the party had seen farther west. The lieutenant give him a pretty good picture and mentioned we might want to be careful to avoid Santa Fe, and maybe Taos, too. It was a pretty tense time between Mexico and the United States right then and he warned us to be careful not to get caught for spies. So far as he known, there wasn't any large force moving through but word was slow getting out of Mexico and the situation could change any time.

We got to swapping lies with the troopers after that and after a while the old man mentioned I was a real escape artist. Wouldn't do but I had to tell them all about my quick exit out of Washington and the only one who didn't seem to think it was downright funny was Charlie. He was glaring at me by the time I was done, and when I asked the troops if they had come across any sporting palaces along the river, he got up and stalked off from the fire.

"What's wrong with that boy?" one of the troopers asked.

"Ain't no telling," I answered. "Sometimes he gets riled up over nothing. Could be his folks getting killed. He seen it happen. He'll get over it."

"Well, if you put a skirt on him, I'd ask him for a dance," one of the other troopers said and we all laughed. Only thing was, I noticed the old man didn't laugh. He stated at the fire a while and then knocked out his pipe and said it was getting time for him to be turning in.

We didn't talk much more after that. When the circle broke up I wandered outside the camp to water the weeds. The moon was just coming up then, about half full, and I stood there a while admiring the way it lit up the countryside. Then I thought I saw a gleam over across the river from where we first spotted the soldiers. I watched for a long time and it never come back, so I figured it must be a firefly between here and there. Or maybe it was the moon reflecting off something or just my eyes playing tricks on me. That happens a lot out in the desert.

I seen Charlie was bedded down close to the old man and I heard them whispering. When they seen me they stopped and I wondered what was so secret, but I was too tired to ask. I told them good night and was asleep five seconds after I lay down.

The soldiers headed east early the next morning and we headed on up the river. We was heading further into the canyon and the walls was getting steeper, but the lieutenant drawed a map to show us where could cross over if we didn't want to follow the water all the way through. He told us following the river could be done, but there was some tight places perfect for ambush near the water if we didn't keep our eyes open.

I noticed Charlie was quiet when we taken off upriver but by the time we made camp that night, he was teasing me again. I thought about asking what got his tail over a rope the night afore, but I figured he would tell me when he wanted me to know. Until then it weren't my worry.

I taken us a while to find a good camp that night. I could tell the old man was a little spooked by the riders we seen watching the troops, and he cautioned me and Charlie to keep a good eye out on our tail. He said not to be obvious doing it and a couple of times I thought I might of spotted something. Yet, I wasn't for sure and when I mentioned it to McAdams, he just nodded and rode on.

We filled our canteens in the river and made camp that night on a protected slope overlooking the river. We was able to get to it without crossing open ground or riding against the skyline and it had a good view of the river valley a good way up and down. It weren't too level a spot, but I've slept on worse and after a cold supper we taken turns keeping watch all night long.

The old man taken the last watch and when he woke me and Charlie, the sky was just turning light. We waited until it was just light enough to keep from stepping on a snake, and Mac told us to lead our horses rather than ride. This meant slower going but it was quieter and made it a lot harder for a bushwhacker to spot us. As it turned out, being on foot saved my life.

We didn't cut no fresh tracks so we stuck close to the water and passed through two perfect spots for ambush afore we decided to take the lieutenant's advice and leave the canyon. Mac didn't talk much, which told me he was worried, and I know I felt like we was being watched. Yet nothing happened until we was getting close to the top of the cap rock.

I don't know why they waited until then and I don't guess I ever will. It weren't the best place to jump us, though it weren't that bad, neither. When I asked the old man about it, he said it was just the way they was, too damned lazy and impatient to even do a good job of bush whacking. Easy money robbing banks and wagon trains made them careless.

I guess he was right. When they finally cut loose, the fool who fired first was in way too big a hurry to take his second shot. So the bullet buzzed by my ear and I hit the dirt with my Colt's up and cocked. When I saw the flash of the second gun, I fired a couple of foot behind it and rolled to my right.

Sure enough, I saw another flash from a different place and a bullet dug a rut where I had just been. I heard Mac's Hawken bark off to my left, but I seen he missed. Yet I also seen a rifle laying in the open where I'd fired and I figured I must of at least winged my man. I cocked my pistol watching for him to reach out to get it.

Then it got real quiet for a while. I looked to my left but couldn't see Mac or Charlie, so I started circling to my right, aiming to get above the first shooter where I could get a clear shot. I found a narrow draw and moved up it, quiet as an Indian. When I found a place I could look out without being seen, I could see the man I shot laying still just behind his rifle. There wasn't nothing I could see of the other man and I decided to move on up the draw.

Just as I was about to move I heard somebody holler off to the right of the man I shot, and it sounded like somebody in pain. Then it got real quiet again, and I slipped on up the draw. It weren't long afore I got to the top and when I peeked over, I saw something move to the left. I ducked right quick and heard the crack of a slug go over my head just an instant afore I heard the deep boom of a Hawken.

I couldn't tell who it was firing, so I eased back down the draw. When I did I almost blasted Charlie coming up the way I had. I give him a quail call and he had his bow up and aimed afore he seen it was me. I ducked and heard the arrow hiss over my back, taking my hat with it. "Damn it, it's me, Charlie," I hissed.

Charlie dropped down beside me, looking like he was about to cry. "It's all right," I whispered. "You didn't know it was me." He nodded and damned if his chin didn't quiver. I was about to say something sharp, but then I remembered he was just a kid. "It's all right," I whispered. "You seen Mac?"

Charlie nodded and pointed over the ridge. "That was him who shot at you," he told me.

"How about the second shooter?" I asked. "You spotted him?"

"He's dead," Charlie told me grimly. "I got him." He held up his bow. I saw blood smeared on Charlie's hand and shirt.

"You hurt?" I whispered. Charlie shook his head and reached down for something at his belt. When he held it up I could see it was a bloody blonde scalp. "Damn, Charlie!" I said. "We're white folks. We don't do stuff like that."

"I recognized him, Jack," Charlie told me. Even at a whisper, his voice was real strange. "He was one of the riders that killed my folks."

"I would of cut off his nose and ears, too!" I declared. "I better let the old man know we're up here."

Charlie nodded and I give a bob-white quail call. There ain't many of those on the high plains and I figured Mac would know it was me if it was him down below. The answer come over to the right and a little above us and a minute later the old man appeared. "I don't think there were more than two of them," he whispered. "I only found two ponies and a pack animal. Either of you hear anyone riding off?"

We both shook our heads and the old man looked at me. "I shot high, Jack," he told me. "You weren't in any danger from me. I didn't know it was you for sure."

I grinned and tried to make a joke, my tongue got tangled. Then the damnedest thing happened. My belly knotted up and I started to dry heave. It was good we hadn't eat yet or Mac and Charlie would of got sprayed.

We made our way down to where the man I shot lay. He hadn't moved that I could see but we slipped up real careful until we got close. Then it was pretty clear why he wasn't moving. My slug caught him just where his jaw hinged and pretty well taken the top of his head off. Right below him, where it fell and slid downhill when he dropped it, was a Hawken rifle like the old man's.

Mac turned the body over with his foot. "Recognize him?" he asked. Charlie looked a little green around the gills but he nodded. "That was a good shot," Mac remarked, but the way he said it I known he was ribbing me.

"That was a damned lucky shot," I corrected him. "I was trying to keep his head down."

McAdams chuckled. "That's one way of doing it, Jack. You want this one, too?" He was speaking to Charlie and pointed to what was left of the man's head.

Charlie shook his head. "He was Jack's kill." Then he taken the bloody scalp from his belt and throwed it on the body and turned away. "Rot in hell," he said.

The old man nodded and picked up the Hawken. He handed it to me. "Spoils of war," he said. Then he chuckled. "Maybe your luck at shooting will improve with this."

Once we collected the weapons and horses, we headed on our way. One thing we found on one of the bodies was a wanted poster from Missouri. None of us had ever heard the name on it, but the rough drawing looked like the man I shot.

What I found interesting was the hundred dollar reward for bank robbery and Mac agreed. "We need to keep alert," he cautioned us. "I don't know why these two are riding separate from the rest, but I figure they're expected back. Someone may come looking."

Surprise

We rode hard that day, topping out of the canyon on the north side of the river and riding north a couple of miles afore turning back west. I guess we must of covered twenty-five miles afore we stopped for the night. What was strange to me was how quickly the canyons disappeared behind us. I mentioned it to Mac and he nodded. "Wouldn't do to come riding through here on a dark night, now would it?" he chuckled.

We traveled across the cap rock for quite a few days, heading back to the river bottom when we needed water and camping on the slopes. We kept a close eye on our back trail and did what cooking we did during the middle of the day, building our fire in low places and using dry buffalo chips for fuel to keep from sending up smoke. At one point we spotted riders along the river, but it was too far away to tell who they was. Even the old man's spyglass wasn't strong enough to see if they was Indian or white men.

"It's getting downright crowded out here," the old man said. He sounded as sore as a sow with a toothache. "I think we may need to lay up somewhere for a few days and let them clear out."

That sounded good to me and Charlie. We wasn't riding hard by then but we'd been in the saddle a long time without a break and our horses could use a rest, too. So we headed back to the river and found us a good spot by a feeder stream half a mile from the river. There was a couple of better spots not far from where we camped, but it was clear they was used quite a bit and we passed them up. Where we made camp it looked like we was the first ones to ever stay there.

One thing I liked about the place was the deep pool fed by the spring. It was a warm afternoon the next day after we stopped and I decided it was time to have me a bath. McAdams had headed out early that morning to try his luck at fishing and Charlie was off messing around with the dog. So I headed for the pool.

When I got to the pool I seen Charlie and the dog had beat me there. Charlie was out in the middle of the pool up to his shoulders in the water and I decided to play a prank on him. So I snuck up and taken his clothes, tying knots in the legs of his pants and the arms of his shirt.

The pup spotted me, of course, and growled. Charlie stood up and whirled around. He must have been sitting on the bottom of the pool because when he stood up I saw the sweetest little set of tits I ever seen. I could also see Charlie didn't have no tallywhacker.

"Gawd!" I said. I was so stunned I didn't have no other words. I never seen a woman so beautiful. I just stood there gawking.

"What are you staring at?" Charlie snorted. "You never seen a pair of these afore?"

I dragged my eyes up to her face. Damned if she wasn't smiling. "You ain't a man!" was all I could manage.

"I never claimed to be," Charlie laughed. "Question is, what are you going to do about it?"

I still couldn't say nothing and Charlie laughed again. "Well, are you going to stand there staring or are you going to come in the water?" She turned around and bent over to wash some mud off her leg and I caught sight of the gates of heaven.

"You're just a kid!" I stammered. Even as I said it I knowed it was exactly the wrong thing. Thing is, I was dumbfounded. Charlie was a good a partner on the trail as any man I know.

"And you're as dumb as a red eared jackass!" She declared, stomping out of the pool and snatching up her clothes. I could hear her cussing me like a mule skinner as she stalked back to the camp. The pup looked at me mournful and trotted after her.

I decided it might be a good time to see how Mac was doing at the river. I headed back to camp to let Charlie know where I was going, but when I told her, she wouldn't say nothing. She wouldn't even look at me, but it was hard to keep my eyes off her. She was sitting there with her pants and boots on, trying to worry the knot out of one of her shirt arms. Her rising beauties was swinging free.

I offered to untie the knot for her but she snorted. "Don't need your damned help," she told me.

Charlie still wouldn't look at me but I saw tears in her eyes. "Look," I told her. "I didn't know. I didn't mean no offence."

"No, you'd just rather spend time with sporting ladies," she snapped back. "I ain't good enough for you."

Well, I guess what I should of done was grab her and hold her until she stopped kicking. Life would have been a hell of a lot simpler over the next weeks if I done it. What I done was try to explain, but the more I said, the deeper I was in horse apples. So I finally throwed up my hands and headed for the river.

Well, the old man must of seen right off I was agitated. More than likely he known why, too, but he didn't say nothing. He just waved when I got there and held up a string of fish. "We'll have good eating tonight," he whispered.

Just at that moment his line went taut and he pulled in one of the nicest trout I ever seen. "Many more like that and we can smoke them for the trail," he said. "So what's eating your packing, Jack?"

"Charlie ain't a man!" I told him.

"I wondered how long it would take you to figure that one," he chuckled. "How'd you find out, if you don't mind my asking."

I told him what happened and when I was done, he shook his head. "Jackie, Jackie!" he said sadly. "For a fellow who knows so much about the wilds, you don't know the first thing about women, do you? You insulted the poor girl in the worst way a man can insult a woman. She offered you herself and you didn't take her."

"She's just a kid!" I protested.

"She's only a couple of years younger than you," he told me. "I know women who've had four children by her age, none of them twins. She's plenty old enough to know her mind." He shook his head sadly. "She's had her heart set on you since the day we found her," he added.

"She's acting like a hussy!" I protested. I don't know where in the world I got that word. I don't recall hearing my mother or pa ever use it. The minute I said it, I knowed it was the wrong thing to say.

McAdams blinked. When he spoke I could see he was fighting mad. "Don't you ever use that word about Charlie!" he hissed. "You might consider yourself damned lucky she ain't ashamed of what the good Lord gave her. For a man who spends his time with sporting ladies you seem damned ready to condemn."

"That's sporting ladies!" I protested. "That's the way they're supposed to act."

"A married woman isn't?" he asked. "What business is it of yours how she acts with her husband?"

"We ain't married!" I told him.

"No, and Charlie's damned lucky if that's the way you think. Do you think she's like that with other men?"

"I don't know," I augerd. "I never seen her around other men."

"I suppose those soldiers weren't men?" Mac asked me. "Did you see her batting her eyes at any of them?"

I had to admit I hadn't. The fact is, Charlie was damned quiet around the soldiers, even the lieutenant that tried to be friendly with her. Of course, he must have thought she was a man. Then I remembered what one of the men said about Charlie, about putting a skirt on him and dancing all night. I also remembered that night under the poncho in the rain.

"Shit!" I said. "Why didn't you tell me?"

The old man rolled his eyes toward the heavens. "It was obvious, Jack! I kept thinking you'd catch on any minute. You have no idea how patient that poor girl has been."

"What do I do now?" I asked. "I just lost my best friend. Next to you, of course."

McAdams laughed. "I'm flattered, Jack, but I'm a little old for you. Just for the record, I ain't a woman, either." He was stroking his scraggly white whiskers. "Didn't you ever notice Charlie never had to shave and never grew a beard?"

I shook my head. I felt like I'd been kicked in the gut by a mule. "Well, don't worry, lad. The fairer sex is very forgiving of us men. If they weren't, the race would have died out a long time ago."

"What do I do?" I asked.

"Don't try to fix it today. Give Charlie some time to get over her disappointment. Go about your business, but be nice to her, no matter how snippy she gets. Then in a couple of days, surprise her by doing something special. Flowers work wonders with women."

I looked around. The only flowers I could see was withered blooms on a prickly pear and I couldn't remember anything else in the last hundred miles. "Got any other ideas?" I asked.

"You have a point," the old man nodded. "Just give it some thought and you'll come up with something." Then he frowned. "I don't like playing matchmaker, but you might want to run what you think of by me first. You don't want to make the hole you're in deeper."

That sounded like good advice to me, though the next few days was a trial. Charlie wouldn't talk to me and always put McAdams between me and her when we sat around the fire. It was on the tip of my tongue to say something a dozen times a day, but I figured I was already in pretty deep and the fact is, I missed the easy way me and Charlie fooled around. The couple of times she caught me looking her way, Charlie glared at me and bunched her fist, and once when she did it, I saw the old man grinning behind her.

"Keep the faith, lad," he advised me once when we was alone. "She really likes you."

"She has a damned strange way of showing it!" I belly-ached.

Things went on like that for a couple of weeks. Then one night after riding all day in a miserable cold rain and eating our supper cold, I had my fill. I cain't remember what Charlie said to Mac. It was something sharp aimed at me and I jumped to my feet and flang my plate down. "Damn it, woman!" I roared, shoving my face right in hers. "If you cain't keep a civil tongue in you head, don't say nothing at all!"

When I said this, Charlie busted into tears and ran out of camp. I started to go after her, but McAdams stopped me. "Leave her be, lad. She's fine. Just sit down and have some more hard tack. Take yourself a deep breath."

"I really messed up this time, didn't I?" I asked a while later after I cooled off. Charlie had come back to camp and the old man and I was off watering the prairie.

"Not at all, lad. Matter of fact, I think Charlie's happier than she has been in days. A woman likes a man with backbone. Let them walk all over you and you'll lose their respect." Even in the dim starlight I could see his grin. "That was the first time you publicly addressed Charlie as a woman. She knows you don't think of her as just a kid any more."

"Women are damned strange," I muttered.

"What's funny is they say the very same thing about us," Mac chuckled. "Makes life interesting."

Like always, the old man was right. The sun come out with the dawn and when I wished Charlie a good morning, she smiled back. Then later in the day she started teasing me again and things was back to normal. Well, almost to normal. There was a difference in the way we looked at each other and the way we talked, and there was a little distance that never had been there afore. It weren't bad. It was just there.

The old man seemed to leave us two alone a lot more after that, making himself scarce and taking the dog with him. It taken me a while to figure this out, and when I did, I mentioned it to Charlie.

Charlie nodded and said she'd noticed that, too, and there didn't seem to be nothing else to say for a while. Then I patted her on the hand and she looked me in the eye. "There's no going back," I told her. "I just want you to know if that happens again, I'm coming in the water."

Charlie smiled, mocking me. "What makes you think it might happen again, Jackie," she asked and there was pure devilment in her eyes.

"Well, a man can always hope, cain't he?" I answered.

"There's no way I can stop that," she admitted, and there was the same smile on her face I'd seen at the pool.

Well, I wasn't about to let the moment pass again, so I got up and set down on the log next to her. My intent was to plant a good one on her but as I sat down, I felt something bite my ankle.

I jumped up and looked down at the biggest damned snake I ever seen. I grabbed Charlie by the arm and flang her plumb across the clearing, putting myself between her and the snake, and I whipped out my knife. The snake taken the chance to head for other regions and I grabbed a dry branch and started to go after it. Damned if the branch didn't turn out to be another snake and I hollered and flung it as far as I could.

Then I heard Charlie laughing and I turned around and seen her all bent over. What made matters worse is that the old man showed up about this time and the pup run after the snake I just flang. "Stop him," I hollered. "I just flang a rattler that way!"

"Looked more like a prairie racer to me," McAdams said and just then the pup come running back with a dead snake in his mouth. When she seen it was a racer, Charlie started laughing even harder and I could see the old man was trying to keep a straight face, too. "Seems like you broke up a promising courtship, Jack," he said, then started chuckling. "It's their mating season."

"The damned thing bit me," I said, pulling up my pant leg. Sure enough, there wasn't no teeth marks, only a red place where I was pinched when the racer struck me.

Then Charlie starts trying to tell McAdams what happened and acting it out. She gets so tickled I start laughing. Pretty soon, we're all at it and when we're done, the old man says, "I'm glad things are back to normal again. Makes camp a lot more pleasant."

When he says this Charlie gives me a look telling me there will be another time. McAdams sees the look, too, but he just smiles and gets a far away look in his eyes. It's a look I seen afore and I know he's thinking about another time and another young woman and the young man who loved her.

We moved out the next morning afore first light but that night Charlie made her bed between me and Keenan. She said there was a lumpy spot under where she slept on his other side, but I couldn't see it and the old man wasn't fooled, neither. He looked at me and smiled.

Then late that night when I was up admiring the moonlight on the prairie, I heard something behind me. It was Charlie and the pup and she didn't say nothing. She just come and stood next to me and put her arms around me. When I was just about to put my head down to kiss her, I seen something. She must have felt my body go tight because she looked, too. "Riders!" she whispered.

"Go tell Keenan," I told her. "I counted seven but there may be more. Looks like they're headed for that camp by the second bend in the river."

A minute later the old man was there with his spyglass. "They went into the grove there," I told him, pointing.

Mac looked through his glass but there wasn't nothing to see. It was a full moon that night and the light was good, and I could see he was troubled. "We better move out," he said. "We still got three hours of darkness."

"You think it's Indians?" I asked.

"Could be," He answered. "If it is, it's a raiding party, coming or going. And if it's white men, they're up to no good."

"Look there!" I said and pointed. I'd seen a flash of light coming from the first camp, the one closest to us. It was just a half mile away and there was four or five other flashes, looking like fireflies in the shadows. A few seconds later we heard the sound of shots.

"We better get going," Keenan said and headed back to camp.

It was good we packed up the night afore because we was moving out ten minutes later. The old man sent me and Charlie ahead, showing me the line to follow, and he came after, brushing out traces of our passing. Once we was a couple of miles gone, he taken the lead again, following the contours of the land and keeping to the low places, and we didn't stop to rest until the moon went down four hours later.

"Get some rest," he told me and Charlie. "We'll move out again when we can see the way. I'll keep watch."

That sounded good to me. I was dead beat, mostly from keeping my eyes peeled for snakes. I found a soft spot in a tall stand of grass and stomped around afore I stretched out. I was surprised when Charlie laid down beside me. "Good night, Jack," she whispered when she snuggled her way into my arms. Without a thought, I kissed her on the forehead but she was out like a light.

Turned out the place we stopped was on high ground not far from a place we could hole up for the day. From there we could see miles and miles back the way we come, and I thought I could see the sun reflecting off the river. I said something about it to the old man and he nodded.

I could tell the old man was worried. He wouldn't let us build a fire and he kept watch all day on the rolling plains behind us. He had me watching to the west and north and Charlie keeping an eye on the land in between. Nor would he tell us much of what was on his mind. "Just be sure no one slips up on us from that direction," he told me. "If you see anything, let me know right away, but keep quiet. There may be trouble coming from that way and I want to avoid it if we can."

It was about half way through the afternoon and I was getting tired of watching empty tan prairie when he give me a bird whistle. I slipped over and joined him where he sat. I could see Charlie laying in the grass on the other side of Mac looking through the spyglass. I shaded my eyes and looked in the direction the glass was pointing.

At first I couldn't see nothing. The glare was bad and the plains was sending up heat waves. Then suddenly, like they was a quarter mile away, I seen a group of riders on the horizon. I grabbed for my rifle but the old man stopped me. "Stay right still," young 'un, he said. "It's a mirage. Those riders are miles away."

Well, I'd seen mirages afore, but nothing like that. "Can they see us?" I asked, whispering.

"I think not, but you never know. We need to keep still in case they can."

That made sense. There's nothing that catches a predator's eye like movement. Unlike deer or rabbits or other prey that has to be on the lookout all around, a predator's eyes both point forward. I don't know a single exception. This tells me human beings are predators, no matter what the gentle folk say. We wasn't worried about bears or wolves or even mountain lions or grizzlies. Those critters can give a man a lot of trouble if they're hungry or mad enough, but mostly they try to keep as much distance between them and us as they can. What we was worried about was hostile folks, and white men way more than Indians.

"I see seven riders," Charlie told us. "I can't see their faces but three of them look like men that killed my folks."

The old man cogitated this a spell. Then he sighed. "I guess we need to go back when they've cleared out. No telling what they did at the grove." He give me a thoughtful look. "You're thinking we shouldn't go back, Jack?"

"No," I said. "Not really. It ain't our business but somebody may need help. I was just thinking of the last time we crossed trail with those bastids. I just hope we find somebody still alive."

"Not likely," the old man said softly. Charlie nodded.

"You sure you want to go with us?" I asked Charlie. "It won't be anything but ugly."

"I can handle ugly as good as you can!" Charlie hissed back.

I looked at the old man but he rolled his eyes, and then shook his head, so I kept quiet. What I was trying to do was spare Charlie's feelings, it being so soon since her folks died and all. From what I would see, what I done was step right in the shit hole again, and I wished Charlie was still a man so I could learn her some manners. "I'm sure you can," I whispered back. "Suit yourself." What I was smart enough to keep from adding was that she would, anyways.

The old man's face was turned toward me, so Charlie couldn't see his grin. What it told me is I must of done the right thing. Still, I felt downright proddy. "I'm going to check the other slope," I said and slipped away on my belly until the plains was out of sight.

Turns out, we hadn't come that far the night afore. Since it was so late in the day we decided to head back at first light and I turned in early.

Mac asked Charlie to take the first watch and while we was off watering the prairie he spoke to me in a low voice. "Don't take it personally, Jack. Charlie's going through a pretty rough patch right now. She isn't upset with you. This just reminds her of what happened to her people."

"I know that," I whispered back. "I was just trying to help."

"Might be more wise to help when folks ask for it." Mac grinned and I could see his teeth gleaming white in the twilight. "Charlie is still trying to prove herself to us. To herself, too."

"She done that at the ambush," I reminded him.

"Yeah, but did you tell her so?" McAdams asked. I had to admit I didn't. "Young folks like her need to be told, and it needs to be true." he added. "You appreciate what I'm saying, don't you?"

Well, he had me dead to rights. When I give it some thought I seen he'd done just that with me all along. Then I got to wondering what else he was doing that I wasn't aware about. So I started watching him more close after that, puzzling through what I seen him do. Turns out, there was a lot more. My first teacher may have been my daddy, but McAdams taken up where Daddy left off and he done it without my realizing. Smart old coot, he was.

Sure enough, when Mac taken the second watch, Charlie found me and snuggled up close. I didn't know how the ground lay, so I played 'possum, acting sleepier than I was, even though what I really wanted was to grab her. Charlie didn't seem to mind but I felt her fighting a giggle, and when I asked her about it the next day she smiled and told me I needed some looser pants.

"I was trying to be a gentleman," I told her. She didn't bother to answer, just snorted and rode off with a grin.

CHAPTER EIGHT

Dust to Dust

We made good time that next morning and when we got to the grove where we seen shots two nights afore, we circled our way in. This time McAdams circled in the other direction. I guessed this was to not make a habit, and when I asked later, he said I was right. Habit can be a good thing if you think things through, but it can also get you killed if you don't.

What we found there surprised us. We was thinking it would be another small party like Charlie's folks, but it weren't. What we found was eight dead soldiers and one dead officer. All of them was in Mexican Army uniforms. Their bodies was robbed and their guns was taken, but there was a leather bound journal near the officer that looked like it was tossed aside when he was plundered. I looked at it but couldn't make heads nor tails of what it said, but Mac told us it was in Spanish.

There wasn't much we could do for the soldiers. They was too many of them for the three of us to bury, so we left them lay. "Not much else we can do," McAdams told us. "I suppose we could burn the bodies but that's going to send up a lot of smoke. We need to find the tenth man, too. He may still be alive. Or they may have taken him with them."

"What tenth man?" I asked.

Mac held up the leather bound book. "From what I can tell, and my Spanish is pretty rusty, these soldiers were escorting a priest to somewhere north of Santa Fe. I don't know why they were this far east but I only read the last few pages. The answer may be earlier in the journal."

"Why would the killers take the priest with them?" I asked. "That don't make no sense."

"That's a very good question," the old man answered. "The padre must have some value to them. I doubt it was for the sacraments."

"What's that?" Charlie asked and I was glad she did. I wondered the same thing.

The old man thought a minute. "There are some church things only a priest can do, like marrying people," he told us. "Those are sacraments."

"You think one of them wanted to get married?" I asked.

"More likely he wanted absolution," McAdams answered. That led to a lot more questions and finally the old man threw up his hands. "Enough!" he said. "I'll try to explain it after supper tonight but right now we need to find the padre."

We spent a couple of hours looking all around the clearing on every side but we didn't find hide nor hair of the priest. Nor did we find any trail leading away from the grove except the tracks the raiders left. One thing we did find was a Bible, tossed aside like the journal, but it was in Latin, or so the old man said. When I tried to puzzle out the words it sounded like babbling to me. Then, when Mac taken the Good Book and tried to learn me how to pronounce the words right, Charlie caught a fit laughing. I could see the old man trying to hold it in, but then he busted out laughing too and so did I. It weren't that funny, but there we was, howling like fools.

This came to mind later and it bothered me. So I asked the old man about it. "I know, Johnny," he said, dead serious. "It may sound strange to laugh at the site of a massacre, but sometimes it's laugh or cry and after what we saw, we needed a little relief. I, for one, think we did better to laugh."

That made sense to me but McAdams wasn't through just yet. "I've seen a lot of good men laugh at funerals," he told me. "When it's time to be serious, they are, but afterwards life goes on and a good laugh is part of life. It's a way of saying we're damned glad to be alive."

That would have done it for me but I saw a gleam in Mac's eye and I known even more was on the way. "Fact is, lad, I had occasion to attend a good Irish wake once, out in the hinterlands of County Mayo. Damned if after the funeral dinner couples started slipping out the door, and I asked the lady next to me what was going on. She was a widow herself and offered to show me. When I followed her through he hedge, damned if she didn't haul me down and have her way with me, right there on the ground in front of God and the full moon."

I saw Charlie coming up behind Mac and tried to signal him to let it rest, but he had a full head of steam going and rolled right on down the track. "Then after she had her way with me, the good widow explained this is customary in back country. As she put it to me, it was their way of telling Death to go get fucked! Now isn't that something, Johnnie?"

About then Charlie giggled and the old man whirled around. As far as I can recall, that was the only time I ever seen him rebarrassed in all the time we rode together. "God in heaven, woman," he roared. "Don't go slipping up on a man like that! You could get yourself shot!"

This only made Charlie laugh all the harder, and then it got me to going, too. McAdams was in such a state he just stalked off and kept to himself the whole afternoon. Yet when he sat down at the campfire that night, he looked at us and started shaking. Then he chuckled, and that set me and Charlie off again, too.

That was later on. That afternoon we sobered up quick enough and rode down to the second camp, the one where the raiders stayed, to have a look around. There wasn't nothing there we could find and the light was failing, so we rode back to where we camped when we seen the attack. When we got there McAdams taken a good look around but it didn't look like no one had been there since we left.

The next morning we chewed over what to do. The thing wasn't none of our business, plain as plain could be, and I said as much. But Mac thought that somebody official needed to know what taken place and Charlie agreed with him. I wondered at the time if she really was of the same mind or if she was doing so to goad me. I think the old man may have thought so, too, but, of course, he wasn't about to say a damned thing.

"I don't like it," I told them. "Seems like we'd be better off just riding on and minding our own business."

"They were the same men who killed my family," Charlie said. "I think that makes it our business. At least, it makes it mine," she added. She give me a hard look that said, "if you aren't of a mind to keep your promise." McAdams kept quiet but I known he remembered what I said the day we found Charlie.

"Cain't we just pass the word along?" I asked. "Seems like if we tell them about it, they'll think we did it. Especially since we have the padre's Bible and the captain's diary."

"There's a lot of truth in what you say, Johnny," Mac sighed. "Yet, even if they don't arrest us for the attack, there's a good chance they will arrest us for being American spies. I am not in any way suggesting we ride into Santa Fe with this. That would be more than foolish."

"What are you suggesting, then?" I asked him. To tell the truth, I was not opposed to going after the bastids. There was nothing I'd like better than seeing them in my sights, but I didn't want to go after them with Charlie with us. I couldn't see no way of leaving her behind, neither, and I known if I even mentioned what was in my mind, she'd pitch a walleyed hissy.

"I think we need to follow along for a while until we have a good idea where they're headed. Then we need to head for Taos and talk to the priest there. After all, it's one of his people they have and I'm sure he will get word to the officials in Santa Fe." He shrugged and I nodded. It made sense that way.

"There is the matter of the priest, too," McAdams added. "If he's still alive we may be able to help him."

"How?" I asked. "They have us outgunned two to one."

"Yes, but with the element of surprise, we can even those odds in our favor," Mac said. "As we saw at the ambush, they've grown careless. They aren't expecting an attack, especially by a smaller number. With the bows we can take out half of them afore they're aware they're being attacked."

It was clear to me he was including Charlie in his plans and I ain't liked this a bit. Since discovering she was a woman, things had changed in my mind. The idea of me getting killed didn't bother me near so much as the idea of her catching it or even getting hurt.

Of course, Mac known what was going on with me. He known I had no leg to stand on, neither. When it came to an all out fight, I'd choose to have Charlie at my side over any man excepting Mac. As the old man would say, Charlie had pretty well proved she had plenty of sand in her craw.

I known Charlie known what I was thinking, too, but unlike the old man, she had no qualms about voicing her mind. Yet she surprised me by letting it pass, though the look in her eye told me I better not press the issue if I didn't want to get dragged over the coals.

"All right," I said. "We'd better get riding."

We watered the horses good and headed back toward the river, where we cut the trail. The gang wasn't trying to hide it's tracks but we lost them two days later when we ran into a line of rain storms that soaked the prairie. By then it was clear they was staying close to the river and McAdams decided it might be good to ride ahead and pick up their trail farther west.

Since we was at a bend where the river bed turned southwest right them, we set a bee line for the setting sun. McAdams figured this would save us a good twenty to twenty-five miles of riding afore we reached the town of Sabinosa, which lies maybe a hundred miles southwest of Taos.

As it turned out, we'd only gone a half day's ride from there when we saw the carrion birds circling south of us. When Charlie spotted them and pointed, I felt my gut twist. Like the two times afore, there was no knowing what we might find.

This time we lucked out. There wasn't no massacre. What we found when we got near the river was only the priest, so bad hurt he was more dead than alive. Somehow he had managed to crawl a quarter mile from where they left him until he found the shade of a big, bushy mesquite. This had kept him from being baked alive and it kept the birds away, though when we rode up a couple of smaller varmints ran off. We could see where one of them had started chewing on the padre's toes but I don't think he could feel them by then. He was that bad off.

Yet the worst part come when we taken the priest's robe off to clean the wounds we could see bleeding through. It was pretty clear the man had been beaten and tortured. Most of the bruises was to his face and belly, but it was the burns to his chest and privates that got to me. It looked like someone had gone after him with a burning branch.

When I looked at Charlie, her face was white as snow, but she never flinched. Using water from the canteen, she bathed the burns as best she could while the old man mixed up something from his saddle bag and began to rub it into the cuts and scrapes. When he did, the padre moaned at first but seemed to rest better, and when McAdams was done with the cuts, he began to work on the burns.

I was left standing with nothing to do, so I told them I was going to keep an eye out if they didn't need me. Mac just nodded his head and grunted and I looked around for a good place to keep watch while Mac and Charlie worked on the padre. There was nothing stirring nowhere that I could see, except for the birds. Even they begun to fly away once we got there and after a while it was like nothing had ever happened. All could be seen was endless rolling prairie, and there wasn't even a cloud in the sky.

I don't know how long I kept watch. It seemed like a long time afore I heard a bird call and looked back to see Mac waving me to come down. When I got there he told me, "Johnny, we're need to move the padre. Could you go and scout us out a camp site not far from the river?"

As it turns out, we wasn't too far from a good enough place. It was small clump of new growth brush by the water, shaded by a single small cottonwood. Judging from the burnt stumps scattered around in the brush, it was once a grove but destroyed by fire, and it looked like no one had camped there for a long while. The grass was tall and bright green and there was brush to hide the horses and shade them from the sun.

When I got back, Mac was surprised to see me so soon. He had seen the brush when we was circling in but thought it too small a clump for a camp. What made it especially good to my mind was it lay at the end of a dry draw and was pretty well hidden from the prairie. It was isolated from anything else by forty yards of flat land, so it would be simple to defend, too.

Mac wanted to put the padre on a horse to move him, but I told him it weren't that far and I could carry him there. When Mac lifted him onto my back, I was surprised how light the padre was. There wasn't much to the man but skin and bones, and it felt like damned little of those. He couldn't have been much more than five foot tall, if that, and I've seen twelve year old boys bigger than that.

Once we got the padre to the campsite, Charlie stamped down a wide bed of grass and laid out a blanket across it. I noticed it was the blanket we slept under, but the padre needed it worse than us. I headed out and gathered some dry deadfall and when I got back, Mac got some water boiling and made up some jerky broth for the priest to eat.

I noticed he tossed some other stuff into the broth and asked him what it was. "I am not sure what the proper name is, lad, but the Indians around these parts call it healing weed. I'll show you what it looks like the next time I see some, but be careful. Too much is worse than none at all. It can kill a man."

When we taken the broth to the padre, we found him awake and Charlie feeding him sips of water. "Gracias," he whispered, thanking us.

"I speak no good English."

"Just rest a while, father," McAdams told him. I didn't know what he said until he told me later. He was speaking Spanish as well as he spoke English. "We will talk later." He handed the brew to Charlie. "Just give him small sips, but try to get as much of it down him as you can. Johnnie and I are going to look around."

The first thing McAdams had me do was to cut branches to wipe out our tracks. "Cut them low, Johnnie," he reminded me. "Hide your work from prying eyes." Then he smiled. "I know, lad, and I mean no offence. I'm telling you what you already know."

"You must be worried," I answered.

McAdams nodded. "This is a good place you found, Johnny, and we can defend it if we have to. I would rather not if we can avoid it. With the padre down we don't have the choice to retreat or make a run for it."

I thought about that later and the old man was dead on, as usual. Having stuck our nose into this business, the padre was now our problem and we had to see it through as far as we said we would. Otherwise, we wouldn't be no better than the men in the gang we was following.

Somehow, our luck held. Part of it was that there was better looking camping spots not too far in either direction, and part of it was a light rain that finished up the work we done in covering our tracks. One morning while we was there we watched a hunting party of six Indians ride by, headed for the camp east of us. It was pure luck we saw them first. One moment there wasn't nothing but empty prairie, and the next, there they was, big as sin and twice as ugly. Charlie was laying there with me, keeping watch in the other direction and she told me later she known something was wrong when I tensed up. She slipped away to warn Mac and the padre, who was having a gabfest in Spanish.

We had a cold supper that night. The smell of wood smoke is as dead a giveaway as heavy smoke rising against a blue sky and we didn't want to encourage any early morning callers. We kept watch that night like we always did, only breaking it up into two hour stretches to keep us more alert. The way it worked out, Charlie and me didn't get to spend more than a few minutes together until almost dawn, when I finally got to the bedroll. Yet she was out like a light and it's just as well. Somehow it didn't feel quite right to do nothing with the padre in camp.

That was our fourth day in the camp by the river. The next day the padre was doing a lot better, but he was still too weak to ride. I taken the morning watch and Charlie come with me, mostly to keep me company. The old man was asleep and the padre was reading his Bible and saying his prayers, so there wasn't much else for her to do. I guess the padre's prayers must have worked, too, because we saw the Indians headed west about mid morning. They didn't seem to be in much of a hurry.

Once they was out of sight, we got to talking about what the padre told McAdams a couple of days afore. The old man said the padre was still a little unclear in his head but he said that him and the soldiers was bringing a map of some kind to the governor in Santa Fe. The map was discovered hidden away in a monastery down near San Antonio, and they wanted to keep it from falling into the hands of Sam Houston and his Texans. The soldiers had cached their guns and uniforms and snuck into the city dressed like monks. With the priest leading them, it weren't that hard and they got away without a bit of trouble.

What made the map so important was it was supposed to show the way to a cave in the north where there was a good bit of gold. It belonged to the monks of a monastery who mined it to support their work converting the Indians. What this support boiled down to was paying off the captain of the garrison to make sure the Indians the monks was trying to convert wasn't run off or killed. It also went for buying the supplies they couldn't make themselves from the governor's quartermaster at outrageous prices.

The abbot realized that a time might come when the governor or the captain would get more greedy, so the gold was kept hidden in a cave in the mountains. Only the abbot and one brother known exactly where this was, but the abbot was wise enough to make a map in case something happened to both of them.

Sure enough, it weren't but a year or two later that the captain rode up to the monastery with twenty soldiers and demanded the gold. The abbot refused and things got nasty. Knowing he would never break the abbot, the captain started torturing the monks one by one, thinking the abbot might tell to save his monks.

It's hard to believe what happened next because the very first monk to be tortured was the one who known where the gold was hidden. He begged the abbot not to tell, and to make sure he didn't break under torture himself, he bit his tongue off and bled to death. So did every other monk who was tortured that day.

At some point, the abbot stood up and called to the captain to stop the torture. Yet when the captain come close to learn where the gold was, what he got, instead, was a curse from the abbot. This made the captain so mad he ran the abbot through with his sword, killing him on the spot. This, of course, ended any hope of him ever getting the gold.

Now when I say a curse was placed on the captain, I ain't talking about a good dressing down in muleskinner talk. McAdams says he doubts the abbot even raised his voice. What he did was to place the solemn curse of a bishop on the captain and his troops, and on the gold itself. The curse was that anyone who holds the gold unrightfully will find himself in a world of trouble, and will suffer in body, mind and spirit until he restores it to the Church.

When McAdams told us this, it felt like a goose walked over my grave. I could tell Charlie was struck by it, too. Then she said, "I hope they burn for eternity in the fires of hell!" It sounded more like a wounded cougar than a human voice when she said it and at that moment I would have hated to of been that captain facing her with a knife in her hand.

Of course, I got to thinking about all this later on. As best as I can tell, all this happened maybe fifty or a hundred years afore we come along. So who knows just how much of it was fact and how much was pure fancy. The question I had and still have is how all this come to be known. Supposedly the abbot and all the monks was killed, so who was left to tell the tale?

When I jumped the old man about this a week or two later, he just shook his head. "Now why would you be after worrying over all that, Johnny? The story had the ring of truth, didn't it?"

"Yeah, it did," I admitted. "On the other hand, some of your better efforts do, too."

Mac grinned. "I take it yours don't, lad?" I laughed and he went on. "Seriously, Johnny, by now it doesn't matter. What matters is blood was shed over something with no more life in it than these rocks. What matters is that blood is still being shed over it. That's the sad truth of it all. That's the curse."

That made a lot of sense, but there was another question eating at me. "The other thing I wondered is if the abbot and the monk died, how can anyone claim to know where the gold is now?"

"That one's easy," McAdams answered. "I asked the padre the same thing. He told me that the map had been sewn into the inner binding of the Bible we found, and it was taken to Santa Fe with all the monastery books after the slaughter." The old man shook his head. "Apparently the captain blamed the Indians for the slaughter and the governor accepted his explanation."

"Well, how did it get to San Antonio?"

"Someone from the order apparently took it there to be repaired and restored," Mac told me. "It wasn't illuminated, but it is very old, so old it was written by hand."

Of course, it would have made more sense to ask the padre about this, but he wasn't with us any more. We stayed in the camp a full week after we saw the Indians, waiting for him to get strong enough to ride and he seemed to get better every day. And when we packed up to head west, he was all right. Yet, two days later he grabbed his chest and fell off his horse. He was dead by the time I got to him and Mac says it was most likely a heart attack.

We didn't really know him, but things was kind of sad for a day or two after we buried the padre there on the prairie. McAdams read from the Spanish Bible and said a few prayers in the same tongue. I didn't understand a word of what he said but when he was all done, my eyes was wet and stinging.

So was Charlie's, and even though she liked the padre, I don't think her tears was for him. I think it was there on the prairie at the padre's unmarked grave that she finally buried her family. When McAdams was done, she started to sing a song so beautiful and sad it like to broke my heart. When I come to think of it a bit later, I decided that it was there on that day that I finally buried my own folks, too.

Chapter Nine

Sabinosa

It was late in the afternoon that we buried the padre but we rode on for a couple of hours afore we made camp in a dry coulee overlooking the river. We carried plenty of water for us and the horses, and from where we camped we could see a fair stretch of the river. It was running to the southwest at that point and we had passed another big stream flowing in from the north. The country was getting pretty broken along the river beds, which made traveling slow, but we was able to stay out of sight. Of course, it worked the other way, too. Anyone out there couldn't see us, but we couldn't see them, neither.

That night Keenan taken the first watch, and I was glad. Me and Charlie done most of the work burying the padre while the old man kept lookout, and I was beat. Seemed to me he used a lot of breath telling us just where he would be, near a little knob maybe a hundred yards uphill. I also wondered why he made such a point of telling us he wasn't coming back until one of us come to relieve him. Then I seen Charlie trying to hide a smile and I knowed.

We was just getting our bedrolls laid out when Charlie told me she needed to find a bush. I told her she might have to walk fifty miles for that and when I asked why she needed a canteen, she give me a strange smile. She told me she needed to clean up and said I might give that some thought, too. She claimed she seen a skunk pass out downwind of me.

Well, I didn't waste no time doing just that and I couldn't see no point putting dirty clothes on a clean body. So I was sitting there in my natural state when I seen Charlie coming back. The moon wasn't up yet, but I seen by starlight she had the same idea about hygiene. Seemed like she was even more beautiful than the day I seen her in the water, and when she sat down beside me and our skin first touched, I exploded.

That weren't exactly what I had in mind but Charlie got tickled. She was trying to keep quiet so McAdams couldn't hear it but she sounded like a hog having a sneezing fit. Didn't help that I taken to laughing and tickling her ribs, but that didn't last long. We ended up face to face with me holding her hands over her head and us looking each other eye to eye. So I kissed her, long and sweet.

Charlie kissed me right back, this time so fierce it startled me. I give back as good as I got and she did, too, and it weren't long afore we was ready to gallop. Then as I was just about to ease myself into the saddle, there come a loud hiss. It was Keenan and when I looked around he weren't twenty foot away. To give the old man his due, he had his hat in front of his face but I knowed he must of seen it all.

"Jack! We got trouble."

Charlie was out from under me in a flash, reaching for her bow and quiver and had an arrow nocked by the time I had my Colt's in hand. "Get dressed," the old man whispered. "We may have to move out soon." Then he turned and crept back to his lookout.

Charlie and me didn't waste no time joining him. When we did, I could see why the old man come and got us. Not a three hundred yards from where we laid I could see a band of riders moving our way. I counted nine of them.

"Comanche!" the old man whispered so soft I could barely hear him. "Use the bows first but wait until I tell you!" I nodded and I could feel Charlie nodding next to me. She handed me one of our bows and a quiver of arrows and I was grateful she thought of it. I'd grabbed my Hawken and the Colt's, but not my bow.

As we watched, I wondered what Comanche was doing so far northwest. We was a long way out of Comanche country and all I could figure was that this must be a raiding party. The old man told me later I was dead on and it was a bunch of young men looking to steal horses anywhere they could find them.

Right then, I thought it was kind of strange they was traveling by night and I couldn't study out why. What I was told is that Indians is superstitious and believe night is when ghosts go out walking around, but Keenan set me straight. "Well, Jack," he told me. "Some do and some don't, just like white folk. There's lots of both that don't countenance ghosts."

McAdams motioned me and Charlie out fifty foot on either side of him and told us to smear our faces with dust. I laid my Hawken to one side and set out three arrows, which is what I figured I could get off afore I needed the rifle. The Colt's was in my waistband in the back of my pants where I could reach it without getting up.

The hardest part of a fight is waiting for it to start, and it seemed to take those Comanche an hour to close the distance between us. Yet they kept coming straight for us and I hunkered down low, wondering just how close the old man was planning to let them get afore cutting loose. I didn't want no fight, but if they was one, I sure didn't want to come in second. I had plans for me and Charlie and I weren't about to let no Comanche spoil it.

The Comanche was less than fifty foot from us when I seen the old man raise his arm about six inches and hold it steady. They was so close I could smell them and I was ready to shoot. When Mac dropped his hand was when we was to fire, but he never done it. Like us, the Comanche was avoiding crossing the skyline when they didn't need to, and just as the old man raised his arm, the first rider turned west to follow the lie of the land. The others followed and it weren't long afore they was out of sight.

Even though they was gone, we kept watch for maybe an hour afore McAdams told us he was going to get some sleep. He asked me to take the next watch and when Charlie didn't get up to go back to camp with him, he started to say something. Then he must of changed his mind because he turned without a word and started to move away.

"We'll keep watch, Keenan," Charlie whispered. "I promise. We won't go to sleep." When she said this Mac turned around and give us a smile, waving good night.

Charlie and I laid there quiet for a long time. Then she bent over and whispered in my ear. "You get some rest, too, Jack. I'm wide awake." I nodded and laid my head down right where I was, using my hat for a pillow. I felt Charlie shift so she could sit up, but I was wrong. I felt her kiss me on the cheek. "There will be another time," she said. "I promise." I remember wanting to kiss her back but I was already asleep.

When Keenan come to wake me up the next morning, it was the pup who done the job, licking my face. The sun still wasn't up yet and there wasn't no sign of Charlie. When I asked, the old man told me she was tending private business.

"I'm damned sorry about last night," he told me. "I was going to let you be but I was afraid the Comanche would hear you." I must of looked surprised because he added. "You know how well sound carries at night."

I rubbed my eyes and stretched. The grass where I was laying was nice and soft, but I was stiff in all the wrong places. "Which way did Charlie go?" I asked. "I got some business of my own."

We ate a cold breakfast that morning and headed west. After checking the trail of the Comanche, who was avoiding the river like us, Mac headed north a bit afore turning west and we kept a sharp lookout. It was clear the raiding party was headed the same way we was and it bothered Keenan until he studied out why they was there in the first place.

Even though the land was getting dryer the more west we went, we wasn't hurting for water and the prairie grass was high. We crossed a few small streams that fed into the Canadian and there was places where high water scooped out deep pools. Mac got us a few fish and they was a lot of prairie hens and rabbits, so we never hurt for fresh meat even though we was only using our bows. It was way to risky to use the guns and wasn't no need to bring down big game. We was traveling light and leaving a cut up deer carcass would be like sending up smoke and leaving a calling card. It would draw birds like stink draws flies and birds can be spotted miles away. No telling who'd show up to see what it was.

Since the old man was always close by, me and Charlie didn't have much time to talk, just me and her. I was watching our back trail while McAdams was taking lead and Charlie was on lookout for game. We was traveling careful, not making many miles in a day but walking long hours, and we was too wore out for much but rest when we made camp. Even the pup was glad to curl up at the end of a day, and he slept right beside Charlie and me until one of us taken watch. Then he'd go with me or her and more than once his nose called my notice to something I might not of seen.

It was about five days after we buried the padre that we come to a place called Sabinosa. The Canadian turned northwest a week or so afore then and at Sabinosa it turned straight north.

There wasn't much to the place. It was just a bunch of mud houses and a couple of corrals, and we bypassed it and laid up to the east of town. Mac had me and Charlie keep watch while he rode in alone to see the lay of the land, and he was gone a long time. When he come back, he was carrying two bags of beans and a sack full of news. He also had two bottles of some kind of cactus liquor and I could smell he'd taken a snort or two.

"This lovely creature is called sotol," he told us, holding up one of the bottles. "It's for us to sip along the way, but you need to watch it. It's got a kick like a mule."

He handed me the bottle I taken a short snort myself. Saying it had a kick was like calling a cyclone a breeze, and I damn near dropped the bottle. It felt like a fire was burning itself all the way down my gullet, but when it hit bottom, it give me a nice warm glow all over.

I offered it to Charlie, gasping for air, but she shaken her head. "I don't want any of that poison!" she declared. I could see she was agitated but I couldn't see what got her dander up so quick. Afore I could ask, she stomped off by herself. The pup give me a look like I'd said something awful and went after her.

I was flat stupefied for a second, but then I started to go after her to find out what was going on. Mac stopped me. "Let her be for a bit, lad. I'm sure she'll tell us when she's ready. In the meantime, I hear the creature calling. Take a sip and pass it along."

I did just that and handed him the bottle. The second snort went down a lot easier, but the kick was even more. I got to feeling so light headed I had to sit down.

"That's enough for now, I think," Keenan said, putting the cork back in the bottle. "We'll be needing to keep our wits about us, lad. That raiding party we saw came through and stole three horses, so we'll need to keep an eye on our own."

I put my hands over my face. My head was swimming. "Man, that stuff is potent!" I told him. "I feel drunk already, on two sips!"

The old man chuckled. "Aye, it is, Jackie. On the other hand, it's been a while since you did battle with the creature. You're a bit out of shape for it, now aren't you?"

"What's wrong with Charlie?" I glanced in the direction she had gone but I couldn't see her no place. "You think we ought to see if she's all right?"

"I think we'd best leave her be," he told me. "As I said, I have no doubt she will let us know exactly what's on her mind. I expect she's known some troubles from someone drinking. Maybe it was her dad or someone else in the family." He shrugged and grinned. "Or, maybe not. It could be she was raised believing in temperance, God help us all!"

I could see the sotol was having it's way with McAdams, too. He looked at the bottle he had in hand and then at me. "You know, Jackie, it's as well to be hung as a goat than as a sheep. How about another nip of the creature?" He uncorked the bottle and taken a big snort, then handed it to me.

I shook my head. Despite the sotol I had a strong sense of something not right. "I'm going to find Charlie," I told him and taken off in the direction she had gone.

Well, it taken a minute to get my feet both going in the same direction and I crawled half way up the side of the coulee afore I got them under me. By then I was worried, but I needn't have. Charlie was just over the top of the rise, setting all folded up and hugging herself, crying her heart out.

I slipped up beside her and set quiet, not wanting to startle her. I thought she hadn't seen me but she had and in a minute she put her arms around my neck, tucking her head under my chin, and still grieving. I didn't know what to say, so I didn't say nothing. It had taken me a long time to learn this, usually by stepping square into a pile of shit by saying the wrong thing, but I did learn after a while. So I just set there holding Charlie until the storm passed.

"Thanks, Jackie," she whispered, wiping her nose on my sleeve. "I appreciate your not asking."

Didn't seem to be nothing to say to that, so I just nodded. And it weren't too long 'til Charlie told me what I wanted to know. "My daddy had a small keg of whiskey in the wagon," she told me. "The men who killed him found it. I saw them drinking it while they raped my momma."

When Charlie told me this, she started crying all over again. All I could think to do was sit there like a stump until she stopped. I felt like crying, too, thinking of how my own family was killed. I held it back but Charlie noticed I was having a hard time breathing. She looked up at me, then reached out and wiped the tears off my cheek. I didn't realize my eyes was leaking.

We set there like that a long time, so long Mac came looking for us. I appreciated he made plenty of noise coming up the rise but it weren't no need. Taking a ride was the last thing on my mind.

Mac set himself down besides us. After a minute he fired up his clay pipe and set there watching the smoke rise. Wasn't any wind I could feel and the smoke went pretty much straight up. "The calm afore the storm," he said, real quiet. "We've got weather coming in before morning."

I looked around and seen he was right. They was a long blue line of clouds coming in from the northwest, what I heard called a blue northern in Texas. Seemed like it was still early in the year for that and I said so.

"I've seen it happen early, Jack," the old man told me. "We're at pretty high elevation here and it could get bad tonight. There is a room for us at a house in town if you want. Trouble is, there's only the one room and we'll have to all stay in it together."

"Shoot, I'd bed down in the barn," I told him. "I ain't thrilled at getting wet." Charlie nodded.

McAdams grinned. "That's the other thing. It is the barn where we'll be staying. That's all there is besides an outhouse and that's too small for us all."

"We could take the barn and you could have the outhouse." Charlie told him. This taken him by surprise and for a second he looked at her like he thought she was serious.

"I guess it wouldn't be too bad if I got the upper floor," the old man grinned. "One good thing about the barn is that we can keep and eye on our horses. I don't think those Comanche will come back, but there isn't much predicting what the Comanche will do."

The next morning we set out not long after daybreak. Sleeping with a roof over my head felt strange after so many weeks on the plains but the hay made a softer bed than prairie grass. Charlie and me burrowed into the pile in the loft and we was lucky not to be under no drips from the rain that come in at midnight. The rain didn't last long but it was cold and it was good to have the pup under the hay with us.

The family who owned barn where we stayed fed us that morning. It was tortillas and warm beans, with a little green sauce to spice things up. It was so good I had trouble not being a hog even though the old man advised me and Charlie not to eat too much sauce. When I asked him why not, he told me I'd find out afore mid day and he was dead right about that. I must of used a bale of prairie grass trying to keep my pants clean. The other thing I found out is why they call chiles the food that warms you twice.

Keenan and Charlie, of course, thought this was hilarious.

A couple of miles north of Sabinosa we come across another river branching northwest. It was called the Mora and Keenan said the man who put us up told him that this was the way we needed to follow to get to Taos. He said it would take us straight through the mountains to a pass we needed to cross. Since it was getting to be late summer, we might find snow, but after we crossed over, any watershed we taken would lead us to the Rio Grande. Taos would be a day or two to the north.

With the rain wiping out old tracks, we had to be more watchful than ever to avoid the Comanche. We wasn't certain they was even headed this way, but sure enough, we cut their fresh trail late that afternoon. A day later we cut the trail of at least nine riders with shod horses and they wasn't no question in my mind it was probably the bunch that killed the padre. It was good to know they was ahead of us instead of on our trail, but it meant having to keep a sharp eye out for them, too.

It did make me wonder, though, why they hadn't showed up in Sabinosa. When I asked the old man about it, he just shrugged. He said a couple of strange riders had showed up in Sabinosa a few days afore us and from what people in town was saying, they was bad hombres. So they was probably part of the gang, out scouting the lay of the land, and I guess they must of figured they was nothing worth stealing in Sabinosa. Or maybe the folks there was too well armed. From what I seen, most of the men I saw carried rifles. I reckon that was because of Indian raids. From what I heard at breakfast, the Comanche wasn't the first.

Once we cut their trail, we followed the Comanche until their tracks headed for the river. It was clear by then they was following the shod horses and I wondered why they was going after what they known was a stronger party. Seemed crazy to me.

"They're after the horses, lad," McAdams told me when I asked. We was stopped for a bite to eat. "They're out for glory, to prove themselves, and if they get away with it, they can claim to be mighty warriors." He chuckled. "Even if they don't, I expect the number of white man will double if they get home to tell it."

"Still don't make no sense to me," I answered. "What they is up to is thieving. Ain't much glory in that."

McAdams give me a look that told me I was full of horse apples. "Depends on where you stand to look at it," he answered. "You and I might call it stealing, which it would be if we did it, but you know, we might be considered worthless drifters back east."

"My folks was respectable church-going people!" I said.

"I am sure they were very good people," Mac said calmly. "But can you claim the same for yourself and me considering the life we've chosen? Jackie, we're drifters. We don't work for a living and we're certainly not good church folk."

"Well, ain't many churches out here," I muttered, but Keenan was right. Even if they was churches, it ain't likely either of us would show come Sunday morning. To tell you the truth, I wasn't even sure what day of the week it was or even what month we was in. It's easy to lose your sense of time out on the plains.

"And what if there were?" Charlie asked. The look on her face was pure devilment.

"Then you and me could get married," I laughed.

"What makes you so sure I'd want to marry you?" she asked and stood up, looking at me like she was buying a horse.

"We better get going." The old man said, laughing.

CHAPTER TEN

Red Hawk

With trouble twice as likely ahead of us, Mac said it would be a good idea to keep traveling north of the river. According to what Lieutenant Peck told us, there was an easier trail on the south side, but no telling what else we might run into there. While all of us would be right happy to take the bandits down if they crossed our sights, we wasn't anxious to catch up with them or the Comanche, neither. Life has enough trouble without looking for more.

Once the river lay between us and certain danger, we relaxed a little and things was a lot more enjoyable. We still had to be careful, of course. Them as ain't can get dead right quick, but there was time to stop and spend an hour swapping tales or admiring the view. The country was getting a lot more interesting and after a day or two there was times we could see a low line of blue on the horizon. McAdams told us those was what the Spaniards called the Sangre Christo range.

When I asked Keenan what the name meant, he said, "It translates to 'Blood of Christ' in English, Jackie." That sounded right strange to me and I said so. The old man looked at me and said, "It wouldn't if you were Catholic, lad. It has deep religious significance to them."

About then Charlie piped up and asked what that was, and I was glad she did. I hated being the only ignorant soul among us. When she did, Keenan shaken his head. "Ask me about it again when we make camp tonight and I'll try to explain. It's too complicated for horseback."

About then the pup growled and we taken a look to see what got his attention. They wasn't anything we could make out in the direction he was staring except part of the stream bed we was crossing. So Charlie and me taken our bows and followed the pup's nose while Mac stayed with the horses and covered us with his rifle. Just in case things got bad,

I had my Colt's in my belt.

Charlie and me was about ten yards from a curve in the stream bed when a horse suddenly popped its head up over the bank. I seen right away from the markings that it was an Indian pony, and when we seen it, we stopped and hunkered down. The horse had a couple of feathers braided into it's mane and I could see some markings and what looked like a rope halter on its head.

All this taken less than two seconds, and I started looking up and down the creek bank expecting to see a Comanche pop up any second. Out of the corner of my eye I could see Charlie was ready to let fly with an arrow and so was I. We was about twenty yards apart by then, so even if the Comanche got one of us, the other one would get him.

Nothing happened for a long time. Then the pony shaken its head and made its way down the creek bed toward where Keenan and the horses was. Yet Charlie and me didn't move. I didn't know but what it was a trick to get us to watching the horse and not looking at the stream bed, and if we stood up, we'd be better targets.

So we watched the stream bed and after what I'd guess was a half hour, I motioned Charlie to start moving up slow like. I done the same and it taken several minutes to reach the lip of the bank. When I did, I seen there wasn't nothing there and no cover on the other side to hide nobody, neither.

Once we seen nobody was there, we headed up the stream bed a ways, but wasn't nothing but dry rocks there. When we got back to where Keenan was waiting with the horses, we seen him holding the Indian pony by the halter and feeding it oats out of his hand. I guess that was the first oats that pony ever eat, unless it was stolen from a white settler, but it didn't take that horse long to catch on.

They wasn't no saddle or blanket on the pony, of course, but I seen a big splash of blood on her shoulder. They wasn't no wound I could see, neither, so I reckoned the blood come from her rider. From the way it looked, he must of fallen forward and rode for a while afore he dropped off. They was that much blood.

"I think you're right, lad," McAdams said when I told him this. "The question is, what do we do about it?" He rubbed his hand over the blood and some of it come off on his palm. "I don't think this blood is an hour old."

"You're saying we ought to go find him?" I asked.

"Aye, that would be the Christian thing to do," he answered.

I happened to agree but I couldn't make no claim on being any Christian. I was baptized when I was old enough to speak for myself, but I had backslid a considerable way. "Would he do the same thing for us, you think?"

"Does it matter, Jackie?" he replied sadly. "Could you live with the thought you might have saved the man's life but didn't?" When he said this, I seen Charlie nodding.

"I'm getting right tired of finding dead people," I told him. "But I think you're right. We cain't do nothing else. This one may get a little ticklish if he's still alive."

McAdams nodded and give me a wry smile. "Challenges, Jackie. Think of them as challenges, man."

"Well, this one might challenge the hair plumb off our heads!" I told him, but he just grinned.

It was late in the day we found the pony, but we backtracked as long as we could. The trail was hard to find since the pony come down the creek bed, and once we found it, we lost it again three times. An unshod pony is right tough to track through high grass and we stayed on foot to keep from being spotted. We was also trying to avoid leaving much of a trail ourselves and that slowed us down considerable.

Since Keenan was our best tracker, he went on ahead with Charlie leading our horses and me following behind her to cover our blind side. What worried me about this was that we was going to be headed back toward the river, and I wondered who might be tracking the pony from the other way. It could be that some of the other Comanche was looking for the rider, too, and if they was, it could get right ticklish, indeed.

We stopped tracking when the light too low to make out much. I heard tell of people who could track by moonlight but that always struck me as stretching the truth. I guess it could be done, but it didn't matter for us. We was in the dark of the moon, and starlight is way too dim to see nothing but big shapes right close.

We was too close to the river to risk a fire that night and the next morning we set out as soon as the light was good enough to track. I had my doubts the rider would be alive by then, and Keenan did, too. Still, we'd come this far and needed to finish the job if we was able. Maybe that was being foolish, but that's the way it was.

We was not a half mile from where we camped when Keenan saw blood on the tall grass. It was fresh, but dried out, and we left the horses hobbled right there and begun circling out from that spot on foot, trying to find some sign of the rider. That must of taken us a good hour and we had give up and was headed back when Charlie damn near stepped on the rider. When she did it weren't twenty yards from where we spotted the blood. As bad wounded as he was, that Comanche had still hid himself in the high grass.

He was still alive when Charlie spotted him, and when Keenan and me come up he had drawed a wicked looking knife and was ready to fight. He wasn't going down easy, even with a bullet hole through his chest, and I had to respect him for that. It made it hard to do anything for him, but I had to respect him for going out right.

Keenan looked at him right hard for a minute. Then he turned to me. "Jackie, does this man look familiar to you?"

I nodded. "Same thought struck me, too. Only place I can think of was when we jumped that bunch afore we got to Texas."

"I think he was the lad who brought the horses back," McAdams said. "I'm pretty sure of it."

"You think he recognizes us?"

"Not in the shape he's in. And looking at that wound, I don't think there's much we can do for him." The old man looked troubled. "I'm afraid we'll only hurt him trying to get that knife away."

Then I had a thought. I throwed back my head and cackled like a fool, just like I done afore when I was acting crazy, and I begun to dance around the Comanche, babbling all kinds of strange noise. When I did, I seen Charlie looking at me and she looked scared, but Mac started laughing and singing like a fool, too.

The Comanche turned to look at McAdams, and when he did I was on him like a cat on a mouse. I grabbed the knife hand and pinned it down, and Mac grabbed the other arm. It didn't take much to take the knife away. The kid was weak as a kitten, and after we disarmed him, we let go and backed off. Mac started to talk to him in a soft voice, making signs that he wanted to see the wound. I don't know if the kid would of let him or not, but he passed out and we was able to clean up the wound.

Keenan looked at me and Charlie when we was done. "I'm glad we came to find him," he told us. "That wound is bad but it's not mortal. The bullet didn't hit a lung or an artery, and it didn't even crack a bone. What he's suffering from mostly is loss of blood."

"So he'll likely live?" I asked. McAdams nodded. "So what do we do with him when he gets well?" I went on. "You think we could ever trust him?"

"It's going to take him a lot of time to get his strength back," the old man said. "I'm afraid we're going to have to take care of him until then. It may be we can get him to trust us afore he's strong enough to do much harm."

I looked at Charlie. "What do you think?" I asked. "This affects you, too."

"I think we took on that obligation when we started looking for him," she said. I seen McAdams nod and Charlie went on. "I guess we could get him back on his feet and give him a choice of going home to his people or coming with us."

"How are we going to get that across?" I wanted to know.

"Oh, that won't be as hard as you think, lad," Keenan said. "We can always use sign. The first thing is to win his trust."

So that's how Red Hawk become one of us. I have to admit it weren't as hard as I thought it might. It taken some thinking and a lot of pointing and repeating, sometimes over and over, but it worked pretty good.

Using point and tell was how we learnt his name the second day after we found him. He pointed to a red tailed hawk circling high and then to himself and give us a word. We couldn't say it quite right, and never could, but we got close enough. That's also how we learnt him his name in English, though most of the time we just called him Hawk. So we was Red Hawk, Mac, Charlie, and Jack. It sort of went together real good.

Like with the padre, we couldn't travel too far until Hawk was strong enough to ride on his own. Where we found him weren't a good spot. It was out in the open with no water, and wasn't much telling who might come following Hawk's trail. So Mac and Charlie loaded him up so I could carry him on my pony in front of me and we headed for a spot we seen the night afore. It was off to the west of the trail we followed and didn't look like much until you got right up on it. There was a spring there and a couple of small trees, and it made a good camp. We ended up staying there most of two weeks, and when it come time, I hated to leave.

One thing I didn't like was how Charlie started acting with Red Hawk in camp. With McAdams, it was just the three of us and things was nice and easy. Charlie was just herself and she and me did a lot of teasing.

This all changed after we found Hawk. Charlie seemed to spend all her time tending to him and it was either Mac or me who went out hunting. When I suggested on day that Charlie come hunting with me, she give me a look like I was stupid. Then I opened my mouth and put my big foot square in it, and she wouldn't even sleep next to me.

When I asked Mac about this, he just shrugged. "Women get odd when they have a child or a sick one to care for," he said. "Give her time and she'll get over it."

"Give it time and I'll get over her!" I declared. When I said this, the old man just shook his head and sighed. He wouldn't talk about it, neither. He said something about young men needing to stretch their souls, but wouldn't say what he meant by that.

I was so riled I wouldn't let it be and Mac finally cut me off. "I gave you my advice when you asked for it, Jack. Either take it or don't. That's all I have to say. So leave me be!"

That's how I come to be caught in the buffalo stampede. I was so worked up over how Charlie was acting I couldn't sit still, so I taken my pony and my bow and went hunting. By then it was late in the afternoon and I told the old man I was going after deer and I might not be back until the next day.

Keenan nodded and told me that might be a good thing. "You need some time with yourself, lad. You might want to ask yourself what is most important to you."

I tried to tell him I already knowed that, but he just held up his hands and shook his head. "Think about it again, Jackie. That's a question a man needs to ask himself every day. Right now your pride's been hurt. You might want to ask yourself what part you had in it. I think you might see you shot yourself in the foot."

Of course, I wanted to know what he meant by that but he shook his head again. "Do you remember the story I told you about Bill, how he put himself in the bullet's way?"

"What does that have to do with this?"

"Well, it's just an observation, and I may be wrong, but you did ask. From where I stand, you seem to be putting yourself in harm's way just like Bill."

I couldn't see no connection, but the old man clamed up tight after that. "Go hunting, Jackie," he said. "Take two or three days or as long as you need to get your soul on straight. We'll be right here when you get back. Or if we have to leave in a hurry, we'll meet you in Taos, if not before. Just stay clear of the civil authorities. They'll arrest you for being an American spy."

So I taken off, not bothering to let Charlie know or nothing. I was still sore as a four-day boil and I didn't see how I could do no good talking to her. I wasn't even sure she cared, and I told myself if she didn't care, then I didn't, neither. That weren't true, of course, but at that moment I surely weren't thinking straight.

An hour's ride from camp, my state of mind had improved considerable. I had to agree the old man was right, just like he always was when it come to people. At least, he was about getting away by myself. A man does need time to think when he gets a kink in his tail. I wasn't sure he was right about the rest of it, but coming from him, I was willing to study it.

I found me a good place to spend that night right there on the prairie and along about midnight there come a rain. It weren't that much, not even enough to wipe out my tracks. What done was to clean the dust out of the air and make it sweet to smell. When it passed I lay there a long while, looking at the stars and breathing in the fresh air, thinking how good it was to be out here on the prairie and not shut up in some town.

CHAPTER ELEVEN

Close Calls

The rain the night afore made the next morning bright and clear. The mountains was close enough now I could see a snow cap on the tallest peaks, and they looked a lot closer than the day afore. I realized they was still a good thirty miles away, but it was hard for me to believe. Seemed like I could almost reach out and touch them. It turned out they was more like sixty miles off and I had to walk a big part of the way.

One thing that surprised me was seeing big bright patches of yellow scattered against the dark green slopes of the mountains. Later I learnt yellow patches was stands of aspens. They look like birch, except the bark don't peel. The dark green was some of the tallest pines I ever seen and the mountains themselves was a lot bigger, and more rugged than any I ever seen afore. The rock looked like dark granite, hard and sharp like flint, but there was streaks of red and other colors mixed with it.

I taken a notion it might be better to hunt as far as I could from camp since I was after deer, so I went on foot an hour or two more, leading my pony and following the draws. I studied out that was where I'd find game, and I was right. Only it weren't exactly the game I was after.

I spotted a likely looking draw and worked my way around to the head of it, always checking the skyline. I slipped over the top and went down until I come to some trees. I tied up my mare so she could graze and nocked an arrow. Then I slipped down real careful like to see what might be there.

Turned out the ravine was deep and wide and I knowed I was in luck when I felt the wind coming up the draw. There wouldn't no game smell me while I was still too far away to shoot. All I had to do was be real quiet and move slow, and my uncle learnt me that when I was barely walking.

Luck was with me more than I thought because I ain't gone ten yards afore I heard my horse whinny. When she did, I knowed she was downright terrified. Them that has been around horses knows what I mean. Horses have different sounds for different things, just like humans have different yells.

What I seen then like to froze my blood, but I didn't have no time to be scairt. There was a full grown grizzly charging out of the bushes and going for my pony. Without thinking, I roared like a bull in rut and headed right straight for the bear. I reckon this saved my horse because brother bear turned when it heard my yell and headed straight for me.

Like I said, I didn't have no time for being scairt or nothing else. I didn't even have time to pull my Colt's. I pulled back the string on my bow and let fly for a spot right under the grizzly's chin. All those days shooting prairie hens on the wing paid off right then. My arrow went right between the bear's collar bone and his neck, and hit him square in the heart. He come to rest two paces in front of my feet.

By that time I had my Colt's out ready to finish the job if brother bear got up and wanted more, but he was dead. I must have waited ten minutes afore I believed it. Then I went to fetch my horse.

As I expected, when I yelled, my pony had broke its rope and run for the top of the rise at the head of the ravine. When I looked uphill to spot her, she was two hundred yards up the slope, standing quiet. What caught my attention, though, was the fact her reins was being held by a mounted Indian. There was three others sitting there, too, looking at me like I was some strange kind of critter they never seen.

There wasn't a whole lot I could do, so I raised my raised my right hand and held it up shoulder high. My uncle taught me that was the sign for peace and I guess it was out here, too. After a minute the Indian holding my pony done the same thing and they began making their way down the slope towards me. Not knowing what else to do, I laid my bow aside but tucked my Colt's in my belt where I could get to it quick. Not knowing nothing else to do, I started carving up brother bear, keeping an eye on the Indians all the time.

By the time they got to me I had the heart cut out and was chewing on a piece of it. I ain't partial to raw meat but I was hungry and it tasted damn good. I skewered the heart on my knife and walked up to the Indians, offering them a slice with my left hand. I was keeping my right empty in case I had to draw real fast, but the ponies shied at the smell of grizzly and fresh blood. The boy with my horse said something sharp and I stopped and waited while they backed off a ways.

When they stopped, they had a palaver amongst theirselves afore they dismounted and tied up their ponies. I taken it as a good sign they tied my pony a little apart from theirs. I'd walked most of the way to where I was and I could walk back to camp even quicker, but I sure hated the idea of losing my mare.

I seen right quick these wasn't Comanche and I was right glad of that. According to Keenan, Comanche don't need much cause to fight and I was seriously outnumbered. With the Colt's I might handle three and still come out alive, if I was lucky, but four was way too many.

I was also glad they was a good bit younger than me. I'd guess the oldest was no more than fourteen and the youngest wouldn't of been much more than twelve. By then I'd been a long time out on the prairie and my hair was down to my shoulders and my skin was dark, so I guess to them I looked like some kind of Indian in white man's clothes. I guess they also figured if I could handle a grizzly with only a bow, I could whip all them and send them home afoot. Like I say, I'm guessing, but the three youngest jumped to it when I signed we needed a fire to cook us up some bear. The oldest was a different story. He didn't do nothing but watch me.

We had us a fine dinner of fresh bear cooked over live coals. It weren't as tough as the one the old man shot the day we met, so it must of been a lot younger. The teeth wasn't yellow and the claws was long and sharp, and I guess I was a lot luckier taking it down than I first thought.

After we eat, we had a talk by sign lingo. I never used it afore, but for Hawk, but I caught on quick. I let them know right quick I was Choctaw, and pointing at myself and old bear, I let them know my name is Bear. Somehow, that didn't surprise them much.

What I come to find out, they was Cheyenne. Keenan told me later this put them a long way from home, just like the Comanche, but didn't seem to me like this bunch was raiding. I think they was just passing through and the old man told me later I was probably right. Comes a time with some tribes that a bunch of young men takes off on a trip on their own and it can be a long time afore they get home. If they make it back, they're no longer considered boys, but full grown men.

Of course, a lot of this is pure speculation on my part. Signing is not too good for details and I never got to learn much else. Our horses begun getting restless and a minute later we heard something that sounded like rolling thunder. When they heard this, the Cheyenne jumped up and made a run for their ponies.

I didn't know what was going on but I grabbed my bow and run to my horse, too. Not knowing where else to go, I rode after the Cheyenne. Looking back when we topped over the first rise, I seen something I never want to see again. There was a cloud of dust not a half mile away and below it I seen a solid wall of buffalo a half mile wide. They was headed right for us.

Well, I taken off downhill as fast as my pony would go. I didn't figure I could outrun them and there weren't no chance I could run around them. So, like Keenan once told me, I started looking for a safe place to hole up until they passed.

As hard as I was riding, I could hear the buffalo gaining fast and I figured my time was just about up. Then my luck held. I seen a big rock sticking up just to my left and I headed for that. Swinging off my pony, I grabbed my rifle and saddle bags loose and pulled my mare into the shelter of that rock.

That rock wasn't much more than a dozen foot wide but there was just enough room for me and my horse. When we got there, it weren't any too soon. A river of buffalo broke on either side of the rock a minute later, running so close I damn near could touch them reaching out my arm, and the sound was so loud I couldn't even hear my horse screaming. It was all I could do to keep her from running out into the stampede.

I don't know how long it lasted. Seemed like it was all afternoon but I guess it was maybe a quarter hour at most. Dust was so thick I could barely breathe and all I could see was my pony with her eyes rolled back and huge brown bodies running by at full speed.

It was just about then Lady Luck got plumb fickle. One of the buffalo stumbled toward my pony and she reared. Wasn't no way I could hold her and she taken off running with the herd. All I could do was hunker down against the rock and be thankful I had my rifle and saddle bags. I could of been killed or maimed or left with nothing.

Then it was over, though you wouldn't know it by the dust. The rolling thunder got further and further away until it died out and my soul begun to settle down. It taken a good while afore I could see too good, and when the dust settled enough, I seen the ground around me torn up like it had been plowed. There was also a couple of dead buffalo on the other side of the rock and I seen even more scattered across the plains. All that was left of the herd was a cloud of dust off to the northeast, and I hoped it missed Keenan and Charlie and Hawk. I hoped, too, my mare weren't trampled in the rush. She was a good pony and I hoped whoever come to find her treated her good.

Thinking about Charlie, I realized I wasn't mad at her no longer, not even about Hawk. Like usual, the old man had been right. Certain things was important and others was not, and I was beginning to see the difference. I guess being damn near killed will do that, and it's a shame it takes something like that to open a man's eyes. On the other hand, I guess I should be grateful having learnt it as soon I did. It saved me a pile of trouble later on.

Looking around, I hated to see all that meat and hide going to waste but without a horse, wasn't no way I could salvage more than I could carry. I didn't have no canteen, neither, so I was going to have to stick close to water or find a way to carry enough to get me across the prairie.

Then I got to wondering how Indians carried water, and that's how I come up with a way. I recalled how the Good Book talks about storing wine in skins and I was looking at all the skins I could ever need. All I need to do was sew it together. I was also looking at all the leather I'd ever need to make a pack to carry what meat would last.

Thinking the hide would be thinner and easier to sew, I picked out a calf and begun skinning it. I was damn near done when I had another thought, so when I finished the calf, I picked out the biggest critter I could find and started carving away at the rear end. It taken a lot of careful cutting and some scraping, but when I was done, I had me a bladder I figured would hold at least a quart. Then I got me two others afore I walked back to the calf and started cutting off the best parts to take with me.

It was getting on toward sunset by the time I finished up but I didn't want to waste no time getting back to camp. Looking at the lay of the land, I decided to follow the buffalo trail until I needed to head east for the camp. What I was thinking was my tracks wouldn't be as easy to spot if I kept to what was left of the grass.

I don't know how it come to happen, but it taken me five days to find my way to camp. I must have rode a lot further than I thought running from the stampede because I ended up way too far north. It taken me two days to study this out and another two day's walking to get to country I thought looked familiar. Then I seen tracks that I thought I knowed. Then I realized whose tracks they was, and when I did, I come to see I done walked full circle. I was right back to where I first started.

Talk about wanting to cuss! Only thing that kept me from kicking my butt clean over the next butte was lack of boots and a good place to stand.

Once I calmed down, I seen what happened. Being on foot I was trying to keep out of sight and forgot to pick a high point to keep me on track. I heard later that the Indians used long stakes to keep on track crossing parts of the Great Plains.

Giving it some thought, seemed like the best course would be heading south and east until I hit the river. Once I was there I could work my way back to camp. I just hoped Keenan and Charlie was waiting for me. I'd been gone a long time and Keenan didn't like to stay no place too long.

Looking around I seen a buffalo wallow about a mile away. It was in the right direction, so I taken off, keeping the sun about the same angle off my right shoulder. This was harder than you'd think since I was following the natural lay of the land, winding around slopes and keeping away from the skyline. Still, I got there and spotted something else to mark my line of travel, and I kept it up until there weren't enough light to keep from stepping on a snake.

Next morning I was up at daybreak and kept on doing this until all of a sudden I known exactly where I was. I looked around a little to make certain, but sure enough, I'd come to the same spot where we found Hawk. There weren't no rain since we did and I could see our tracks real clear. I could also see dried blood when he laid.

Thing is, I could also see some other tracks there, and this worried me. There was two riders on shod horses and they was headed toward our camp. I couldn't tell how long back they come that way, but their tracks was a lot clearer than them we made. So I reckoned it weren't too long. It could of been that morning.

Seeing all this, I taken off for the camp at a lope, trying to keep to cover but not wasting time. It weren't that far from where we found Hawk and if there was a fight, I wanted to get there for it. I was afraid them two riders might be sneaking up to bushwhack Keenan and Charlie right then and I was hoping I weren't too late.

Turned out I had no cause for worry. When I got to where we taken Hawk, there weren't nobody around and it looked to me like it was at least two days, maybe three, since they broke camp. The riders was there, too, but I could see their tracks was fresher than the ones Mac laid down. What I couldn't puzzle out was that there was a fourth horse. When I left there was only the two horses Mac and Charlie rode and the pack mule.

I filled my water bladders from the spring at the camp and taken off following the tracks again. This time I taken it a little slower. I wasn't too worried about Charlie and Keenan at that point, and I'd been traveling on an empty belly for two days. While I could of gone a couple or three more days without eating, I was starting to feel weakness in my legs and I needed to find food soon. Wouldn't do anyone no good for me to show up for a fight and not have the strength to do nothing.

About a mile out of camp I nailed me a prairie chicken and eat it raw. It does taste a lot better cooked, but I didn't want to take time to build a fire and cook it. I didn't want to risk someone smelling the cooking, neither. Of course, by then I was so damn hungry it didn't bother me much at all. That fool hen tasted right good.

I found a spot where the riders camped just when it was getting dark, and I stopped there for the night. I figured I'd come about twenty-five miles that day and I was plain beat. I'd shot another prairie hen not long afore sundown, and I eat that one raw, too. It was young and tender, but it didn't taste as good as that first one.

I taken off tracking again at first light. My legs was telling me I had run them too far, but after a while they stopped hurting. The trail Mac and Charlie left was getting harder to follow and I almost missed the spot when Mac turned off and the tracks disappeared. Thing is, it weren't anything I seen that let me know. I'd traveled long enough with Mac that I known right away this was exactly the kind of place Mac would of used to hide his tracks.

Of course, the two riders had missed the turn completely and gone on straight along the line Mac had been tracking. I decided to follow them a while to make sure they was out of the picture afore I come back and picked up the trail I was sure Mac taken. By then I had a pretty good idea where Mac and Charlie was headed and I figured I could cut cross country to meet up if I had to. They wouldn't be too far from the river.

That turned out to not be the smartest thing I ever done. I followed their tracks for a couple of miles to a place they stopped. They known by then they lost the trail because they started circling to pick it up again. It would have made a lot more sense to go back a ways first, but these riders wasn't that good.

I figured for sure they wouldn't pick up Mac's trail again, so I headed back toward the turn-off. I was in a hurry then because I was at least two days behind Mac and Charlie and I wasn't as careful as I needed to be. Coming around a bend in a water course, I found them sitting on their horses and waiting for me.

I didn't have much chance to do nothing, neither. One of them had a rifle pointed straight at my chest. "Drop that rifle!" he yelled and I laid the Hawken down right gentle. "Toss that bow, too!" he told me and I did. "Now come over here!"

I was glad he said that because I was trying to figure how I could move in closer without getting myself shot. I was also glad to see he weren't as careful to keep me covered with his rifle. I walked toward them and stopped about ten foot away. "Well, looky here," he said to his partner. "It looks like an Injun but it's wearing white man's clothes. What do you suppose it is?"

"Must be a half breed," the other man said, spitting into the dust at my feet after he said it. He had a rifle, too, but it was laying across his saddle and not pointed at me.

"You got a name, boy?" the first man said.

"Jack," I told him.

"A half breed for sure," the second man said. "Why don't you shoot him and let's get on our way."

"I want to have a little fun first," the other one said. When he did, he turned his head to look at his partner.

That was all the opening I needed. I throwed up my hands and charged the horses. This spooked them and they reared up, almost throwing the riders. When they did I reached behind me and pulled my Colt's out of my belt, dropping to one knee and firing. The first round got the first man in the belly, knocking him off his horse, and my next shot caught his partner in the arm. He tried to turn to ride away but my third shot got him just under his ribs and taken him down.

When I turned to check on the first man, he was trying to reach his rifle. I guess he must of been a dozen foot from me. I taken aim and shot him straight through the head.

I gathered up the guns and went through their pockets. There weren't much there except for a wanted poster in the second man's shirt pocket. This one was from New Orleans and whoever drawn the picture got him dead right. His name was Jones and he was wanted for murder. There was a reward, too, but like the one afore, I known I wouldn't be collecting it. Yet Jones did have a Colt's like mine, so I taken that instead. I also folded up the wanted poster and put it in my shirt pocket. I figured it might come in useful, for wiping paper if nothing else.

The horses had run off when the gunplay started, but they didn't go far and I was able to catch them without no trouble. The saddle bags paid off a lot better than the men's pockets. There was biscuit makings and beans, and lots of ammunition for the rifles. I also found a sack of silver coins, maybe fifty dollars worth, some flint and steel, and a spy glass like the one Keenan used. There was also a rain slicker and a couple of blankets tied on the saddles and I was right glad to find them.

I give some thought to what to do with the bodies and I decided to leave them lay. It weren't like burying Charlie's folks or the Mexican soldiers. It was more like shooting a varmint that was after the chickens. A man might drag it off to keep away the stink but he sure wouldn't trouble to bury them.

The other consideration was that I was right keen to catch up with Charlie and McAdams. The longer it taken me to find them, the harder it would be, and I had no idea where the old man might head after Taos. On foot it was all I could hope for was to not fall behind more than I was. With two ponies to ride, I figured I could make a lot of miles a day and join up with them pretty quick.

Three days later I lost the trail and couldn't never find it again. After most of an afternoon spent looking, I finally give up. I had no earthly idea where Taos was, but I figured I could find somebody could point me the right way. So I turned my ponies west and headed for the mountains.

CHAPTER TWELVE

Valmora

etting to the mountains taken me four days. I could of made it faster but I wanted my horses rested and well grazed in case I had to run for it. To give them devils I shot their due, they chose good horses and they taken good care of them. The one I was riding was a big gray gelding and he was strong and fast. The other was a chestnut mare and it surprised me to find out she was even faster.

Late in the second day I come on a group of buildings. I kept an eye on it a while afore I rode up, and I couldn't see no sign of life there. Taking a peek through my spy glass, the place looked even more deserted, and there was black smoke stains where it looked like the roof burnt out. Circling the place out of sight of the house, I taken a look from the other side. All I seen was more smoke stains and a broken down porch, and even the rails around the corral was missing.

Something about that place felt real strange and I couldn't see no way I needed to find out why. So I slipped away real quiet and kept going. Yet that strange feeling I had wouldn't go away, and I kept a sharp eye on my back trail. I circled back two or three times just to make sure, but I didn't never see nothing but what might of been dust a long way back. Of course, it might of just been a whirl wind, too.

That strange feeling stayed with me that night and all through the next day. When I stopped to rest I was careful to find a place I could defend and I had both Colt's close to hand. I didn't bother to break out my bedroll, neither, and I didn't lay down or do much sleeping. I sat with my back to a rock and taken quick cat naps, and afore I left the next morning, I checked for tracks. There may have been some there, but if there was any, I either didn't find them or couldn't see them. By the time I got to a settlement late the next afternoon, the bad feeling was gone. I never figured out what it was, but I was sure of one thing.

I had no reason for riding up to that burnt out house and I was damn glad I didn't. There was some that told me later that what I was feeling was the ghosts of people killed there, and maybe they was right. I don't know and I don't care to look into it too much, neither. There may be such things as ghosts, but seems to me a man is best off leaving other people at peace, be they the quick or the dead. Of course, them as ain't quick is dead!

Valmora was the name of the town, though I never learnt it until later. I could see it was a good bit bigger than Sabinosa and I circled around it until I found a rise where I could use my spy glass. The first thing I seen circling around was a bell tower sticking up, so it had a church. Looking through the glass, I didn't spot nobody looked like a soldier or any kid of civil authority, as Keenan called mayors and judges and folk like that. Now that didn't mean there wasn't none there, but at least I didn't have to fret about a whole swarm of troops.

I camped out on the prairie that night not far from a dry creekbed and headed in to scout out the town at first light. One thing I was after was something to eat asides prairie dogs and rattlesnakes and half cooked beans. Might not be a store there, but I figured I could find someone to sell me something. Some of the money I salvaged was Mexican pesos and I figured that was good here.

Slipping into town without being seen wasn't hard at all. Most of the buildings was mud houses and was built not too far from the river. Most of them faced each other around a town square and I found a line of bushes running toward the back of one of them.

I was standing behind a bush and thinking to walk up real easy to the back of the nearest house when the back door opened. A man come out in a long night shirt and made a bee line for the outhouse not five foot from me. He was rubbing his eyes and wasting no time getting there, so he didn't see me.

Once he shut his self in, I started to walk to the house but I had a notion that might work better. I seen he was a white man when he was walking to the outhouse and I figured he spoken English. That was one thing as had me worried, finding somebody could understand what I was saying.

So I walked up to the outhouse and knocked on the door. The man inside answered in Spanish, but it sounded like an American voice.

"Excuse me," I told him in English. "I didn't mean to disturb you. I didn't want to walk in without knocking."

"A man of manners," the voice told me. "It sounds like you're from Arkansas."

"Well, I guess it's kind of obvious, ain't it?" I allowed. "It sounds to me like you come from back East."

"Connecticut, in fact," the voice said. "I won't be long. I'd advise you not to go into town until I'm with you. Let me finish my business and I'll tell you why." The next thing I heard was a blast of gas that like to blowed the door off the outhouse.

"Amen!" I said. "That's the way I vote, too."

Well, that tickled the Yankee and he broke out laughing. I broke a little wind back at him and he laughed again. "Don't do that," he said. "Or I'll never get my business done."

I had to agree it's damn near impossible to laugh and take a dump at the same time. "All right," I told him. "I ain't in no rush."

When the man come out I seen he was about the same age as me. He offered me a cup of coffee and I was right glad to take him up on it. While we was sipping it he told me he was Sam Watrous and had left Connecticut to make his fortune in the west. "I heard there was gold near Taos, so that's where I came," he said. "I saw pretty quickly that the only gold is in the pockets of merchants and the big land owners, and they weren't letting go of much of it."

"I hear tell that mining's a pretty hard way to make a living," I told him.

"That it is," he replied. "I tried my luck around San Pedro but it didn't work out. I did better as a store clerk before, but it's hard to get ahead that way. Then, too, I'm a man who likes to work for himself."

"Me, too," I told him. "What are you doing now, if you don't mind my asking?"

"I'm looking for land around here," he answered. "There isn't a really good general store anywhere around here, so I thought I'd farm until I had enough money to build one. There's a place not too far from here I've got my eye on. It's on the Santa Fe trail and I think it would be an excellent place to build a store. What about yourself? What brings you to Valmora?"

"I'm just seeing the country," I told him. "It's right pretty out here."

"That it is," he answered. "You wouldn't be interested in settling around here, would you? I could use some help."

"I appriciate the offer, but I cain't. I was with a couple of partners and we got separated about a week back. I'm trying to catch up with them."

Watrous looked at me sort of strange. "You party wouldn't be an old Scotsman and a young woman, would it?"

"Was his name McAdams?" I asked. Watrous nodded but didn't say nothing. "How long was they through here?"

"It's been three days," he answered me. "I wondered why the young lady was passing herself off as a man. I also wondered why she was so sad." When he said that I known he wanted to know if there was anything between me and Charlie.

"Well, her folk got killed not long back," I told him. "There was a gang of outlaws attacked their wagon party."

"Oh. Well, that's the thing I wanted to tell you before. A band of rough thugs came through here about ten days ago. They shot and killed one of the townspeople here before we drove them off and feelings are still running high. I didn't want someone to mistake you for one of them."

"I ain't, but how can you tell for sure?"

"For one thing, you're a lot darker than any of them. You could pass for an Indian, but I knew before I ever saw you. You have good manners. I can't imagine one of those thugs actually knocking on an outhouse door." He smiled. "They didn't seem to have much sense of humor, either. The old Scotsman did."

I smiled, thinking of what Mac would say about being called the old Scotsman. I could see Watrous wanted to know more, bringing McAdams up again. Yet, I didn't know him all that good and I didn't rise to the bait. "Where can I buy some food around here?" I asked. "I could use some other things, too."

Sam smiled. "Well, friend, you've come to exactly the right place. I've been saving stock for my new store and trading out of the back of a wagon. I don't have a lot of inventory, but you're welcome to look it over. This house is my warehouse."

"You take pesos?" I asked.

"Pesos or dollars, it's all money to me," he replied. I could see he was wondering how I come to have pesos but I kept my peace.

I bought a bag of corn meal from him and another one of beans. I would of taken a bag of flour, too, but that was sky high. When I asked him about it, Watrous told me corn and beans was raised close by. Wheat flour had to be hauled in by wagon from Missouri. He said he had come to prefer Mexican tortillas or cornbread, and later taken me where I could buy tortillas.

I also sold him a couple of rifles I collected from the men who tried to shoot me. They was Hall rifles, breech loaders, and in good shape, and Sam was happy to get them. I known he was wanting to know how I come by them, but he didn't ask and I didn't offer.

"These are old military rifles," he told me, showing me the stock plate. It read Harper's Ferry. "A lot of people don't like loading at the breach."

"Comes in handy in a fight," I told him. I known he was trying to push the price down even afore he made me an offer, and I was pushing back.

"Yet, you carry a muzzle loader," he shot back.

"Mine is a Hawken," I reminded him. "Says so right on the stock. They ain't many of those around. It spits out a .54 caliber ball same as them."

We haggled it back and forth a while afore we come to a price we both thought was fair. Then we eat dinner at the tortilla lady's house, and it was even better than the food I eat at Sabinosa. It was just as spicy, too, and I eat too damn much. I known even as I eat it what I was in for the next day, but that didn't stop me.

Sam told me drinking a pint of milk would help and our next stop was for milk. All we could get was dairy goat milk. That had a right strange taste, but it done the trick. Next day I weren't bothered hardly at all.

Watrous told me I could sleep at his place if I cared to but the day was getting on and I wanted to be on the trail. When I told him that, he kind of smiled and nodded. "I'd wager it's not that old Scotsman you're anxious to see."

He was still looking for information without asking. I just shrugged and told him it was no bet and he asked if I known how to get to Taos. "What makes you think I'm heading to Taos?" I asked him.

"That's the direction the Scotsman set out," he said. "Taos is the only place worth getting to along that trail unless you live in Mora or one of the other villages. There's a short cut that will save you at least a half day's ride if you care to take it."

I allowed as that might be useful to know and he told me what to watch for and where to turn. "I wish I could take you there myself," he added. "I'm afraid I have business I need to tend here."

I was just as glad. Sam Watrous is a good man, but I think I might grow tired of his company on the trail. He liked to talk too much, though I guess Keenan might say the same of me and all my questions.

Sam's biggest drawback was that I didn't think he fit too good in wild country. It weren't that he was lacking in courage or all them things that make a man worth knowing and fit to ride with. The thing is, Sam were a townsman and a shop keeper at heart, not a plainsman or mountain man. As the Good Book puts it, that's where his treasure were, so there was his heart, too. With me and Keenan, our treasure was wild country.

I thanked Sam for his hospitality and loaded my pack horse. When I left town, I headed out to the east to throw off anyone who might be watching. I didn't have the feeling there was, but weren't no telling. It pays a man to be careful.

It taken me the rest of that day and all the next to get to the mountains. After being out on the prairie so long, heading up the river into wooded high country seemed like I was being swallowed up at first. Then I got used to it and after a while I come to like smelling the pine and listening to the sound of the stream I was following.

The trail I was following was well wore into the ground. It struck me that following so close to the stream might not be a good idea, and when I seen a game trail leading up the slope on the side, I followed it. Sure enough, that trail come to a fork up amongst the trees about forty yards up the slope and I taken the branch that followed the contour of the land.

It was cooler there, being on the north side of the river, and afore long I was putting on the serape Sam talked me into buying. What I liked about it was it kept me warm and left my arms free. I also liked it being dark green, the same color as the pines, with gray and brown woven in so it blended into the scenery.

It weren't long after that I spotted a couple of riders making their way downstream. They wasn't paying much attention to what was on the slope above them, and where I was standing I could see them a lot better than they could see me. It helped that I was on foot rather than mounted just then and I taken care not to move too much.

I taken my spy glass out of the saddle bag and give the men a good looking over. When I done so, I was glad I ain't met them along the stream. They had the same hard look as the men I had to shoot. I couldn't tell what all goes into that look to save my soul, but I know it when I see it and these men had it. They may not of looked much different from me or Keenan after three months on the prairie, but there weren't nothing civilized about these men. I was given no doubt they'd just as soon cut my throat as look at me. They was the kind to take pleasure in it, too.

I seen the men was talking about something as they was riding. At least, they was moving their mouths like they was, but there weren't no way I could hear what they was saying. The noise of the stream and the wind moving up the canyon carried away even the sound of their voices.

I guess I could of tried to read their lips, but I ain't too good at that and I didn't want them to get the feeling they was being watched. People ain't any different from game that regard, and if you stare at somebody long enough, like as not they'll look around to see who is looking at them. So after the first gander, I spied on them out of the corner of my eye. Then after they passed by, I waited for a spell afore I moved on.

Seeing them two men got me thinking if I maybe needed to find a different way to Taos. That trail along the river seen some pretty good use. If I'd known the country, I would have. But the last thing I wanted was getting myself lost in these mountains. I was feeling the need to catch up as quick as I could. Keenan and Charlie was all the family I had in this world and I damn sure didn't want to lose them.

The trail I was on kept drifting up a bit at a time and it weren't long afore I was maybe three or four hundred foot above the river. When I come to the spine of a high ridge, I seen I was doing a lot more traveling than if I followed the river. I also seen the ground was a lot flatter on the south side of the river where the main trail run.

I was about decided to start working myself down and finding a faster trail when I seen something. It weren't much, just a couple of busted tree branches laying on the ground in a uncommon way, but I recognized them soon as I seen them. They was laid that way by Keenan and I figured he put them there to let me know this was the trail they was following. Sure enough, there was a single track in some soft dirt on the trail about a hundred yards down from the ridge. It were a track I known as well as I do my own hand, and I known Mac put it there for me to see.

I was being careful to hide my own tracks, so I bushed it out with a pine bough afore moving on. Weren't no use letting someone else know other people was using the trail, too. I also started watching for more sign, but the only place I seen it was where the trail branched.

I weren't in near the rush I was afore. Knowing Charlie and Mac was on the same trail, I also known they was traveling slow, too. We wasn't in no haste to get nowhere and the only worry was getting across the mountains afore snow closed the passes. Still, I didn't waste no time. The sooner I caught up, the sooner I'd see Charlie, and I was keen on seeing her. I hoped she'd cooled off by then and was as keen on seeing me.

That afternoon the trail come to a steep canyon and started drifting down towards the river. There was sign pointing that way, so I crossed the river rode up the main trail for a couple of miles where I come to a wide valley leading north. It was tempting to follow the valley north, but the sign showed Mac kept heading west and he was keeping clear of the main trail. He was also not hiding his tracks.

I give this some thought. I known he was trying to tell me something but I couldn't study out what. So I rode my horses right over his tracks to confuse anyone following us. When his tracks disappeared, I started hiding mine, too. I hadn't no idea what Mac was up to, but I trusted his judgment. I never known him to do something but for a reason.

It weren't much more than a mile after that I come to a settlement the main trail went to, but I seen Mac circled around town and I done so, too. We was following the river pretty close at that point and crossing a lot of crop fields, but weren't many houses along there. When we come to one, we always passed it by.

We done that for a couple more days. Traveling through the mountains was slow. Keenan was being careful to avoid ambush and other travelers, which taken more time, but the trail he was following was exactly the way Sam Watrous told me and it seemed like I was gaining on them a little. Then I come across some horse apples the second day and didn't seem like they was more than a day old, maybe less. Since them was the only horse apples I come across up to then, I figured Mac meant me to find them.

There was only one place I wondered about. This was where the trail

I was following left the waterway and headed up the mountain sides. Sam Watrous told me this would happen, but the landmarks he told me to watch for didn't seem quite right. Where Mac was headed seemed like straight up the mountain, though he was following a game trail. As usual, he would be riding off to one side to hide his tracks, which accounted for me seeing almost nothing but deer tracks on the trail.

That bothered me some until I remembered I wasn't after going to Taos. I was wanting to catch up with Charlie and Mac, so I followed the trail he laid out for me. Turns out later that Mac was this way once afore and known a better shortcut.

When I topped out over the highest ridge, climbing hard for a couple or three thousand foot, I was breathing hard. What I seen then like to taken away what breath I had left. It was a bright clear day and the aspens up high was bright yellow. They give off a soft gold light, almost like they was set afire, and I found it peaceful. The air was so clear it seemed like I see damn near forever and the edges of the mountains as far as I seen was razor sharp. To the north there was a watershed I figured led to Taos, and to the west I seen a good sized settlement ten miles up the river I had been following. I even seen what might be the shortcut Sam told me about. It were five miles up the river and the way Mac come were a damn sight shorter. Yes, we had to cross over a mountain, but we would of done that either way we taken. So this turned out the quicker route.

I taken out my spy glass and looked to the north. When I done so, I spotted three riders moving along the high ridge above the water shed I was planning to follow. I didn't get more than a quick look because they was crossing a clearing they couldn't get around on foot, leading their horses, and I seen they was leading a pack horse, too. I had a strong feeling this was Mac and Charlie and Hawk, but I still couldn't study out where they come up with a fourth horse.

I was right happy to see them. I figured they was about six or seven mile ahead and it was getting pretty late in the day. There weren't no chance in hell I could catch up with them that day. Traveling at night in mountains you don't know ain't only foolish. It's downright crazy. Had I known the country, it might be different.

The sun being so low in the west give me an idea. Taking out my knife, I tried to use it to signal them other travelers, trying to make three flashes and then three more. I done this twice, and the second time I done it, I seen the last of the riders stop. So I done this a third time but there weren't no comeback. This didn't surprise me none. For one thing, there weren't no sunlight on that ridge to flash back. For another, they wouldn't know if it was someone signaling or accidental flashes. At that distance, I was damn lucky if they seen my signal even once.

I didn't waste no time following after. It was getting pretty cold up that high and I wanted to get as low as I could afore stopping for the night. So I led my horses on foot until I couldn't see not more and made camp right where I was. Turns out I was damn lucky. Fifty yards more and I could of walked off a hundred foot drop.

Like I said, it was cold and I was tempted to build a fire. Yet a man in the wilderness alone has to be thrice as careful as a man with two partners, so I didn't. A couple of hours later I was glad I ain't. The smell of wood smoke waken me up. When I got up and looked around, I seen the light of a fire not two hundred yards downhill and maybe a couple hundred more west. Looking through my spy glass, I counted five white men, all armed, and I didn't know but what there wasn't more.

I set there studying this out for a long time, wondering what they was doing here. This damn sure put a kink in my plans to catch up and I wondered where them men come from. I hadn't cut their trail the day afore, so they must of come up from another direction. Then it struck me the three I seen down the water shed might have been part of this party rather than Mac and Charlie. I didn't think so, but it did mean I best be real careful passing through.

I studied the men some more through the spy glass and it didn't seem to me they was just passing through. What I seen of their camp looked like they was thinking to stay a while and I wondered if they was miners looking for pay dirt. They could have been that, but they could have been outlaws, too, and I had to act like that's what they was. I known I could handle two men in a fight because I done it, and maybe I could take on three without getting myself shot. Five was just plain too many.

Somehow I taken the notion to get a closer look at them men. Looking back, of course, it were a damn fool idea, but having two Colt's pistols with twelve shots as fast as I wanted them made me plumb dim-witted. I was a pretty damn good shot with my Colt's but I wasn't no two-gun shooter could knock silver dollars out of the air with either hand. I can shoot all right with my left hand but I ain't never shot with both hands at a time. So what in the hell was I thinking to risk having to fight off five men most likely as good as me?

That was later. Right then taken a look seemed like a good plan. So I tied up the horses and got rid of everything on me that might make noise. Then I put on my softest pair of moccasins and slipped off in the darkness. I was damned lucky I didn't fall off that mountain.

It taken me at least a half hour to make it to the edge of their camp. By then the moon was up over the mountain and a little light made it through the trees. The fire had burned down and from what I seen, three of the men had done gone to bed. The other two was drinking something from their cups and talking so quiet I weren't able to make out what they was saying. So I slipped in closer to snoop.

When I was able to make out their words, it didn't take me long to find out they wasn't miners. One of them was bellyaching over his cut of the loot they taken off some poor soul on the main trail two days back. The other man wasn't too happy having to spend so much time waiting there in the mountains for someone to get back. I guessed it was the two men I seen on the trail. He was for heading to Taos where the rest of the gang was getting ready to go north for the gold afore winter set in.

Wasn't either one of them listening to the other too close and it struck me these men was drunk. Their voices sounded like it and I seen the neck of a bottle catching the glow of the fire. It was setting right next to one of the men but it were too dark to see how far it was down. Seemed reasonable to think the others probably headed for their blankets with a belly full of liquor, too.

I was studying what to do when a sixth man I ain't seen afore walked up behind me and tripped over my feet. He fell toward the fire and landed in it, but didn't take him long to scramble out the other side. When they seen this, the other two men took to laughing so hard one of the other men woken up. When he seen the third man laying there cussing and trying to get up, he put his head down and went back to sleep.

The man who fell had to of been drunk, too, not to see me laying there. He shaken his head, trying to get his wits about him, but when he tried to get up, he kept falling back down. He finally got his self on his feet, cussing like fury, and turned toward me, trying to see what tripped him. When he done it, I seen his face for the first time. He had to of been the ugliest man I ever laid eyes on and falling on his face weren't no improvement. There were a scar run from the hairline above his right right temple clean across his face, running across his eyebrow and nose and barely missing his left eye afore it stopped level with his mouth.

He was standing on the other side of the fire from me with the light in his eyes and I laid real still, hoping he couldn't see me. I known he must of because he went for his gun. When he done it I cut down on him, but he was weaving and my shot caught him high in the gut, not far under the heart. He went down like a sack of potatoes.

The two men sitting by the fire was stunned for a second but then they went for their guns, too, and I taken them out, both straight through their chest. By then the three men in their blankets was grabbing for their guns and jumping up and I just kept on firing. One of them got a shot off at me, but it went high and I put a ball through his neck. He must of been dead afore he hit the ground.

I moved away from where I laid and switched guns, but it weren't necessary. The three by the fire wasn't moving and only the ugly man on the other side of the fire was still alive. Like I said, he was shot in the gut and I known he wouldn't last out the next day. When he seen me watching him, he reached for his rifle but he were too weak to lift it off the ground.

I didn't know but what there might be other men close by so I moved to a deep shadow and set for a long spell, listening and waiting and reloading my Colt's. When the moon shown me I'd set for an hour, I circled the camp real slow, going from shadow to shadow. Weren't nobody I could see or hear or smell, so I went back to the fire and gathered up all the guns I could find. There was quite a few, including three more Colt's and a case of breech loading Hall rifles like the Army used. I wondered if them last was stolen and almost left them behind. One other thing I taken off one of the men was a good holster for the second Colt's. There was a good belt I taken, too, and I was right proud to have them both.

Wasn't no coals showing from the fire by then. But the moon was pretty high and I could see almost as good as day while I went through the bodies. I didn't bother trying to see what I was getting. I cut the arm off a shirt on one of the bodies and made me a sack to hold it all.

The man who I gut shot watched me but I didn't bother him none. When I was done with the bodies and was about to head out he spoke up. "Damn your eyes!" he says to me. "Finish the job! Don't leave me here! Kill me!" His voice was so weak I could barely hear him.

I shaken my head. Killing in the heat of a fight is one thing. Killing in cold blood were something I never wanted to do, even when it might be a mercy. "Like them women you raped on the plains?" I asked.

"That wasn't me!" he told me. "It was the others. I swear!"

I walked across the clearing to where them first two men was laying. Their bottle was still there, close to full, which surprised me, and I carried it over and set it down next to the gut-shot man. I brung him a cup, too, and set it down filled half full. Drinking with a belly wound ain't good for you but that didn't seem to matter considering he were dying.

The ugly man grabbed the bottle by the neck and pulled it to his lips. Seemed like he could barely lift it. "For God's sake, help me!" he says.

I started to give him a hand but thought better of it. I taken a rifle barrel and pushed his blanket aside. Underneath it there was a wicked looking knife. I knocked it out of his reach with the rifle barrel and picked it up. When I done it, the man started cussing me. There weren't no doubt in my mind he'd have stabbed me a dozen times if I'd got close enough to feed him a drink.

I found six horses and a pack mule tied up near camp. I loaded the mule with the rifles and the provisions I found in camp, but I couldn't study out what to do with all the horses. Ended up that I untied them and turned them all loose. Seemed to be the best thing at the time. I had a spare horse and a pack mule and the only thing six more horses would do is slow me down. I thought about taking them to Taos to sell but I didn't have no bill of sale and I sure as hell didn't want to be taken for no horse thief.

CHAPTER THIRTEEN

Taos

The night was getting old by the time I got back to my camp, so I loaded up my horses and headed out. The light was good enough then and I was still way too wound up to rest. I figured them other two men might be back any time and I was wanting to put as many miles as I could behind me come sunset. I also figured someone might of heard all the racket I made the night afore and come looking.

I made real good time that day. The trail wandered around the crest of the divide a long way as it headed down hill and I come to the ridge where I seen the three riders by noon. Turns out it was only about five miles from where I spotted them.

Not wanting to cross the clearing like they done, I dropped over the slope and found my way through the trees. That weren't easy. The slope was rocky and a lot steeper and the horses didn't like it. I had to pick my way real careful but it didn't cost me much time.

When I come to the other side of the clearing through the trees I was damned glad when I spotted a couple of branches the old man broken and left on the ground to let me know I was right behind them. I also seen the trail was well traveled through here and I known I was on the main cutoff to Taos Sam Watrous told me about. From what he said me, it weren't more than a half day's ride on in and I figured I'd find Keenan and Charley waiting for me someplace around there. Knowing Mac, it wouldn't be in town.

It was dark by the time I rode in and I was beat. Not knowing where to look for Charlie and Mac, I rode around the settlement until I found me a nice soft place under a cottonwood by the river and hobbled the horses so they could graze. Then I rolled myself up in a couple of blankets and slept like a rock.

It was the smell of cooking that woke me the next morning. The sky was just getting light then and when I looked around I seen I wasn't forty yards from a mud house I never seen for the bushes. A Mexican man come out just then and when he seen me, he looked me over right good. I must not of looked too bad because he come over to where I was and said something.

I didn't understand a word he said but it sounded like Spanish. So I asked him if he spoke English. He shaken his head and said something but waved me to follow him to his house. His eyes got wide when I buckled one of my Colt's on my belt and stuck the other in my waistband in back, but he didn't say nothing. I guess maybe he was scared to at that point.

The house was only two rooms with a mud fireplace in one corner of the main one. There was a hand made wood table and a couple of chairs in the middle of the room and a small wood pie chest against one wall. When we come in a woman was cooking tortillas on a flat stone near the wood fireplace. The stone was resting on a bed of coals and she was using a flat wood paddle to turn the tortillas.

The woman looked up when I come in but didn't say nothing. The man said something to her in Spanish and she nodded. The next thing I known, she was handing me a tortilla fresh off the stone and it was so hot I damn near dropped it. The woman smiled and pointed to a pot of beans sitting in the corner of the fireplace. They was warm and I helped myself, careful not to take too much so I could roll them up in the tortilla.

There weren't no sauce but them beans and tortilla was one of the best tasting meals I ever had. I was tempted when they offered me more but I could see they was not that well off and shaken my head, rubbing my belly to show I was full. I did know how to tell them thanks, and said "gracias," but when I tried to pay them from the few Mexican coins I had, the man wouldn't take it.

I don't like to be beholden, so I taken one of the knives I got off the men on the mountain and laid it on the table. "Gracias," I said again, patting the knife and pointing toward the woman. She looked at her husband and he nodded. I pushed it across the table to her and she smiled. I known she was glad to have it because the one I seen laying by the fire was worn so thin it was like to break just looking at it.

The man and woman talked together again for a minute. Then the man got up and waved me to follow him out of the house. When I got outside, I started toward my horses but the man said something and shook his head. He pointed toward a house about fifty yards up the creek and waved for me to follow. "El jeffe viva alli," he told me. I didn't understand but I figured there were someone else he wanted me to meet.

I was loath to leave my stock, especially with a load of rifles in the pack saddle beside the mule. Having them on me was worse in some ways than having six extra horses if I got tangled up with the law. Yet I studied there wasn't no better place to leave them, so I followed the Mexican.

Another Mexican answered the door and him and the man I was following talked for a bit. I heard them use "jeffe" a couple of times. Then the man who answered the door disappeared back inside while we waited. I wondered who Mr. Jeffe might be. Turns out the word means boss.

A white man come to the door afore long. He were thin and about my height, and he wore his beard shaved except for a big moustache. His eyes seemed to stare right through me and he looked like a man you'd want on your side in a fight.

"I'm Carson," he told me. "Miguel tells me you camped on our fields last night."

I give him my name. "Jack Bear," I said. "I'm just passing through. It were dark last night and I didn't realize I was on somebody's land."

Carson looked me up and down real careful. "Well, you don't look like a robber or killer to me, despite those guns. Care to tell me how you come by them?"

"I won one in a card game on a river boat in Arkansas," I said. "I taken the other off a man that tried to kill me."

Carson nodded. "Mind if I look at one?"

I handed him the one out of my waistband at the back, butt first. "Take a shot if you want. All six tubes is loaded." When I done it there was this voice in the back of my head told me I was crazy.

Carson looked over the Colt's. "All six cylinders loaded means you're expecting trouble. Yet you just handed me a loaded pistol." He looked at me gravely. "You don't look like a fool. Or crazy, either." He handed the pistol back. "Let's sit a spell and have some coffee. I'd like to hear what brings you to Taos, if you'd care to tell me."

That coffee on top of the tortilla and beans tasted so good I thought I'd died and gone to heaven. I told Carson I was partnered with two other folk and we come west to see the country. "I heard tell of it so much I wanted to see it for myself," I said. "I was lucky to partner with Mac. He's been out this way afore. It was damn bad luck getting separated by the stampede. I'm supposed to catch up with him here."

Carson looked at me strange. "You call him Mac. I take it he's a good bit older than you?" I nodded. "I don't suppose he's a crusty old Scotsman whose first name is Keenan, is he?"

I allowed that was exactly who my partner was and Carson grinned. "I didn't know that old bear was still alive. He's a friend of mine." He looked at me serious. "I think there's a lot you're not telling me, Jack."

"I'd just as soon you get it from him," I answered. "I don't mind your knowing, but part of it is his business, too. No offense, I hope."

"None taken," Carson told me. "I'm surprised you've told me as much as you have. I assure you it will be held in confidence." He studied me for a minute. "I suppose you wouldn't mind a little help finding McAdams."

"I'd appreciate it," I said. "He warned me to stay away from the authorities here."

"He was quite right. You might be arrested and shot for a spy. Things are a little tense right now over Texas." He nodded. "The Mexican government is pretty sore over the treaty Santa Anna signed. We're a long way from Mexico City and things are not as bad here, but I expect war to break out before long."

We fetched my horses. Carson looked them over and liked what he saw. "Those are fine horses. Do you mind my asking where you got them?"

"Out on the plains," I told him. "A couple of outlaws tried to kill me."

"You were riding the mule?" he asked. I shaken my head and told him I was afoot and he give me a strange look. "You were on foot and overcame two mounted outlaws?"

"Yes, sir, I done it," I said and told him how it taken place. "They was a little too cocksure of their selves."

"You're lucky to be alive," he assured me. Then he give me a hard look. "I hope you're not yanking my rope."

"No, sir," I said. "I'm telling you the honest truth."

"Well, there's something you're not telling me," he said. "It's none of my business, of course, but I am curious. You didn't steal that mule, did you?"

I shaken my head. "No, sir, but I know damn sure you won't believe how I come by it. I have a hard time believing it myself."

Carson nodded but said nothing more. We saddled up and he rode with me through town. I was thinking it might be better to slip around and see the lay of the land first, but Carson wouldn't hear of it. "I'm known and well respected here," he told me. "If you try slipping around, someone will spot you for sure. This way shows you have nothing to hide. You'll be all right so long as you are with me."

Turned out he was right about that. He even introduced me to the local capitán, who asked me what brung me to Taos. I told him I was hoping to find a party to travel with to Montana and maybe Oregon. When he asked how I known Carson, I told him we had friends in common. Carson nodded and the capitán let it be. I known he was still suspicious, but Carson was married into one of the main families in Taos.

We didn't spot Mac or Charlie or even Hawk nowhere, so Carson asked me if I'd like to see the Taos pueblo. I had to confess I ain't had no idea what that was. "It's where our local Indians live. It's a settlement that goes back several hundred years, maybe more."

That seemed as good a way to pass the time as anything I had to do, so we rode out northwest of Taos. When I seen it, I found it amazing. There was mud houses stacked two and three stories high, like city hotels, and there was quite a few of them, too. What startled me was seeing cactus growing up on top of some of the houses.

We was sitting there on our horses looking when I heard a meadow lark call. Now I ain't heard one of them since I got to the mountains and I had a good notion who it was. Sure enough, when I looked around, damned if there weren't Mac, riding out from behind some brush and grinning from ear to ear. Right behind him were Charlie, headed for me at a dead gallop, and when she got to me, she like to broke my neck hugging me.

"So it wasn't you Jack was so anxious to find," Carson told McAdams, shaking his hand. "It's good to see you, Keenan."

"The pleasure's all mine, Kit." the old man told him. "It's been a while."

We ended up riding back to Carson's place. Once we was there, Carson introduced us to his family and we set and talked a spell. At least, Carson and Keenan did. Charlie and me was sitting side by side and she was holding my hand so tight I lost feeling in it. Hawk just set there and watched.

After a while Keenan asked me what happened since I seen him last. I told about the stampede and losing my bearings on the plains after my pony run off. Then I told them about being braced by the two outlaws and meeting Sam Watrous in Valmora.

Carson allowed as how Watrous was a good man. "You have to keep your wits about you trading with him," he said. "He won't cheat you but I don't know that I've ever met anyone sharper at making a trade."

Turns out, the pony made it back to camp all bloody from a horn cut, and Keenan and Charlie spent two days trying to find me. Charlie thought you were dead, for sure," the old man said. "When we didn't find a body, I wasn't so sure. You must have found the sign I left." I nodded. "That was you signaling from the mountain, wasn't it?" he asked and I nodded again. "I thought so but I wasn't sure," he told me. "We stopped and waited for you but after all that shooting on the mountain, I thought it best to come on here. It wasn't too many miles and I knew you'd find us if it was you."

"Who was doing all that shooting?" Charlie asked me. "It sounded like it was coming from near where you were. We heard seven shots."

I allowed it was me and it wouldn't do but I tell them all about it. When I was done Carson shook his head. "That's quite a story," he said. "Six shots and six dead men. That's rather...incredible."

"The lad's telling the truth," Keenan assured him. "I've never known him to lie about something like this. He's a dead-eye shot with that Colt's." He looked at me sort of strange.

"I told you I was having a hard time believing it, myself," I said to Carson. "I wouldn't believe it neither if someone told me he done it. All I wanted was to get the hell out of there. That drunk tripping over me was what set it off. He were drawing down on me and once I shot him the others was going for their guns, too. Didn't see I had much choice."

"Neither does a lightning rod," the old man said and Carson nodded.

"You seem to draw trouble, lad."

"I sure don't set out looking for it," I told him. "I don't see no use in trying to run from it, neither."

"That seems to be my fate, too, Jack," Carson said. He sniffed the air. "I think dinner's about ready. I hope you'll do me the honor of joining me and my family."

Truth is, all that killing was beginning to bother me. It was nine men on this trip, and afore that I taken out seven vigilantes that killed my folks. It adds up to a lot of lives taken, even if them killed was worse than snakes. I know some might say what I done were like killing snakes, but the fact is it weren't snakes I killed. I hoped it wouldn't be more killing afore this trip was done, but I known there would be.

After dinner Carson sent a couple of men to round up them horses I turned loose. Then we set and Mac and Carson talked a spell longer. Mac was doing most of the talking, telling Kit what all happened to us across the plains.

Listening to McAdams, I recalled something I needed to tell them about what I learnt snooping on the outlaw camp. "I forgot to tell you the rest of that gang is here in Taos," I said. "They're waiting here and getting ready to head north."

"Those were the men who killed Charlie's folks and tried to ambush us later," Keenan told Carson. "Judging from their tracks, they are also the same ones who killed the Mexican army detachment and tortured the padre. One thing we need to do here is get word to the proper authorities about what happened. The trick is doing so without getting arrested."

Carson nodded. "Why don't you leave the Bible with me? I can talk to the padres and they can pass the information to the capitán."

"We think the outlaws have a map where to find the abbot's gold," the old man added. "I think that's why they're heading north."

Carson give this some thought. "I wonder how many there are. If I add it right, you all have thinned them out by ten men." He looked at me. "And Jack took care of nine of them."

"Weren't my choosing," I told him. "I'd been proud to share."

Carson shrugged, "I'm not one to point a finger, Jack. I've killed more than my share, too. Six at once is rather remarkable."

"They'd of got me if they hadn't been drunk," I answered.

"No offense, but I have my doubts about that," Carson said. I seen Mac nodding. Charlie didn't say nothing but looked real serious.

I was glad when the conversation changed. After a spell, Charlie and I give them our excuses and taken a walk down by the creek. Somehow we wound up down to the horse barn. There weren't nobody there so we took to tossing down some fresh hay from the loft. Then we set down on the hay and talked a little.

"I thought you were dead, Jack," she said. "When your horse came back with blood all over it. What made it worse was us fighting before you left. I couldn't even remember why I was angry."

I known why I was but this weren't no time to get into it and it didn't matter no more. What mattered was Charlie so I just give her a hug and told her how much I missed her. Then I kissed her and wasn't no time afore Charlie was showing me just how much she missed me. Of course, I was showing her right back and pretty soon we didn't have no clothes on to speak of. Not long after that I was as close as a man gets to heaven in this world. So was Charlie.

That's about all I'm going to say about me and Charlie that afternoon. I don't mind talking about my times in a sporting house, but me and Charlie was something different. The only thing I will add is that I had never, ever found nothing like that time with Charlie in a sporting house. And from that day to this, it only got better.

We stayed a whole week in Taos. On Carson's advice I mostly stayed out of sight and, of course, Charlie kept me company. We spent a lot of time in that barn, so much so that Keenan taken to giving the meadow lark song afore he come in to check on the horses. He was sleeping up at Carson's house and Hawk had his self a spot down by the creek.

It was the fifth day we was there that Carson and McAdams took a couple of the horses up to the town square to sell. Charlie and me went along to look around and I used some of my pesos to get her some new clothes at the general store. I learnt she had a taste for sweets and I got us a big bag of candy for the trail.

The big surprise for me at the store was we run into Sam Watrous. He were the clerk there and he told me his business in Valmora had been picking up a load of supplies for the owner. I had a good chuckle because some of the supplies I seen behind the counter was the rifles I sold him. I suspect a lot of the supplies he had gathered up in Valmora he bought with his own money and sold to the store in Taos.

Sam and I was standing there swapping tales and haggling over Charlie's new clothes when I happen to see her face. She looked like she was seeing a ghost. Yet when I looked, I never seen nothing out of place.

When I asked what was wrong, she pointed. "See that man standing over there on the other side of the square?"

I looked where she was pointing. "That tall Mexican fellow?" Watrous asked. "That's Ben White, one of our local ranchers."

"No," I told him. "I think she's talking about that rough looking character that's talking to him." I recognized the man right away. He was one of the two man I seen on the trail when I left Valmora and took the trail into the mountains.

Charlie nodded. "He's one of them, Jack," she said. "He's a member of the gang that killed my family."

"You want to have him arrested?" Watrous asked. He looked worried.

"Wouldn't do no good," I told him. "They wasn't in Mexico when it happened and it's her word against his." I looked at him right serious. "I need you to keep this under your hat. I don't want them knowing anything about us, not even that we're in town."

Sam looked relieved. He told me he'd keep it quiet and he brung us our horses around to the back of the store. So we slipped away and headed back to Carson's place.

We was near the outskirts of town when we passed by a sporting palace. I known what it were, of course, but I kept my eyes on the trail ahead. Then I seen something out of the corner of my eye. I turned to look and damned if it weren't that respectable looking woman who almost got me shot back in Arkansas. She were talking to a customer on the porch and I known who he were, too. Because it weren't no customer she was talking to. It were that ugly looking character that damn near shot me.

They was talking and I didn't think they seen me. So I turned to look at Charlie like we was talking as we rode. When I done it, she give me a look that cut me to the heart and kicked her horse into a run. I started to follow but decided that weren't a good notion. I didn't want to do nothing that would draw attention.

When I got to the barn Charlie was sitting in a horse stall bawling her eyes out. I tried to talk to her but she pushed me away. I decided it might be a good idea to give her some time to cool down. So I unsaddled our horses and brushed them down.

When I come back, Charlie weren't crying no more. "What's wrong?" I said, but I had a pretty good notion without asking.

I think I rather taken a bullet than the look she given me. "You snake!" she declared. "You know what's wrong!"

That was right but she needed to say it out loud. "Why don't you tell me?" I said. "Then I'll know for sure."

"You were staring at those whores!"

"No, I ain't done it," I told her. "I were ignoring them."

"I saw the look on your face, Jack! You were lusting after them!"

"I ain't done it!" I declared. "I was just looking at one of them!"

"That's just as bad!" I think if she had a gun in her hand right then, she would of shot me. "So go on! Get out of here! Go find that sporting woman you're lusting after!" When she said this, Charlie busted out crying again.

"I'm going to say this just once," I told her. I were shaking like a leaf and I wanted to cuss, but I tried to keep my voice calm. "I was looking at the man as well as the woman. They was the ones who tried to kill me back in Arkansas. I told you about that."

"You told me and all those soldiers!" she said. "Are you going to tell them about me, too."

"I may if you try to kill me," I said, trying to get her to laugh. "I don't think they'd believe me, though."

That weren't the best notion I ever taken. Charlie looked like I hit her and run for the hay loft. When she got up it, she pulled the ladder up after and wouldn't say nothing else. After a while I give up and went for a long walk down by the creek.

Charlie didn't come to supper that night. Carson asked after her and I told him she weren't feeling good. He nodded. "Sometimes the ladies don't," he said and shrugged. "We got you a good price for the horses."

That taken me by surprise. "They wasn't my horses. They was there for the taking."

Carson looked at the old man again. McAdams grinned. "The lad has a point, Kit. He only told you where they were. It was your people who went to claim them."

Carson looked at me and then at the old man. Then he eat a couple of bites afore he spoke again. "It looks like we might have an early winter this year. All the signs are there."

Keenan allowed as he'd seen them, too, and Carson went on. "Any idea where you might be wintering this year? You're welcome here, of course. It's a sight to see come Christmas."

"I'd like to do that, Kit," Mac told him. "Yet, I think we need to move on. I hear a lot of war talk and if that gang is in town, I think I need to keep Charlie away from them. There's no telling what she might do if she saw one of them."

"We did," I told them. "Charlie spotted him when we was in the general store. He was talking to Ben White."

Carson give me a look. "How do you know Ben White?"

"Sam Watrous told me who he was. I seen the man Charlie spotted down near Valmora last week."

"So the gang probably knows that someone killed six of their number," the old man observed. "It was a good thing you left the horses on the trail, Jack." He turned to Carson. "I hope this doesn't cause you trouble, Kit."

Carson shook his head. "Not at all. When my men found them, these horses were running wild. They weren't branded or wearing a halter. They weren't even shod. So for all anyone knows, they could be Indian ponies."

"It's strange they weren't shod," Keenan said. "Maybe that's where they got them, off some Indians."

Carson shook his head. "They're too good for Indians to let go."

"Maybe the owner's couldn't do anything about it," Mac answered. "It may be they were dead."

I taken a plate of food down to the barn for Charlie, but she still weren't talking to me. I slept on a pile of straw near the horse stalls that night and a couple of times I woke up hearing her crying. Seemed to me a lot more was wrong than her just being mad at me. She was good about getting over that pretty quick.

Next morning I seen the plate of food were still where I left it and Charlie didn't answer when I called. I seen the ladder was down from the loft. I shinnied up it and poked my head over the top, but weren't nobody there. I headed for the house, thinking Charlie gone there for breakfast, but she weren't there, neither.

When Keenan seen my face, he filled a plate and excused his self from the table. Carson didn't say nothing for a while. Then he looked at me and said, "God and the ways of women, Jack." It must of been clear I didn't get his drift because he added, "No man can understand either one."

"Amen to than," I told him. Then I asked him how long he been in New Mexico and we got to talking about this and that. Pretty soon Keenan come back and joined us, and when breakfast was done we headed for the porch for a cup of coffee like we always done.

After a while Mac told me I might want to check the horses, and I taken the hint. Sure enough, Charlie was waiting for me when I got to the barn. She didn't say nothing, just grabbed me and hugged me so tight I could hardly breathe. "Please forgive me, Jack," she said real quiet.

"There ain't nothing to forgive," I told her. "I can see how you might of thought what you did. I was off base saying what I did. There's no way I'd tell nobody nothing about you and me."

"I know that, Jack," she allowed. "I knew that then. I just went crazy."

"Mind telling me why?"

"It was seeing that man on the square. When I did, it was like the whole thing happening all over again, the day my folks were killed." Her face was white as a sheet and I could feel her shaking in my arms.

"The same thing happened to me, Charlie," I told her. "I know what you mean. I used to dream of the militia killing my folks. It was like I was right back there again."

"This wasn't a dream, Jack," she told me. "You don't understand. I was wide awake and it was right there in front of my eyes. One minute I was in this world and the next I was right back then." She started crying.

"I understand, Charlie. I weren't dreaming the first time it happened. It was just like you said, like I was in two worlds. One was now and the other was then. I could even smell the blood."

"The first time?" Charlie pulled back a little and looked at me. Doesn't it ever go away."

"It ain't never gone away for me," I told her. "It don't help much to fight it, neither. What helped was the first time I told Mac. After that it got a lot less bad."

"Hold me, Jack," she said. "Don't ever let me go." Then she started to tell me about it. By the time she was done we was both crying. To this day I don't know which one I was grieving for most, her and her kin or me and mine. Or maybe I was grieving the fact that in the five years since I was sixteen I'd killed sixteen men. Yes, they was all bad men who got exactly what they had coming, but I couldn't deny the fact each and every one of them was some mother's child.

The seventh day we was there, Charlie and me headed for the barn after dinner. We was too whipped by grieving to do nothing but sleep in each other's arms the afternoon and evening afore. Yet we was young and full of fire and by the time dinner was done, we was both ready to make up for lost time.

When we excused ourselves, Keenan allowed he'd take his afternoon nap on the porch after a pipe or two of tobacco. We was laying there quiet, taking a breather, when we heard a meadow lark. Sounded like it come from up toward the house so Charlie give one back to let Mac know we heard. We got three more back right quick, which meant it were urgent, so we got on our clothes headed that way.

We was half way there when I turned to her. "Are you going to marry me, Charlie?" I asked her.

She got this devilish look on her face. "I don't know, Jack. Are you asking me to marry you?"

I allowed as I was and she give me that same devilish look and pretended she was giving it some thought. "Well, it is the best offer I had all day. So I guess I better take it."

"I don't want any guessing, woman," I told her. "I need a 'yes' or a 'no.'"

"In that case, I will," she said. "I will marry you, Jack."

I stopped just long enough to give her a big kiss and hug and we headed for the house to see what Mac wanted. When we got there I seen he was right agitated. "Pack up, Jack," he told me. "Carson just got word the capitán is rounding up his troops. Someone claims we stole the horses Kit sold. We've got to leave now!"

CHAPTER FOURTEEN

On the Run

Well, I had no fancy to be in a Mexican jail or shot for a spy or hung for a horse thief. I damned sure weren't going to let nobody arrest Charlie. I had five Colt's and a case of rifles, and I was ready to take on the Mexican army. So Charlie and me didn't waste no time. We run back to the barn and was packed and ready to go inside ten minutes.

Mac joined us and we headed due east of Taos and into the mountains. When we crossed over the first ridge maybe thirty minutes later, the old man stopped and taken out his spy glass. I taken mine out, too, and when I looked back towards Carson's place, I spotted a whole bunch of riders gathered around the front of Carson's house. I give my glass to Hawk so he could take him a look, too.

"Kit will delay them as long as he can," McAdams told me. "But they'll be after us before long."

We taken off again up a good sized canyon but it weren't long afore Mac turned us north up a rocky ravine. It were deep enough to hide us if we led our horses and when we come to another ravine leading east, Mac turned us that way. We kept doing this, winding ourselves north and east until we couldn't see to go no further. When we stopped, it were in high country and I'd guess we was about six or eight miles northeast of Taos. It were late in the day when we started and we was mostly on foot, so that weren't bad for a few hours' travel.

It were cold that night. With no fire, I was glad to have Charlie next to me in our blankets. Don't get me wrong. I'm right proud to have Charlie next to me any time, but that night it kept us both warm. I had my back to the cold and we was like two spoons in a drawer, but she had the pup under the blanket on her other side, too. So she were the warmest of us all.

There was a dusting of snow on the ground when we got up the next morning. It made the going slippery at first but the sun burnt it off by mid day and we was able to travel faster. Since we was leading our horses instead of riding, I warmed up right fast and weren't long until I had to take off my serape. Charlie taken it then but she shed it pretty quick.

We wasn't long on the trail afore we run into a large canyon running to the east and Mac taken that. He told us where we was headed was a river valley on the east side of the mountains. He was thinking we could follow that north until we could cross back over the mountains and follow the Rio Grande valley into Colorado.

We made good time traveling up that canyon. The middle of the afternoon we got to where it turned north and Mac found a game trail that led to a good place to make camp that night. We was able to build a fire and I cooked up some biscuits and bacon and made us a pot of coffee from the supplies I taken off the outlaws on the mountain. I found lots of sugar to go into our coffee and even Hawk taken a cup. It weren't bad eating seeing we was on the run.

It taken us several more days to get through the first range of mountains, but we wasn't moving fast. We didn't come across no sign of no one else and from what I seen, didn't look like nobody been up that way in a long time. A couple of days the old man stopped early and went fishing, which got us fresh meat. Then Hawk brung down a young buck and we had meat for several days. Cool as it was, it didn't go bad and we damn near had more than we could eat.

When we topped over the last ridge, we come out over a long, wide valley between two ranges of mountains. There were a stream running down the middle of the valley but we didn't go all the way down. Mac figured we best stick to the lower slopes to steer clear of any Indian camps. It was the Utes and the Jicarilla Apache we might of run into, and he didn't want to mess with neither of them. The Utes had a reputation of being downright unfriendly to folk they seen trespassing and Mac said other Apache didn't have much use for the Jicarilla. Neither did most everybody else, either. He told us they was good basket makers but notorious thieves.

So we stayed on the upland slopes, traveling north until we come across a good place to camp. It had a spring and it didn't look like nobody never been there. It was low enough to be warmer and easy to defend, off to one side of a deeper canyon and one of them places where nobody would think to come. There was just enough game, but not too much, and Keenan found good luck fishing in the river below us.

We was there four days and on the second day Mac come to me. "Let's take a look around, Johnny," he said. Him calling me Johnny instead of Jackie told me he had something he needed to get off his chest. I known it was personal because the old man was unsettled. Nobody didn't know him wouldn't see it, but he were.

"Charlie mentioned you might be making plans," he said. I told him she said she would marry me and we agreed to let her tell him. He give me a grin and relaxed a bit. "Well, then. You understand that changes things a bit, don't you?"

"Yeah," I answered. "Some time I guess we'll need to find us a place to settle and raise kids. I know how to farm. My daddy taught me and he always made a crop, even in dry years."

"That's very good," he told me. "Yet, I don't see you as a farmer. I have not doubt you could do it well, but I don't see you being content with it. Of course, I could be wrong. People do change. Not often, but they do."

"What are you saying?" I asked him.

"I'm not concerned with what lies that far down the road. I'm thinking about this winter. We need a place to hole up and you and Charlie will need your privacy."

"We're doing all right," I told him, but he shaken his head.

"Trust me on this, Johnny," he said. "Charlie may not have said anything but women like their own nest."

"Yeah," I said, "but that's for raising chicks." Then I heard what was coming out of my mouth and I caught his drift. "Oh. You think there's a baby coming?"

"Sooner or later there will be," he said. "Unless you've been doing something to prevent it." When he said this, he was looking off at the mountains. "That's none of my business, of course," he added.

Well, I hadn't been doing nothing to prevent nothing. Charlie and me ain't had opportunity to do much since we left Taos, and we only done it a few times there. Well, more than a few, to be honest, and then again the first night we was in this camp. So it were possible we was already too late to prevent nothing.

"You think she's carrying my child?" I asked him.

"I have no idea, Johnny," he told me. "I think it may be too early to tell, but that isn't my business. I can tell you what to look for if you want to know, but I'm not your doctor."

Then I got real scared. "We're a long way from no doctor," I told him. "You think we ought to head back to Ft. Smith?" Neither my brother or my sister was brought into this world by no doctor, but I known lots of women died having children. Thinking of losing Charlie that way were downright scary.

"I can't advise you on that," he told he. He was looking at me again. "I lost a wife in childbirth and she was tended by a doctor. On the other hand, I took an Arapaho woman for my wife and she had three children in a skin tent. I know Charlie had younger siblings and I'd think that if Charlie is like her mother, she wouldn't have a problem. I think the trip back east might be harder on her than carrying a child."

I was right agitated and the old man seen it. "I'm not telling you this to scare you, Johnny. Yet, you're planning to be her husband and you need to be aware how things are. Talk to Charlie about it. See what she wants." He smiled. "That's the best advice I could ever give you. Always listen to your wife, even when you think she's wrong. Then, when she's wrong, be man enough to admit it's your fault. It will always pay off."

So that night we went for a walk and I talked to Charlie about it. I done so afore things got too far, and the old man was right. It paid off right then way more than I would of ever thought, and it never stopped paying off down the road. After those days in the hay loft I never would of thought it could get any better, but was I ever wrong.

Next day we talked to Mac about where to winter. As he seen it, we had three choices. One was to stay right where we was and build us brush wikiups like the southern Utes done. Yet we was on a north slope and at high elevation, so it would be colder there and winter would last longer. There wouldn't be much game up there, neither.

Of course, we could of stayed in that same area and done the same thing in some other camp lower down. Then game would of been more bounteous and winter, shorter. Yet the chance of being discovered by hostiles were greater. With a belly full of killing like I had, I'd rather of faced winter than hostiles. I weren't going to let nobody harm any of us if I could help it, but it weren't unmanly to shun places where I might have to shoot my way out.

Another choice was to head east to the Santa Fe trail and find us some place to hole up near there. I suggested Valmora, which was fifty miles to the south of us, but Keenan weren't too warm on that. It was a long way from Taos, but the capitán known we was headed east and might have soldiers waiting for us there.

We was sitting on the east side of a ridge and facing toward the valley while we was talking. Suddenly Keenan told me to get out my spy glass and then he pointed to where the river flowed into a canyon. It was four or five mile directly east of where we was standing and with the glass I seen an Indian camp not far from the canyon. Yet when I looked at it without the glass, I could barely make it out for the haze. I give the glass to Charlie and she taken a look, too.

Mac couldn't tell what kind of Indians they was, but it were risky finding out. They might treat us good or they might not and weren't no telling which way they'd might go. Hawk being with us made it worse. Comanche wasn't too well liked by nobody.

So it looked like the only good choice we had was heading east. We would rather of followed the valley north until we crossed over to the Rio Grande watershed, but I spotted what looked like another camp to the north. There was no telling how many more they might be up that valley. It looked like a popular place to winter.

Heading east, it looked to me like our best bet might be crossing the valley three or four mile south of the camp and working our way north through the mountains until we come to the river. Keenan didn't like that much but there weren't no other better choice. He was worried that once we was in the mountains we might get lost and be forced to winter in high country. Yet it was either that or stay where we was, and Charlie was for moving camp. I was, too, once we spotted that Indian camp.

Of course, I known part of what was behind her choice and it tickled me. Heading east we'd hit the Santa Fe Trail and wintering somewhere along the trail, we might come across a preacher headed west. Staying where we was, there weren't no chance.

Since the moon weren't much past full, Mac thought we might be best off crossing the valley by night. I could see Hawk didn't like it much. Some Indians think ghosts are out by night and it ain't wise to tangle with them. I think Hawk held with that notion but he come along, anyway. I think it was because he didn't want us thinking him a coward. I don't know for sure because he weren't talking that good yet, but that's what Charlie said and the old man agreed.

We spent the next day getting ready to travel. Come sundown we turned in to catch some rest and it were getting on toward midnight, or maybe an hour afore, when we headed out. The moon was high, almost as bright as day, and we was careful to keep to the shadows. We had the ponies' feet bound so there wouldn't be no shod tracks, and we was leading them on foot. I figure it was that what saved us.

We was half way cross the valley and close to the stream when the old man held up his hand and stopped us. We froze, holding the noses of our horses so they wouldn't whinny, and it was lucky we was in the shadows of a stand of brush. Not a minute after Mac stopped us I seen riders moving by no more than thirty yards away. The moon was bright enough I could see they was Indians, but I didn't know what kind. Later Hawk told us they was Ute and Mac figured it was a war party. Hunters don't go out in the middle of the night except for possum and there sure wasn't none of them around that country.

The war party was moving slow and headed south, and it taken them a while to get far enough away they wouldn't hear us. We waited a good while after that afore we crossed the stream and made for the mountains. I was keyed up all the time, wondering if they seen us and was circling back to attack. I seen Mac was worried, too.

The ravine we was headed for was perfect for ambush and Mac must of thought so, too. He turned north a hundred yards afore we reached it and passed up two more arroyos. I was wondering if we was heading all the way to the river, but he took the next one and I was damn glad to be out of that valley.

One reason Mac taken the arroyo he done was that it was dry with a hard, rocky bottom. It was also wide enough to let in moonlight to see by and it taken us exactly where we was wanting to go. Looking at a map years later on, I seen it saved us considerable traveling.

What was strange about it was that Mac didn't know the country no better than me. Yet, I seen him do this a lot of times afore and after and I never known how he done it. All he ever said was he listened to something in his mind that always told him the right way. He said it were sort of the way geese always fly north to the same spot every year. I heard it called instinct, and I guess it was. He had it and it worked damn good. It saved us a lot of grief.

We was in high country afore we stopped to rest. The moon was going down and it was too dangerous traveling more. Since we was on the other side of the mountains from the sunrise it was a good while afore we could see good enough to travel again. I reckoned we only come six or eight mile that night but it weren't likely we'd find trouble where we was.

It weren't far from where we was camped to the top of the divide. When we got there what we seen was worth the whole hike up the mountain. The sun was up a good ways and just starting to burn off the haze gathered in the canyons below us. Yet it was high enough I could see Keenan had done it again. We was standing maybe five hundred foot above a stream bed fed by a spring and it led down to the deepest canyon in the range. It were a mile or two below us and I figured that were where the river we was looking for flowed.

Sure enough, we followed that creek bed straight down and come to the Cimarron River just where it made a horseshoe turn and headed north. We was on the south side of the river, which were good since the slope weren't as steep and we would travel a good ways from the river. It made our travel a lot slower but that weren't all bad. About the last thing we wanted was to run into Indians living close to the river. We never seen none, but it didn't mean they wasn't there.

We only made about eight mile that day. That afternoon we come to a deep canyon Mac didn't care to pass through, so we was forced way high on the mountain. Then we come to a wide valley where we seen Indians camped along the river on the other side. It was a large camp, having maybe two dozen lodges, and we didn't care to come calling. Looking through his spy glass, Keenan reckoned they was Ute.

So we stopped there for the night. The next morning Mac found a game trail that led us down the slope and east through some low hills. This were out of our way a little, but it kept us hid. Yet it were there we run into trouble.

Keenan was leading with Hawk right there with him, and it was when we come around a bend in a dry creek bed we seen a Ute dressing out a deer. He were twenty yards off at most and I don't know why he didn't hear us coming. Maybe it was because the wind were blowing our sound back up the draw.

The Ute seen us about the same time we seen him and taken off running. Keenan rode after him like a shot, intending to pull him down afore he got to his pony and went for more Ute. Mac would of done it, too, but Hawk let fly with an arrow and brought the Ute down. The Ute tried to get up but fell down, and he were dead by the time we reached him.

Hawk started to scalp the Ute but Keenan held up his hand and stopped him. He broken off the arrow right at the skin and signed Hawk to help lift the Ute onto his horse. Then Mac tied him on good and we headed east again at a fast pace with the Ute tied over his horse.

We kept riding hard through the hills until we come to a deep canyon maybe five miles from where we chanced on the Ute. Where we stopped were at the edge of a good drop and Mac and Hawk untied the dead Ute and dropped him over the edge. Afore they done that, the old man done something strange. He hand signed Hawk to go ahead and scalp the Ute, which he done. Then Keenan thrown the busted arrow shaft after the body and turned the Indian pony loose.

"They'll have a hard time puzzling that one out, won't they?" Mac said. "Assuming they ever find him. Do you two understand we had to do what we did?"

"I don't understand about the scalping," Charlie told him, speaking for me, too.

"Well, according to Hawk's way of thinking, it was his kill and so it was his scalp to take. It's a matter of honor among his people. I prevented it back there because I didn't want to leave a blood trail for his kin to follow. Doing this will buy us at least a couple of days' time to clear out of the country, maybe more. They'll have a hard time following any trail we left and a harder time finding him. But we best be off."

I was wondering why we freed the horse, too, but I ain't never got a chance to ask. Only thing I could study out was that the pony was old and real poor. He would of slowed us down and wouldn't even been fit to eat. This way if the horse made it back the Ute would know something happened. Even if they tracked it back to the drop-off, they'd think it was the Comanche that killed the man. The arrow was one Hawk made his self.

We had us a few more hours of daylight left and we rode on until we couldn't see. We was on the west side of the mountains by then but it were still too dangerous to travel at night. We didn't need one of our horses stepping into in a hole and breaking a leg, or falling into a dry gulch. So we taken a rest until the moon come up. Then we rode on in the night until we passed a rock Mac called Indian Head and finally come to the Santa Fe trail. After that we rode a few miles until we found a good place to stop. It were hard on us and hard on the horses, but we was fifteen to twenty mile from where Hawk shot the Ute, and maybe more. Any trail we might of left would been lost on the main trail.

We rode on for two more days. The horses was tired and so was we, and we didn't push it. The afternoon of the first day a rain storm come along. It didn't last too long or rain too hard, but it were enough to settle the dust and wipe out any tracks we may of left. I was thankful there weren't no lightning and no hostiles. Matter of fact, we didn't run into nobody on that stretch of the trail.

The second day we come to a place McAdams known from afore. He called it Willow Springs and it didn't take much time to puzzle out how it got its name. Hawk and me started to cut some willow branches to make arrows, but Mac told us to be quick about it and be sure to hide our cuttings. The springs was well known for a watering place and he wanted to make for another place he known about not far from there.

The place where Mac took us didn't look like nothing from the valley floor. This didn't surprise me none because that's the kind of place Mac liked to camp, but this one was better than most. It looked like a dry canyon until we got there but there was water in it. Only the water didn't come from no spring. There was a natural basin the water carved into the rock when it rained and it held enough water to last us a long time. Yet the best thing was we didn't see no tracks there but game.

We set up camp on a wide shelf above the basin. It was wide enough to give our horses some graze and we made our camp behind a big rock to one side of it. Couldn't nobody see our fire from there and it weren't too far to the top of the ridge. From there we could keep an eye on the comings and goings down at the willow spring. It was only a couple of miles as the crow flies. As the buzzard flies, I guess it'd be more like twelve mile.

Anyway, we made our camp there and that night we talked about where we needed to go from there. "I figure we're close to seven thousand feet here," the old man told us. "I've been told that Willow Springs never freezes over. Here we're about three hundred feet higher, so we might have to break ice or even haul water. I doubt there will be as much snow here as on the high peaks above us and we should have plenty of game to eat. The trouble is that we'll leave sign pointing to this place that even a blind man could read."

"What about grazing?" I asked. "Seems to me that could be a problem, too. There's not much grazing up here."

"What better choice do we have?" Charlie asked. She was looking right tired and I seen the travel was wearing her down. Come to think of it, the old man was looking pretty worn, too. Hawk, he looked pretty much the same as always.

"We could push north to Bent's Fort," Mac told her. "They charge pretty high tariff but thanks to Jackie we have plenty of goods to barter. Or maybe I should say he does. He won them."

Mac looked at me and it taken me a second to catch his drift. "No," I said. "We're all partners. Share and share alike. Even the money I got."

"I thought it was that way, but I didn't want to presume," Mac told me. "The Bents are honest but they charge what the traffic will bear. On the other hand, out here rifles are always good for trade."

"That sounds like a safer place to winter," Charlie said. "What would keep us from it?"

"The pass over the mountains," Keenan said. "It's a good twenty miles long and a thousand feet higher. It's a lot colder and we might get caught in a snow storm. Then after that it's a good eighty miles to Bent's Fort. That's across the plains and we could get caught in an early blizzard. If we did, it would be much better to be in the mountains."

"How much chance of that?" I asked. "It's cold up here but it don't seem that late in the year." The truth is I'd lost all track of days and months.

Keenan smiled. "I had to ask Carson what day it was, myself. He told me it was October 30 when we got to Taos. By my calculations, that would make today November 21. We'll reach the winter solstice in a month."

"Another month and it'll be Christmas," I said. I had no notion what a winter solstice were. Come to find out, it's the shortest day of the year.

Charlie looked sad. "We always kept Christmas," she said so soft I could barely hear her. What I seen was the tears this brung to her eyes.

"We'll do it this year, too," I told her. "My family done so, too, and that would be good. I don't know how, but we'll puzzle it out. What did your folks do?"

We got sidetracked for a while talking about that. Keenan just watched and listened, smiling at us like I never seen afore. After a while he pulled us back on track. "It's good to have something to look forward to," he said. "However, Christmas is several weeks away. The question we need to decide now is where we're going to spend it."

"I think the weather's going to be whatever it turns out," I said. "I think we ought to get on across. What about Indians?"

"That's always a possibility either way we go," Keenan told us. "I don't think we'll see any around the pass this time of year. Wagon traffic is over for the winter and most bands will be in their winter camps by now. We might run across a hunting party either here or on the other side. On this side it will probably be Utes."

"What about on the other side," Charlie asked.

"That's mostly Cheyenne and Arapaho," Mac said. "I don't think we'd have much trouble with them. The thing is, once we get to the plains, we don't have much natural cover. We'd have to be very careful crossing."

"I think I'd rather be in a storm in the mountains," I told him. "What I hear is that it gets pretty bad on the plains."

"It does," Mac said. "I've done it a couple of times. Even at Bent's Fort it won't be a picnic."

"What about wintering on the other side?" Charlie asked. "Couldn't we find a good place in the mountains?"

Keenan nodded. "We could. The thing is, I don't know the mountains on that side as well. I think most of the best wintering places are probably well known by the Indians. We might have trouble finding a place."

"It's sounding like we better winter here," I told them. "I don't like it but I reckon it's the best choice we got."

"One thing we can think about is finding a band of Arapaho on the other side and wintering with them," Mac said. "I know some of them pretty well, though the people I knew were north of here a good way."

Well I remembered that's what he said his wife's people was, Arapaho, but I ain't learnt nothing more about her until later. It taken a bottle of rot gut to loosen Keenan's tongue enough to tell me and Charlie about it. Turns out his wife died of the cholera. He told us a lot of his Indian kin did. They caught it from trade blankets.

I looked at Charlie and seen this talk about wintering with the Indians scared her. She hid it pretty good, like Mac can, but I known. "You decide," I told her. "My vote is what you want."

"I want us to get married," she told me and turned to Keenan. "Do you think there might be a preacher at Bent's Fort?"

Mac shaken his head. "I doubt it. There might be but not many of them come this way. There's not much business for them out here. I'm not saying there isn't need, just not much call." Then he smiled. "Most of the mountain men do things the Indian way."

"That's all right with me," I said. "I think a medicine man's as good as a preacher."

I seen right away Charlie didn't share my point of view. The old man must of seen it, too, cause he jumped right in. "No, Jackie, that was good for then, but not for now. You need to follow white man's rules. The Indian way will be gone before too many more years. There just are too many white people coming into the country and all of them are hungry for land. That's the future of this country and you and Charlie need to find a preacher or a judge. You need to get a paper from him, too."

Charlie was nodding along even as he said it, so I seen I was outvoted from the scratch. Not that I cared. Wouldn't no piece of paper make me more married to Charlie than I was already and I told them so.

Then I taken a notion. "You're the captain of this party, Keenan," I said. "Why don't you marry us? Ain't that legal?"

Well, you'd of though Mac swallowed a gnat when I said that. I never seen him afore or since at a loss for words like he were then. I taken him a minute to see I were out to get his goat. "Ah, Jackie," he said, sounding sort of mournful. "What a terrible way to sneak up on an old man."

"Old man, my foot!" Charlie said. She were as tickled as me. "Who's been running us up and down these hills like a mountain goat? Jack's right. You've got a Bible. What more do you need?"

We ragged him about it a while longer. Then we set and looked at the fire a good spell. Somehow a decision got made because after a while Charlie looked at Mac and said, "We better get some sleep. We need to get an early start in the morning. I'd like to get as far as we can tomorrow. We can make a decision once we're on the other side."

CHAPTER FIFTEEN

Firefight

As it turns out, the decision where to winter got made for us. It was strange how it come to be, but I'm getting ahead of myself. A story's always best when it's told like it happened.

We was up afore light the next morning and up the first slope by the time the sun come over the mountain. What was worrisome to me was who we might run into up on the pass, even this late in the year. I didn't want no part of a Ute hunting party. I'd seen enough fights to have my fill, and it ain't no sin to avoid trouble.

Mac must of felt the same because he kept us off the trail as much as he could. When we couldn't get around sticking to the trail no way, he sent me or Hawk out on foot to scout it first. We couldn't make as good time this way but we wouldn't ride blind into no ambush, neither.

It was cold when we started out that morning but it was a lot colder on top of the pass. We wasn't that much higher than where we started, maybe a thousand feet or a little more, but there was a strong north wind up there. It sucked the heat right out of a man, no matter how many blankets he wore. So by the time we reached cover on the downhill slope, I felt froze through.

The trail over the pass weren't too bad and we made good time, considering. I guess if we was traveling by wagon it could of gotten right ticklish, but leading our horses, it weren't no trouble. There weren't that much snow and what there was were mostly powder. Hadn't been for the wind, it would of been a perfect day.

We was most of the way over the pass and looking for a place to spend the night when we heard shots. They was coming from not far ahead of us and the old man sent me and Hawk on ahead to see what it was. Him and Charlie taken cover with the horses in a good spot where they could cover the trail coming and going. I given Charlie two of the Colt's pistols and taken the other two with me. I taken the Hawken, too, but I didn't expect to use it. We wasn't stalking and if somebody jumped us, they was in for a nasty surprise from my Colt's. I'd given Hawk one of the Hall rifles after we left Taos, but he weren't much of a shot. It was his bow he taken with him and he was damn good with that.

It was a lot farther than I thought to the shooting. The wind was blowing in our face and it carried the sound our way, so we didn't see nothing at all until we'd gone almost a mile up the trail. By then the shots was getting spaced out and when we got there, it was just like I figured from what we heard. There was three men with rifles on high ground and they had somebody pinned down in an open spot. When I taken a look through my glass, I seen it was five Indians pinned down. There was a woman and two children amongst them and somebody was laying real still on open ground. The only man I seen was armed with a bow. I seen he weren't young, neither. His braids was almost pure white.

From where we was, I could see all three riflemen and I seen where their horses was, too. I signed Hawk how I wanted to sneak up on them, and we set off. He taken the far rifleman and I taken the first and there weren't no problem dealing with neither. They was focused on the Indians and never saw us coming. We didn't even have to fire a shot. I taken my man out with my knife and Hawk used his bow.

The third man was a problem. He was in plain sight to where I was but weren't no good way of sneaking up on him without getting shot. So I taken the Spencer and lined him up in the sights. He never moved after I pulled the trigger.

I guess there's some who would fault me for stabbing one man in the back and shooting the other one like that. I guess such folk ain't never been in such a situation. Them bastids wasn't men in my book. They was varmints. Anybody that would bushwhack a family like that don't deserve nothing better. They was lower than rattlesnakes to me and the world were a better place without them.

Truth is, I known this afore I ever laid a hand on the first. I cut their trail as we was stalking, and I seen them tracks afore. I first seen them tracks where Charlie's folks was murdered, and I seen them again where they ambushed the Mexican soldiers. So they reaped what they sowed, and there were justice in it. I was their Angel of Death, and I didn't lose no sleep over it, neither. It were like killing a mad dog. Tired as I was of killing, I don't see I had much choice. Neither did Keenan.

After I shot the third man, I gathered the horses and walked down to the third man and taken his rifle. Then I hollered and thrown him down in the open where the Indians could see him, and I stood up and held up my hand. About then Hawk shown up, too, carrying another rifle, but when he raised his hand, I seen he was holding a fresh scalp. Then he give out the most awful war scream I ever heard.

I think it were the war cry that convinced the Indians we was friends. The old man stepped out of cover and raised his hand, but I seen he weren't so far he couldn't jump back right quick if we was fooling him. When he done this, we walked down to them, leading the horses. I were careful not to make any sign that might be taken as hostile. Even so, I kept my shooting hand free so I could grab my Colt's right quick if I needed it.

I seen the Indians was uneasy over the fact Hawk was Comanche. I guess they taken me for the half breed I am. So I pointed at myself and told them, "Choctaw." I pointed at Hawk and said, "Comanche." Then I pointed where we come from and held up two fingers. "Wicasu," I told them, using the only Indian word I knowed for white man.

The old man nodded and walked over to where the woman was trying to help the man on the ground. The man was breathing, but just barely, and I could see he weren't long for this world. When he seen me and Hawk, he said something. Later I learnt he was thanking us for saving his family and asking us to care for them.

Just then we heard shots coming from back where we started, and me and Hawk taken off at a dead run. When we got to the horses, we jumped on and rode like the devil for Charlie and Mac. As we done so, we heard more shots. Some was the deep boom of the Hawken, but most was the sharper crack of the Colt's.

I think it was riding so hard that saved us all. When we come riding in the gang must of thought it were two of the three men attacking the Indians. I had my Colt's in my hand and shot the first man square through the chest. The second turned to shoot me but grown one of Hawk's arrows through his heart. The third taken aim but was brought down by a shot from Mac's Hawken, but the fourth got a shot off afore I rode him into the ground. I thought he was aiming for me and missed, but it turns out he taken Hawk straight out of the saddle.

The fifth man must of had me dead in his sights. I seen the hammer drop and thought I was gone, but nothing happened. The man was smart enough to hold aim, thinking he had a slow misfire, but when I looked at his rifle later, I seen he got so rushed he forgot to cap the nipple afore he fired. I figure that's why I'm here telling this now.

Right then I seen the man fall to the side just afore I rode him down. I wheeled to finish him off, but he weren't no danger. There were blood coming out of his gut and I known he taken a ball through the liver. When I turned to look, I seen Charlie, laying there bleeding with a Colt's still smoking in her hand.

I looked around right quick, but weren't no more of the gang left. So I lit out for Charlie, thinking she was dying. Seemed like it taken me forever to get to her. When I did I seen she were wounded bad, shot high through the chest and bleeding like a stuck pig. Yet, the ball were high enough it missed her heart and lung and it passed right through.

Yet, as I was holding her and trying to get the bleeding stopped, Charlie told me, "I'm all right. Check Keenan! I saw him go down."

Mac was wounded a lot worse than Charlie. He taken a ball through the leg and had lost a lot of blood. The leg was broke just below the knee and he might lose it to gangrene, but what worried me was the head wound I seen. His scalp was laid open for three inches, with bone sticking through and when I first seen it, I were sure he was dead. Then I seen him breathe and I done what I could to stop his bleeding afore I went to check Hawk.

Hawk were sitting up holding his side when I got to him. When I looked at his side, I seen the bullet carved a groove across his ribs. It were bloody and right painful, I'd guess, but Hawk didn't let on none.

Hawk said something while I was tending his wound and got to his feet, pointing. The old man from the Indians we rescued was standing there with a bow in his hand, looking around. He pointed at one of the outlaws and said something and I seen the man was moving. So did Hawk. He drawn his knife and walked over and finished the outlaw off. Then he scalped him and give a war cry, and damned if the old Indian didn't join him. Then him and Hawk made sure the rest was dead.

Turns out the old Indian known a lot about healing that I didn't and we was lucky to have him there. He sprinkled Mac's head wound with something and packed it with moss and then shown me how to set his leg. I pulled it whilst the old Indian set it and made a splint and it were a mercy Mac was still out. It would of been damn painful.

When he was done with Mac, the old Indian treated Charlie. Turns out his name was Raven and he was known amongst his people as a healer. I ain't known that then but I seen Charlie trusted him. I could tell he done a good job on Charlie and Mac, and even Hawk somehow known it was all right to let Raven tend his ribs. Maybe it was killing a common enemy that done it.

Once we was done tending our wounded, Raven went back to his family and Hawk and me started looking for a place we could make camp. Then Raven showed up again with a horse and a travois and signed me to help him load Mac on it. Then we helped Charlie onto a horse and we taken them down to where the Indians was. While I done this, Hawk rounded up all the horses and followed us down.

That were how we come to winter with the Arapahos that year. Raven taken us to a good campsite I would of never known was there. There was lots of willows nearby and by the time we got to camp, the woman had started making a wikiup out of bent branches and buffalo skins. Me and Hawk joined in and afore long we had a good sized lodge that would shelter us all. There weren't much room with all of us in it, so Hawk and me slept outside that night.

The next morning we went with Raven and done a funeral the Indian way for the man that was killed. Turns out he was Antelope's husband and the father of her children. I couldn't understand anything was being said but Mac told me later what it was and why it was done like it was. Seems to me a right decent way to honor the dead.

After that I taken Hawk and we went back to search the bodies. When we done so I seen there was birds circling. That got me thinking that it was birds that led us to find Charlie and the Mexican soldiers and the Padre. I didn't care to think of someone finding us like that. So when we was done searching the bodies, we stripped them and taken ropes to drag them into a deep canyon. Then we covered them over with rocks too big for scavengers. It would have taken a bear to move some of them stones.

It was mid afternoon afore we got back to camp. When we got there I seen Mac was awake and sitting up. Him and Raven was sitting there jawing in Arapaho like two old men swapping lies. Come to think, that was what they was, two old men. I don't know if they was swapping lies right then, but they sure done so over the winter to come. I ain't never decided which of them were the most outrageous. They was both of them full of moonshine.

I learnt the woman was called Antelope. She had food for us to eat, and after we was done, me and Hawk helped her start a second lodge. We made this one out of willow branches and some canvas we found in the outlaws' mule pack.

When we got done with the second lodge the next morning, we had a tight wikiup that kept us out of the weather all winter. Later on we killed two buffalo and made a third, smaller lodge using their hide. That one was for me and Charlie and I've slept in a lot worse houses afore and since. Raven given us his blessing and said some prayers over us, and that's where we spent our first winter as man and wife.

There ain't a whole lot to tell here about that winter. The first lodge was used by Antelope and her children, and as a place for us all to eat when we couldn't be outside. Charlie stayed with Antelope and her children until our lodge was built and I slept with the men in the second lodge. Raven slept there with us, too. I think it was mostly to be with other men to swap tales and smoke his pipe.

Along about the middle of the winter, Charlie asked me if I would mind us staying a few nights in the lodge with the children. When I asked why, she just smiled and told me Antelope needed some privacy. When I asked why Antelope needed privacy, she told me I'd see. She was right, too. I known exactly why when I seen Hawk come out of our lodge the next morning.

Weren't all that long afore Raven given his blessing over Hawk and Antelope, too. After that Hawk started dressing less like a Comanche and more like Arapaho. I guess he never did get back to his Comanche people. Last time I seen him, him and Antelope had grandkids.

I see I'm getting way ahead of my story again. It's been a long time in the telling and I'm getting tired of talking. Living it was different from telling it. I never got tired of living it.

One thing I need to tell is we found the abbot's treasure map on one of the outlaws me and Hawk killed that day on the pass. It was on one of the men that shot Charlie and Mac, along with a lot of Mexican pesos. With all that money, we figured him as leader of the gang, and we come across a wanted poster on him, too. The reward was a lot more than for the others, and according to the poster, I could see why. We saved the world a lot of trouble by killing him.

That ain't why we done it, of course, but he surely got what he had coming. As Keenan put it, "Ever there was a man born to hang, it surely was him. You and Hawk were only the rope that swung him."

We done a lot of talking that winter about that, me and Mac. All the killing weighed heavy on my mind. I was twenty-three years old and I'd already taken the lives of twenty-one men. Knowing I didn't have no choice didn't help much. The fact was that they was dead by my hand. Being only the rope ain't much consolation.

"Jackie," Mac told me, right stern. "You have to let go of that! It can kill you if you don't. Do it for Charlie's sake, if not for your own. She doesn't deserve to be a widow."

"I ain't going to shoot myself over it, Keenan!" I told him.

"No, but it may cause you to hesitate a fatal instant in a fight forced on you," he told me. "Even if it doesn't do that, it can kill any joy you find and drive you to despair. Do you want to rob Charlie and yourself of the joys of life? Let the dead bury the dead, man. Consign them to the mercy of God and let them rest in peace."

That didn't make much sense to me at the time. Over the years studying it out, I come to understand how right Keenan were. Holding onto grief only breeds more grief. While I don't hold much with religion, I had faith in the old man and I done what he told me. I went to the top of the tallest mountain I could find and talked about each of them I killed to Whoever might be listening.

When I was done I asked for peace, for me and for them, too, just like it says to do in the Good Book. It helped considerable, and after that I found myself doing this, talking to Whoever might be there from time to time when my spirit was troubled. To this day I ain't seen no burning bush nor got no notion how this works, or why. It just works for me and I always find a feeling of peace.

The other thing we done a lot of talking about that winter were the abbot's map and what to do with it. Didn't none of us want no part of that gold. The padre said it were cursed and from what I seen, the curse run true. Them outlaws taken the map to steal the gold. Now they was all dead, every last man. So didn't none of us want to go after it for ourselves. It weren't ours and it weren't like the money we taken off the outlaws.

One thing we talked about was taking the map back to the monks and let them find the gold. Thing is, we didn't have no way of knowing who they was. I guess we could of just given it to the first priest we come across, and that might of done it. Only, that were right risky about then. Carson thought war was likely between Mexico and the Americans, and it were too risky to head back to Taos or even Valmora.

"I'm sick of talking about it," I said one day. "Why don't we just burn the damn thing and be done with it? That way ain't nobody will ever be cursed by that gold again."

"I'd do so in a minute if I thought it would work," Mac told me. "I'm as sick of it as you are, Jack. Somehow, I don't think it would. I think this map was given to us for a reason, and I think it's up to us to get the gold to its rightful owners."

I looked at Charlie, but she weren't saying nothing. This told me she agreed with Keenan but didn't want to say it. "You mean we ought to go looking for it?" I asked him. "Wouldn't that bring the curse down on us?"

McAdams nodded. "That would seem to be a risk, wouldn't it? On the other hand, if we weren't planning on keeping it ourselves, I don't think we'd have to worry."

"Seems to me that gold was a curse on the abbot, too," I said. "It got him and his monks murdered. It even got the padre we found killed, him and every soldier, too. I say we burn it. It never done nobody no good."

While it don't happen often, ever once in a while I say something that Keenan ain't thought of yet. This was one of them times and he were man enough to own it. "I never considered, that, Jackie," he said softly. "The last thing I want to do is bring trouble on you and Charlie. Maybe you're right. Let's think on it a few days."

"What if someone finds it later on?" Charlie asked. "Wouldn't the curse be on them, even if they didn't know about it?"

"That's beyond me," Mac answered, stirring up the fire and lighting his pipe. "I wouldn't think so, but the whole idea of a curse still working after all these years seems strange to me. I don't know if there's anyone on this good green earth who can answer that. On the other hand, I think it's up to us to make a decision what to do. I don't know why we were given this responsibility, but I think it's ours. I don't think we can dodge it."

"Well, let's study on it," I said, lighting my own pipe. "Like I said, I'm sick of talking about it. Why don't you run out one of your tall tales?"

"Tall tales?" Keenan said, pretending he were hurt. "Why, Jackie, have I ever told you anything but the pure truth?"

"I reckon not," I said, leaning back and getting comfortable. "But I like the way you dress it up for church."

CHAPTER SIXTEEN

Winter's End

We had a hard winter that year and the thaw come late. There was a couple of false springs when the snow melted back some, but each one was followed by a blizzard. One of them lasted five days and by the time it was done, I was feeling half crazy. When we come out we seen snow drifts high as the trees in some places but none of them was close to us.

It was a couple of weeks afore Christmas we holed up for the winter and by the old man's reckoning, it was the first of April by the time we broke camp. Some ways it felt like the longest three months of my life, but in other ways it was the most peaceful. There wasn't no shortage of game and me and Charlie helped Antelope butcher and make jerky out of a horse that was killed by a stray shot in the firefight.

I wondered why Raven and Hawk didn't help us but Keenan told me later that a lot of Indians consider such work unmanly. "They don't see it as unmanly to help eat it!" Charlie jumped in. "What do they do when there isn't a woman around to do it for them, starve?"

The snow weren't too deep to walk in until later in the winter and we passed time making snow shoes for when it was. They wasn't nothing fancy, willow branches and rawhide, and we didn't use them too much, neither. Walking on them was hard work and I kept getting my feet tangled. Charlie and Mac thought that was real funny and even Hawk broke a smile, but I noticed he never tried it himself. At least, he didn't while I was looking.

Keenan and Raven, was full of stories and that helped us pass the time, too. Mac's stories was always good, but I liked the ones Raven told best. Some of them was short and to the point, but some of them wandered clear around the mountain afore it was clear where they was headed. That didn't really make no difference. Raven had a way of telling stories that snuck up and grabbed you and wouldn't let go until he was done.

Yet what really grabbed me was how every one of his stories give a different slant on looking at common things. One evening we was talking about mountains and he started telling us about a strange peak way north of us. He said his people called the Bear's Tipi because of the deep grooves running straight up it and there was a story how it come to have it's name. As he told it,

A long time ago when the world was very young there were seven sisters who went out to pick berries one day. Their mother told them to be careful and watch out for bears since bears love berries. She also told them to be home by sunset because bears often like to hunt at night.

Yet, the berries were so good and so many the girls forgot all about keeping watch. They quickly filled their baskets and if they had gone home right then, everything would have been all right.

Yet those foolish sisters didn't go home with their full baskets. The berries were so sweet that they ate and ate until their fingers were stained with berry juice and their bellies were so full of sweet berries they couldn't keep their eyes open. So they lay down by the spring that fed the berries and went sound asleep.

The sun was going down when the oldest sister woke up. When she did, she saw a great bear coming from its cave to eat berries. She woke the others quickly and they began to run away, but the bear was between them and the way home. So they ran to a steep mountain they thought the bear couldn't climb and they climbed to the top.

The bear was right behind them but he couldn't climb as fast as the sisters. He had been eating too many berries and was too fat to climb fast. Yet he was very strong and began to claw his way up the mountain. His claws dug in very deep and left deep marks in the rocks.

The sisters saw the bear would soon get them so they cried out to Earth-maker to drive away the bear so they could go home. Yet Earth-maker was far away and couldn't get there fast enough, so he sent a great whirlwind to lift the sisters up from the mountain and save them from the bear.

The whirlwind came quickly from the south but he had to cross

a desert with lots of magic cactus, the ones some peoples call peyote. This magic cactus made the whirlwind very drunk and when he came to the mountain and snatched away the seven sisters, he became frightened of the bear, who had clawed his way right to the top of the steep cliffs surrounding peak.

So the whirlwind grabbed the sisters and lifted them up with all his strength, but it was too high. When he threw them, it was too hard and they began going higher and higher into the sky. They went so high the whirlwind couldn't reach them but he yelled very loud and told the sisters he would come back to get them later when he was strong again. He told each one to build a fire so he could see them when he came back, and then he went away.

Yet even the strongest whirlwinds have a very short life and the great whirlwind that saved the sisters died that night. So he never came back to save them. Nor did anyone else, even though they kept their fires burning. You can see them to this day in the night sky, burning below the three bright stars in a row. And you can see the claw marks in the mountain that the great bear made trying to reach them.

The strange thing is that when we went out later that night, Raven pointed out the seven sisters in a cluster just where he said they would be. It was a long time afore I got up to see the Bear's Tipi but it was worth the whole trip just to see it. It was just like Raven said, marked by deep grooves in the rock going straight up to the top, but it didn't look like no tipi to me. It looked like the Earth-maker having fun showing off. Thirty years later Richard Dodge come through with the US Geological Survey and called it the Devil's Tower, but I don't know why. The Arapaho name fits better.

Raven also told a lot of stories about Kawuneeche, who white folk know as coyote. Seems all the Indians had stories about old man coyote and them was the ones I liked best. One I remember is when all the animals come together for a Great Council, and I recall Mac smiling when Raven mentioned the story. I known he'd heard it afore but later he told me Raven told it even better.

...Even though the lodge where they met was very large, the animals were told to leave their assholes outside so it wouldn't stink so bad while they talked. So they left them in a great pile outside the

door. Yet while they were talking, Kawuneeche snuck up and stole their assholes, and ran off and hid them.

When the animals found out who did this, they were very angry. They went to Coyote and demanded that he give them back their assholes, but Coyote refused. So Badger clawed Coyote's eyes out while Bear held him down and they told Coyote he would not get his eyes back until he returned all the animal's assholes.

Coyote promised to give the assholes back, so he was given his eyes so he could find the place where he had hidden them. Sure enough, he found it and gave them back, all except the dogs, who were all off chasing their tails. So Coyote threw the dogs' assholes into the air where they were all caught by a cloud of gnats, and the gnats were sent to return the dog's assholes.

The gnats did this, but gnats are not very smart. They became confused and gave the wrong assholes to the wrong dogs. This caused a lot of confusion among the dogs and to this day you will see all the dogs sniffing each other, trying to find the right asshole.

Not all our stories were like that. A lot of them were about things we come across just trying to stay alive. Raven wanted to know every detail of my fight with the outlaws in the mountain and when I was done, he said something in Arapaho I didn't understand. I was getting pretty good at ciphering out things he said by then, but he used some words I never heard and he spoke quite a while.

When Raven was done, Mac told me what it meant. "He said you are very close to the Earth-maker's heart, like a favorite son. Now he understands how you were able to kill so many enemies when you rescued him and Antelope, and then me and Charlie. He says the badger medicine is very strong in you. I don't know if you've ever come across a badger, but you don't want to, believe me. Even the bears avoid them like poison."

When Keenan told me this I looked at Charlie. She was nodding her head and I had no notion what to say. Keenan seen it on my face and nodded. "Carson said the same thing, lad. He may not have used the same words but that's what he meant."

"I hate the killing," I told him. "I hate being good at it and I hate what happens inside me when I don't have no choice."

"I know, lad, you don't get hot. You go cold as ice until it's done." He sighed. "That's what makes you so effective. You know you could get killed but you also know the only way to live is to fight your way out as efficiently as you can. You do it better than any man I know."

Well, the man had me pegged. Then I had another notion. There was only one way he could of known. "That's how you get, too, ain't it?" I asked him and I seen the answer in his eyes.

"I live right now," he told me. "I smell the flowers and enjoy my food, and I never kill when I can avoid it." Then he sighed. "I hate it as much as you do, Jack. I wish it weren't necessary and I try to avoid situations where I may have to kill. The thing is, so often it's forced on us. The only alternative is let ourselves be killed and we can't do that, not when someone else is depending on us."

Anyway, that's how I come to be called White Badger among the Arapaho. By the time the story circulated amongst the Arapaho camps for a couple of years, it come back to me as sixteen men me and Hawk killed on Willow Springs pass, armed only with a knife and a bow between us. I never told Raven this, but I found it sort of awkward. It's hard living up to a reputation you ain't earned.

Anyways, that's how we passed the winter and I was damned glad we wasn't out on the plains. It got so bad out there a lot of buffalo died. This helped not having to hunt them come early spring, but I hate to see good meat go to waste. Of course, Keenan pointed out it weren't going to waste. The coyotes and birds need to eat, too.

There was also people that got caught out on the plains by the false springs, too. Or maybe it was greed that killed them. After a long winter spent in Bent's Fort, three freight wagons set out hoping to get to Santa Fe ahead of the rest and get higher prices. They was a week out of Bent's Fort when there come a three day blizzard that covered the wagons with wind packed snow and froze most of their livestock.

One man lived to tell about it but he weren't much use as a teamster after that. Frostbite taken both feet and most of his fingers. Yet the way he told it, it were a blessing. His partners was dead and the iron and most of the dry goods they was hauling come through the blizzard fine. After selling off his goods, he had enough money to start a bank, and when I seen him several years after, he looked right prosperous. He had to get around on crutches and stumps, but he done right good and could hire people to do what he couldn't. Strange how things works out.

Charlie and me done all right, too. After all them months on the trail, it was good to have our privacy. We done a lot of making up for lost time, but come spring, there weren't no baby on the way. This made Charlie sad but I was just as glad. Even with Antelope to help out as midwife, I was worried about Charlie having her first child way out there. I also known we'd be on our way afore long and Charlie would have a lot better time on the trail not carrying a child.

The thaw weren't done afore Hawk come in one day and told us there was wagons coming up the trail from the north. So Keenan and me rode out to look them over. When we seen it was families in wagons, we rode on up to talk a spell.

Turns out it were five families in four wagons and they was full of war news. Seems like Texas was admitted into the Union that winter and was a state now, and these people was headed this way looking for free land to settle. According to what they said, there was so many people like them in Westport, Missouri, it was hard to buy a wagon or horses to pull it. I learnt later it was hard to find anything from St. Louis west that spring. What with wars and crop failures in Europe, there was thousands of new settlers coming into the country every day, and they was every one hungry for land.

The other thing they told us was that American soldiers was headed our way. They hadn't seen no soldiers, not in any numbers, but that was how the talk at Bent's Fort was running. The Mexicans was not happy at Texas being admitted to the Union and had threatened war. So it only made sense to the people doing all the talking that American troops would be heading down the trail to Santa Fe afore the year was out.

It sounded to me this was what them folk wanted to believe and it also seemed to me there was something not quite right about them. One thing I seen right off was there was way more women and children than there was men in the party, and what men there was didn't seem too glad to see us. They wasn't exactly unfriendly but I got the feeling they would of been just as glad if they'd never laid eyes on us.

The men seemed to thaw a bit when we told them about the trail ahead, but it was only the men who was talking to us. The women and children kept their distance, which struck me as strange, too. Everywhere I ever been the kids crowd as close as their folks would let them, and while the women folk might not say much, they hung close listening. News was always welcome and travelers generally stopped a while to visit and swap what they learnt along the way.

This bunch was different. They was glad to hear it weren't that far to Willow Springs, but they wasn't too anxious to offer much back except war news. They did tell us what we asked about their trip out and trail conditions, but their information was right sparse when it come to details and there was some long silences. These folk didn't seem to like wasting words and I couldn't swear that more than the two oldest men even known how to talk at all. The rest just kind of looked at us like we was some strange kind of critters they never seen afore and never said a word. It weren't a half hour from when we stopped until they was moving on again.

The whole thing left a bad taste in my mouth and I was glad we didn't tell nothing about ourselves, neither. I don't know how it would of hurt, but I was still glad we didn't. As Mac said later, it's hard to trust people who is so full of distrust theirselves.

Thinking about all them people lined up in Missouri to come this way bothered me and Keenan and me spent time chewing it over on the way back to camp. I told him I was damn glad him and me come west when we done so. Sounded to me like it wouldn't be many years afore a man couldn't ride across the prairie without stumbling over a hundred other folks.

Keenan allowed I was right but said it might take a little longer than I reckoned. "It's a big country, lad," he said. "There's ten times more of it than I've ever seen, and there are places even wilder than here. Yet, I'm afraid you're right. Should we live so long to die of old age, it will happen in our lifetime." He looked kind of sad when he said it. Then he grinned. "That is assuming we both live so long. The point is we're here now and we need to enjoy it while we can."

Well, I damn sure couldn't auger with that but my mind was still unsettled over how unfriendly them folks was. I said as much to the old man and he said they struck them the same. "I'd guess they're Mormons, Jack," he told me. "They have the manners and the look. If they are, you can't blame them. The last few years they've been run out of a lot of places."

"They sure caused a ruckus in Missouri," I said. When I said it, Mac give me one of them looks that tells me he thinks I'm full of shit. "Well, didn't they?" I asked him. "The way I heard, they was trying to take over the state and it got so bad the governor had to hand down that order to shoot on sight."

"It depends who you talk to, Jack," he replied. "The way I read it, most of what they did in Missouri was in self defense. On the other hand, they are certainly not the easiest people to live with and they don't seem willing to back away from a fight, either. They seem to like it from what I've seen. To be fair, most people from Missouri are no different. I suspect that may be true in Arkansas, as well." He was grinning when he looked my way.

"I can't auger with that," I told him. "That's how I am, except for liking it. What I don't understand is why people can't just leave each other alone. Seems like they always got to peck at each other like chickens. Then they go and blame each other and lie about it!" I was surprised to find myself getting so hot over it. What was in my mind was the look on the faces of the men in the wagon while we talked. It was like they was looking down on us like we was no better than dirt.

Keenan didn't say nothing to that. He just nodded and let me stew in my own juices, which I done right good. "Who the hell do they think they are looking at us that way?" I asked.

"I don't think it was just us, Jack," Mac told me. "I suspect one of the reasons those particular folk left Bent's Fort so soon was that they did the same sort of thing with other people. They don't seem to be blessed with an abundance of tolerance. I also think that may be why they got run out of Missouri and why they've had so much trouble other places. Some people are so convinced they're right that there's no reasoning with them and that's been my experience with Mormons. Of course, I'm equally sure some of their Baptist or Methodist neighbors took exactly the same stance over what they hold true. That's been my experience of them, too."

"How the hell is a man supposed to know who to believe?" I asked him. "Seems to me any one of them is pretty much as full of shit as the next!"

The old man nodded again. "When you figure that one out, Jack, I'd like to know, too. I've been studying on it for sixty years and I'm no farther along than when I started. The best I can do is listen to all the facts and try to winnow the truth. It's not easy."

"A neighbor back in Arkansas once told me, don't believe anything you hear and only half of what you see!"

The old man give me a strange look. "That's probably a good rule if you never want to be fooled," he told me. "On the other hand, it's a pretty dark way to live, and a pretty lonely one, too."

I asked him what he meant. He taken a while afore answering, long enough I thought he wasn't going to say nothing more. Then he said, "You remember me telling you about my partner, Bill?"

"The one that put himself in the way of the bullet?"

"Yes, that's the man. If you cut through everything else, the thing that made him that way was how he chose to see things. Yes, his step-brother and his wife made a fool of him, but what he refused to see was he helped them do it. I'm sure there were signs there all along but Bill chose to ignore them. Then after it happened, Bill still made the same choice. Rather than choosing to learn a lesson and get on with his life, Bill chose to chose to see himself as a tragic victim. There were other ways he could have looked at it, but that's what he chose and he never could give it up."

"How else could he look at it?" I wanted to know. "They betrayed him, pure and simple."

"Yes, they took advantage of his sweet nature and betrayed him all right. Yet after it was over he could have looked at it as a stroke of good luck. He could have admitted he made a rotten choice in the woman he chose for a sweetheart, and he could have seen the whole thing as an easy way to get out of that bad choice. Yet, he didn't and you could say that right then he chose to end any chance he had at a happy life."

I was confused and Keenan seen it. "Listen, Jackie, have you ever known anyone who always expected the worst to happen?" I told him I had and he asked me, "What kind of life did they have? Did good things or bad things tend to happen to them?"

I thought about it a minute. "I'd have to say their life was truly a veil of tears. Seems like something was always going wrong."

"Yet, there were still a great many good things that happened to them, wasn't there?"

"Well, maybe not a great many, but a lot."

"The point is that good things and bad things are going to happen to us all. Yet if we're always looking for bad things, this makes it harder for good things to happen."

"Seems mostly like a matter of bad luck," I told him.

"No, Jack, there's no such thing as luck, only possibilities, and these tend to even out. My point is that someone who expects bad things to happen cannot see that the good things that happen far more often than the bad. They see the bad and they expect bad and they make choices that bring about more bad rather than the goodness that's right before their eyes."

I shaken my head. "I ain't saying you're wrong but I'm going to have to study on it. There is a lot of bad things that happens and there is a lot of bad folk in this world that can't be trusted."

"Fair enough," he said. "However, I don't think that being suspicious of everyone like the folk we just met fits you and it's not the way you approach people. Everything I've seen of you tells me you're a fair man who has a good sense of people. You have a pretty good sense of who you can believe and who you can't. It seems to me you made a decision to believe me when we first met. You did the same with Charlie and Carson, too. The point is that if you hadn't made that choice you wouldn't have a wife and a couple of good friends you didn't have a few months back. No, make that five good friends if you count Antelope, Raven and Hawk, which I think you do."

Well, I couldn't auger with that. The old man had me cold and he known I known it. "One of these days I'm going to get you back," I told him and he laughed.

"Jack, it's too beautiful a day to be like those folk in the wagons. Life is just too short to be twisted into knots by something we can't do a thing about. Maybe that's a lesson that comes with living longer than most." Then he grinned. "The best way to do that is to always be late for your own funeral."

I had to laugh. He was right. After a winter like the one we passed it was too pretty a day to spend in a shit hole. "I guess if other folk want to peck each other's eyes out, then it's their business," I told him. "To hell with it!"

"Now you're talking," he said. "That's the shortest prayer I know." Then he pointed to a clump of green peeking out of a snow bank. "Are those wild flowers? They're the first ones I've seen. I bet I know someone who might like a few." I did, too, so I stopped and picked a few for Charlie.

That evening we was talking about what to do about finding the gold. It was pretty much the same palaver we had afore but this time Raven said something in Arapaho to McAdams. I was to the point where I could follow a lot of what Raven said, but I didn't understand. "He's asking what we're talking about, Jack. I think we need to tell him." He could see I wasn't too happy with that notion. "You don't have to worry about him getting greedy. Gold doesn't mean anything more to him than a pretty rock. You can't eat it and it won't hold an edge."

"You can buy horses with it," I told him, but I seen how I was wrong about that even afore I stopped talking. "On the other hand, you can also get yourself killed trying to trade with greedy white men." I taken the map out of my possibles bag and handed it to the old man.

"You've been hanging around me too long, Jack," McAdams laughed. "You're answering your own questions as fast as you ask them." He shown Raven the map and the two of them talked back and forth a long time in Arapaho. I caught a word or two here and there but they was going at it too fast for me to keep up. I had the sense Mac was telling Raven the whole story, including how we come by the map.

When they was done, Mac summed it up for me. "Raven wonders why we don't just burn the map and forget the gold. He says too many people have died over it. When I told him that's what you wanted to do before, he told me you are very wise for a young man."

"Maybe you should just toss it into the fire, then," I said. "It would save us a pile of trouble getting it back to its rightful owners. We could get killed doing just that." I looked at Charlie. "I got way more to lose now than I ever did then."

Mac nodded. "That's still one possibility, but hear me out. Raven knows where the monastery used to be and he is willing to help us find the cave where the gold is hidden if we're crazy enough to try. I still think we have been given the responsibility, so I think we need to find it if we can."

Raven and me jabbered back and forth through Mac. To give the old man his due, I'm pretty sure he didn't spare himself using milder words than Raven and me done. I was right frank and Raven was, too, and I could see even Charlie was coming around. Both me and Raven thought

Keenan was crazy.

"Are you sure you don't want to claim some of this gold for yourself?" I asked Mac right out. "I can't figure why else you'd be pushing so hard to find it."

"Not at all, lad," he told me. "On the other hand, I think it could do a lot of good in the right hands. I find myself thinking about that orphanage Sister Carmelita runs back in Arkansas. I can't help but think how many children that gold could feed and clothe."

I still didn't like it, but Mac had a point I couldn't get around. It was the only reason I could see for going after the gold. "How would we get it to them without getting killed?" I asked.

"Wait a minute," Charlie jumped in. "Remember what Jack said when we first talked about this? Even if we got it back to Arkansas, how can we be sure we wouldn't be bringing a curse down on the orphanage? Maybe we ought to burn the map, Mac. Look what it's doing to us, and we haven't even found it yet."

Raven said something to Mac in Arapaho and the old man talked to him in Arapaho a while more. When they was done, Keenan told us what was said. "Raven thinks Charlie is right. The gold is already having a bad affect on us." He handed the map back to me. "It's up to you, lad."

I leaned forward and held the map over the hot coals of the fire. I intended to drop it, but somehow I couldn't. So I folded it up and put it back in my pocket. "I don't think it's mine to burn," I told the others. "I think what I need to do is to figure out some way of getting it back to the padre's order. Let them decide what to do."

Raven nodded when Mac told him what I said, but Charlie looked troubled. Still, she didn't say nothing and when I got to my feet, she did, too. "All this talk is vexing," I said. "I think I'm going to stretch my legs and turn in."

Afore I went to sleep that night, I hid the map in my Bible just the way the abbot done a long time back. Charlie helped me and when we was done we walked out to look at the stars a while. It was the dark of the moon and the sky was clear that night, and I don't think I ever seen so many stars afore, or stars so bright.

Or maybe I never noticed. Coming after all our talk about the map and the curse that went with it, I thought about how many people had died because of that gold. Then I thought about all the men I'd killed since coming west and wished there'd been another way. All this rode heavy on my mind, but I remembered what Mac said that afternoon and it helped. Setting there with Charlie, watching the stars and talking about what troubled me seemed to wash the poison from my soul. Charlie didn't say nothing, just listened, and Whoever might be out there must have been listening, too. When we turned in that night I slept like a baby.

CHAPTER SEVENTEEN

Summer Hunt

Even with the hard winter we had, spring come quickly that year. A few days after I hid the map in my Bible, Raven was thinking it was time to break camp and set out to find his people again. Their winter camp was a good ways north of where we was, and they would be moving out to follow the buffalo afore long. He was anxious to join them afore they broke camp.

Raven asked if we would be coming with him and Mac and Charlie and me talked about it. Even though he was Comanche and his people wasn't too friendly with the Arapaho, Hawk had decided to live with Antelope's people. By then, Antelope had a new baby boy and had started another one with Hawk. She'd also made him some new moccasins and buckskins and he didn't look much like Comanche no more. At least, he didn't to me. Raven said he done so.

"I'd favor going with Raven," the old man told us. "There's some new country I'd like to see and I have nowhere else I need to be. It would be safer traveling through Cheyenne country if we did."

I looked at Charlie. "Going with Raven would mean we'd have to put off getting married," I said.

She give me a smile and said, "Jack, I think of you as my husband right now. I am your wife and having a preacher man say some words over us wouldn't make that any more true. Not for me. Does it make any difference to you?"

I give that some thought. "As long as we're living out here, it don't make no difference to me. When we go back east, I think it would be best to find a preacher. That way there wouldn't be no question."

"Then why don't we go with Raven?" she said. "He's given us his blessing and to me that's better than any some preacher we don't know could ever give. When we get to his people's camp we can see how it suits us. These folk are my family now."

"If I might have a word, lad," the old man broke in, "I think it would be a wise thing to go with Raven. From what we heard from the Mormons, it's pretty clear there's going to be war in this part of the world pretty soon. I'd just as soon steer clear when it happens."

I couldn't auger with that. I couldn't see no way this was my fight and I didn't want to be pushed into a corner where I had to shoot or be shot. So two days later we all headed north. All our horses come through the winter in good shape and was ready to be moving, but we walked and led them instead of riding. This was mostly because all our gear was packed on two travois and there ain't getting into no hurry dragging one of them.

Even so, we kept our riding stock saddled. There was no telling what we might come on, so Hawk and me rode out ahead as scouts and flankers. Keenan and Charlie taken turns watching our back trail and wrangling the rest of our horses. Raven, riding the fastest horse we had, rode between me and Hawk and showed us the way.

This might seem like we expected trouble, but we didn't. We was just being ready if trouble come calling and it paid off. Hawk spotted a Ute hunting party the second day out and we took a different way. Another time I spotted a grizzly and we was careful to circle around downwind so we didn't have to tangle with that. The last thing we wanted to have to do was use our rifles and it would of taken that to down a grizzly without risking being killed. Being as early as it was, brother bear had just come out of hibernation and was bound to be hungry, and we had a lot of fresh meat on the hoof.

It taken us a full ten days to reach Raven's winter camp. That's what the folk there called theirselves, Raven's Camp, not for Raven but because that was the name of the first head of the band. Aside from the Ute and the Grizzly, we didn't see nothing but game and lots of wild country.

We was keeping to high ground where there was still patches of snow on the north slopes and in the coulees we crossed, but from where we rode, we seen lots of green pushing its way up in the valleys. There was some places we could see fifty miles across the prairie to the east and at one point we spotted a wagon train making its way toward the pass where we wintered. It were a long train, twenty six wagons we counted through the spy glasses. It didn't look like they was pushing too fast, neither, and I seen the reason trailing behind. There was maybe fifty or sixty head of cattle they was bringing along.

Two days afore we got to the winter camp we come to a river and turned west following it's south bank. We was still keeping to the high ground a good ways from the river. We was in Arapaho and Cheyenne country then and there weren't as much danger of running into hostiles, but there weren't no place in the west that was altogether safe. So we kept to the high slopes and keep close watch for any sign of danger.

When we turned west, Mac told me and Charlie that he thought we was following the Arkansas river. "I've never been this far west," he told us. "Yet I'm pretty sure that if we followed the river downstream fifty or sixty miles, we'd come to Bent's Fort. Remind me to ask Raven when we make camp."

When we asked Raven that night, he told us Keenan was right. He also told us it might be a little risky for a small party heading that way. Comanche was known to come that far north, raiding for horses and hunting buffalo. With so many horses, we'd be quite a prize, and I didn't fancy having my fresh scalp dangling from some young warrior's belt.

We was about a half day out when we come across a hunting party from winter camp. It was mostly young men, but they recognized Raven a long way off and one of them rode ahead to camp to let them know we was coming. The rest was happy to break off the hunt and ride in with us. I could see they was curious about me and even more about Hawk, but like most Indians they held their peace and kept their ears and eyes open. That's one thing a lot of white folk could learn from Indians.

There was quite a ruckus when we rode into camp. People was glad to see Raven and Antelope, and there was a lot of yelling and milling around. There was lots of hands to help set up lodges for us and by the time the sun set there was plenty of fresh venison roasting over the fire. I started to offer some of the food we had, but Raven shaken his head and I got the idea it was bad manners. Later the old man told me I was right. We was guests and not accepting hospitality would of been insulting.

After sundown the whole camp gathered around the fire to eat, and when we was done, weren't much left except bones for the dogs. Even them was pretty well stripped. Then Raven stood up and everybody got quiet. He began talking, and from what I caught, he was telling the camp about their travels. When he come to the point where they was ambushed, he pointed at me and Hawk and he must of spent a quarter hour just talking about the fight. From what I could tell, there was about twice as many outlaws as I remembered, and be damned if me and Hawk ain't strangled about half of them with our bare hands. I asked Keenan about this later and he told me I was right.

Then Raven told them about blessing me and Charlie and how we decided to come to winter camp with him, and there was lots of grins and whoops. He already done told them I was a mighty warrior from the Choctaw nation, but then he told them how he come to give me the name of White Badger. Seems like it come to him in a dream one night many days afore we met. His dream told him he would meet a white badger who would come to his aid when he was surrounded by strong enemies, and when he told it, things got real quiet. People looked at me different after that, almost like they wasn't sure what I'd do next. On the other hand, that's the way badgers is.

After Raven was done, Keenan got up and told them how we come to meet. The way he told it, the bear was eight feet tall and weighed eight hundred pounds, with claws a foot long. He told them he shot the bear while I was sleeping because he was afraid there wouldn't be enough left for breakfast if I woken up and went after it with my knife. Then he told about Hawk shooting the Ute we come across, only it were three of them, and all of them seven foot tall.

When he was done, he started talking about Charlie and what a warrior spirit she had. He told them about how she killed four armed bandits who tried to ambush us with her bow, and how she scalped them when she was done. When he told that part, there was lots of war whoops and I seen Charlie looking down and blushing. Yet she seemed to like it, too, and I had to agree with Keenan. Charlie's got more balls than most men twice her age.

When McAdams finished talking, Raven nodded to me and I got up and told them an outrageous story about how Keenan sent me out running one day without telling me why. I told them I heard him shoot when I was about a half mile off and how I heard the bullet ranging over my head. Then I ran another half mile and found a dead antelope shot right through the head. Then I seen another one a hundred yards away, shot straight through the heart with the same bullet.

That didn't take no time and I could see a lot of the folks didn't know what to make of that story. I didn't know what else to say, so I stole one of Mac's stories and told them about how Big Gas come to bend over facing away from the campfire. By the time I was half way through everybody was smiling and some of the older kids was giggling, and by the time I was done, they was all laughing hard.

What was funny about the whole thing was I did it all in Arapaho without having to ask Keenan for very many words. I had no notion I could speak Arapaho that good until that night, and even Keenan was surprised. He didn't show it much, but I known he was and he told me so the next day.

The other strange thing was that Hawk didn't say nothing that night and Raven never asked him. I didn't catch it at the time, but when I did, I wondered why. The only thing I could figure was because he was Comanche and Keenan told me later some of Raven's folk got their nose out of joint because Antelope taken up with him. They was also upset she done it so soon after her husband died. So I guess Hawk was just laying low until they got over it and got used to having him around.

It was a good thing we come to winter camp when we done so. Every year there was a gathering of bands of Arapaho for a big buffalo hunt and Raven's people was getting ready to head out for that. Two days later and we would of missed them. We would of caught up pretty quick but it wouldn't of been quite the same. We'd still be welcome, but traveling like that don't allow time for much visiting, not like we had the first night we was in camp.

One thing that was slowing us down was all the winter kill we found out on the plains. A lot of the meat was too ripe for eating, and the ones that died was the old and sick, and tough to chew. Yet the hides was still good and we spent a lot of time salvaging them. It were hard work, and sometimes right aromatic, as Mac put it, but it give me and Charlie a chance to get to know some of Raven's band better. By the time we got to the gathering place, we was part of the band. It helped considerable we known Arapaho ways by wintering with Raven and Antelope. It also helped that we was close to Antelope's two boys. To them, me and Charlie was like a second mother and dad.

I never known how many bands was at the gathering we was at, but after spending most of the last year on the plains, it seemed like a whole town full. It also seemed like every one of them wanted to meet White Badger, though they didn't make a big whoopee over it like white folks sometimes does. There was a lot of time spent visiting and catching up with news from other bands and by the time we broke up into small bands again, seemed like I known half the people at the gathering. Then, when we come back for the late summer gathering, it seemed like a family reunion to me.

The only thing I didn't care for too much was how the stories of White Badger and Hawk kept growing. Yes, it was good for Hawk. People was a little in awe of us and being part of the legend, he become part of the tribe. I mostly found it embarrassing being brought up the way I was. On the other hand, Keenan and Charlie found it hilarious. The old man didn't tease me much about it, but Charlie did. Every once in a while when she thought I was taking myself too serious, Charlie would look at me with a grin and say, "How many is it now?"

This bothered me at first. I didn't like thinking about how many men I'd killed. After a while, though, it bothered me less and less, and I come to see it as Charlie's way of reminding me to find the sunny side. By the end of the summer, I was grabbing an outrageous number out of the air, like 1483, and firing it back at her. Either that, or I was claiming it was Hawk that done it all. It helped take the sting out of the memory.

Looking back, that summer of '46 was one of the best I ever had. We worked hard but it seemed like play, bringing down buffalo two hundred yards off with the Hawken's and riding in close with the bow and arrow. Seemed like me and Charlie grown closer every day, hunting and skinning and riding the prairie like we was born to it. Some of the men looked at us kind strange at first since she didn't stay home with the other women, but once they seen how she used a bow and a rifle, they accepted it. They even given her a name for it, Kills Bull Woman.

After living through one buffalo stampede, I was real careful to make sure Charlie and me was on the right side of the herd when we was hunting. I started to say the safe side of the herd, but when you're hunting buffalo, there ain't no safe side. They can be stampeded this way or that, but there's not much telling when the herd's going to turn, or which way. And if you crowd them too close, they'll charge. When they do, it's a good idea to have a fast horse. There ain't no shame in running away from sixteen hundred pounds of death on the hoof.

One of the strangest things we seen that summer was a white buffalo. It was late in the summer and Charlie and me was hunting with a couple of young Arapaho. A lot of the big herds was scattered by then and we was tracking a small group of maybe a dozen grown buffalo and about half that many calves. When I first spotted it, I thought the white buffalo was a big horse that somehow come to range with the buffalo. Then I taken out my spy glass and seen the hump, and when I let the youngsters look through it, they wasn't sure what to make of it. The things are so rare it scared them, though they didn't say so, and when we started stalking the creature, they was glad to let me and Charlie take the lead.

Now I don't hold with a lot of nonsense about spiritual hocus pocus, but that white buffalo seemed to know we was there. We stalked it most of the afternoon but we wasn't never able to get closer than a quarter mile afore it moved off. That weren't too much for the Hawken, but ever time we got anything near close, the critter started moving and it put every bit of cover there was out there between us.

I give this some thought and come up with a plan. I had Charlie and the youngsters stalk it so that it would naturally move off to the right. While they was doing this, I moved straight to the right a few hundred yards and started circling slightly to the left. Looking at the lay of the land, I known pretty well where the buffalo would go and I found me a place where I'd have a good close shot. The last thing I wanted was to wound the critter and to have to track it by night.

Well, it weren't too long afore buffalo started moving out of a coulee right where I figured they'd come out. I was set up for an easy shot by then. It was about fifty yards and I had the Hawken propped on my jacket on top of the big rock I was laying on. So I let the others drift by and lay there waiting for the white one to come out.

Only, the white buffalo never done so and after a while I begun looking around. Then I heard something snort and I looked over my shoulder. Standing there not fifty feet from where I was laying was the biggest buffalo bull I ever seen. It was pure white and I was close enough to see it had almost colorless eyes. It was looking right at me like it was considering what part of me to stomp first.

Moving real slow, I swung my rifle around, expecting the bull to charge at any moment. I known I'd have only one shot and I picked a spot where I would surely hit the heart. I known that might kill the beast without stopping it and I hoped I had enough time to scramble over the big rock where I was laying. It weren't a lot of cover but it might be enough. It ain't a good idea to be under a ton of anything when it hits.

I don't know to this day why I didn't just fire afore the bull charged, but I didn't. It just didn't seem like the thing to do and after a couple of the longest minutes I ever lived, the bull turned and begun to walk away. I thought about taking it then, but it just didn't seem right. About then the bull stopped and looked back at me. It was like it was telling me that if I was going to shoot, then I needed to make it a clean kill.

When I didn't do nothing, the bull snorted and took a piss. I dropped my eyes and seen the biggest pair of stones I ever seen on any critter, and for some reason, this tickled me. I laughed out loud and lowered my rifle. When I done so I seen movement off to my right, and there was Charlie and the two young men. She had a bead on the bull and the youngsters both had an arrow ready to fly.

"Hold on!" I said in a loud voice. "Let him be." I was looking right at them by then and when I seen them lower their weapons, I turned back toward the bull. It was gone, like the earth opened up and swallowed it whole. Yet when I went over to where it stood, I seen the biggest set of buffalo tracks I ever seen afore or since. There was also the biggest puddle of piss you ever seen.

By then Charlie was standing next to me. When we looked at each other, it was like we reached agreement not to talk about this until we was by ourselves back at camp. The youngsters was too shook to say nothing and I didn't encourage them.

Looking back, not talking to the youngsters may of been a mistake. By next morning there ain't nobody hadn't heard about White Badger and the white bull. Nobody said nothing to Charlie or me except Keenan, but we kept getting strange sideways looks. "I don't know how you do it, lad," Mac said, giving me one of his wry grins. "You seem to provoke the damnedest things. These folk wouldn't be surprised if you sprouted wings and flew off to the mountains."

"I don't understand what happened, neither," I told him. "I had him dead in my sights but I known it would be wrong to shoot. I'm damned if I know why, but I'm glad I didn't."

"Killing a beast that magnificent would be wrong," Keenan answered, nodding. "From what Charlie told me, it looked like white bull won the stalking match. He had you dead to rights first."

I nodded. "He did. I don't know why he didn't stomp me flat. Maybe that's why I didn't shoot."

"From the way folks around here are telling it, white bull was scared to tangle with White Badger," he chuckled. "Your reputation seems to have outstripped you, Jack. From what those youngsters said, that bull was bigger than a house."

"Well, he had the biggest set of stones I ever seen," I told him. "I seen smaller muskmelons back in Arkansas."

"Don't get caught up in your own legend, Jack," McAdams cautioned me. "Consider being alive this morning a gift from Mr. White Bull and Whoever is running things."

I allowed he was absolutely right.

Of course, the story grown like a weed, and by the time the bands got back together for the last fall hunt, it were outrageous. When Raven asked me about it, I told him that me and Mr. Bull didn't want no part of one another. I had a new wife and he had lots of new calves to make and we agreed to have it out some other season. I was pulling his leg, but Raven taken me serious, and after that the legend grew some more. That's what it were by then, not just a story, but a legend.

We done so good that summer that Raven's band decided to head for winter camp early. We had enough dried meat to carry us through even the worst winter and I think most everyone was ready to do something besides butcher buffalo and scrape skins.

Once we was settled in at the winter camp, Mac and Raven and me headed into the mountains. Mac wanted to try out a couple of trout streams afore they froze and I was ready so see some new country. I think Raven just wanted to get away from the women and children for a while. Sometimes a man just needs time to be with other men without having to worry about nothing in particular.

It taken us two days to get to the streams Mac wanted to see, and the fish was almost jumping out of the water for us to catch. Raven shown me how to tickle trout and there ain't nothing better than mountain trout taken to the fire right out of the stream. We eaten our fill and dried a whole lot more for the winter, and over the campfire we told some outrageous yarns.

One night when we run out of things to talk about, Raven asked me if I wanted to find the gold. I told him I didn't have the map with me, but he said it didn't matter. He known the place it shown and we was within a couple of days of reaching it.

I given this a lot of thought afore I answered. Neither Mac or Raven said nothing whilst I cogitated. When I did, I allowed it wouldn't hurt to find the gold just to know for sure if it was there. Finding it didn't mean we had to take it, but I was curious if it was real.

Knowing what I know now, I wish to hell I'd said, "Hell, no!" Only I didn't, and like a damned fool cat, I let curiosity bring me a pile of troubles. Maybe that weren't the worst decision I ever made, but it bought a load of grief.

Anyway, that was later. The next morning we cached our dried fish in a high tree where even a small bear or some other critter couldn't reach it. Then we headed upstream.

The country we went through was some of the prettiest I ever seen, but it was clear we didn't have much time to look around. The snow was settled in on the high peaks, and was moving down the mountain. While there weren't much chance of us getting caught by an early storm, there weren't no use risking it, neither. There was plenty of places we could hole up, but we damn sure didn't want to be forced to winter up there.

Truth is, I was missing Charlie pretty bad about then.

We got to where Raven said the monastery ruins was about noon the second day. We was at a higher elevation then and it was cold when he shown us what was left. It weren't much, just the bare walls of a church and a couple of other buildings. The walls was made of rock and could of been used to rebuild he place, but the roof was long gone. I'd guess it was wood with wood shakes when they built it, but weren't even any beams left. Could have been they was scavenged for dry wood but it's more likely they just rotted.

We was in Ute country by then, so we camped that night inside the ruins without a fire. It was cold, a lot colder than winter camp, and the next morning there was a light frost. We was lucky we was on the east slope because when the sun come up, the frost burnt off fast and things warmed up right quick. Even still, it seemed like it taken me until high noon to warm up and I was ready to head back to winter camp. I said as much to Raven and Mac, but they wanted to spend at least another day looking.

The way things turned out, the gold was easy to find. It wouldn't of been while people was still living in the monastery, or even in the spring after the leaves come out and the brush was thick. Or if I ain't seen the fox pop out from behind some rocks, we could of spent months searching them canyons and come up with nothing.

What grabbed my attention was that I couldn't see where the fox come from. There was a big rock sticking out of the side of the mountain, maybe four or five foot high. It had a big bush that was losing its leaves in front of it, and behind that big rock was some smaller rocks and a little more brush. The thing is, there weren't no other cover for twenty yards around that rock. So I figured them rocks was the fox's den and I only looked out of curiosity. Wasn't nothing about that particular pile of rock and brush that caught my attention except the fox.

Even then I wouldn't of given it a second look except for something I seen through the bush. It was some shadows that could of been a couple of big cracks in the rock, but I somehow didn't think it was. Sure enough, it weren't no cracks. While the stone was pretty weathered, it looked like them lines was chipped into the rock, and they was in the form of a long T. Sticking straight up from the top of the T was another mark that was way more weathered than the rest and I couldn't quite make out what it was.

I wouldn't of thought anything about it but when I looked around to the back of the rock, I seen what looked like the opening of a small cave. It was big enough I started to go in but I thought better of it. Afore I went in I wanted someone to know where I was, so I went and fetched Keenan and Raven.

When we all got back, I shown Keenan the marks on the rock and he nodded but didn't say nothing. Neither did Raven but when I stooped to go in, Keenan stopped me. "Just a minute, lad," he said. "Things are not quite what they seem." Standing to one side he pulled on a small rock over the opening, and a whole bunch of rock come tumbling down.

"Now, let's see what lies behind this," he said, and begun pulling rock away from where it fell.

I just stood and watched him. Had I gone in like I started, I could of been buried alive with no one knowing where I was. I felt a shiver go up my spine, like a goose walked over my grave and I known there was something very wrong about this. "Maybe we ought to let it be," I said.

Keenan was too busy flinging rocks out of the way, but Raven heard how I said it and give me a serious look. I said it again in Arapaho and he nodded. There was something about this that weren't right and Raven felt it, too. Somehow Keenan missed it. He was too busy moving rocks aside and looking for gold. Looking back, I'd have to say the curse was already working on him. When I asked him about this a good bit later, he agreed it was. Yet, by then it was too late. At least, that's what I think but I'm getting a good way ahead of myself again.

There weren't as much rock over the entrance to the cave as I'd thought, and it weren't long until we seen why. What I spotted may of started out as a big cave cave with a smaller mouth, but someone dug it out and cut timbers to brace up the entry. What caused the cave-in was a couple of the braces was completely rotted away, leaving only loose rock and dirt barely holding things up. When Mac pulled out the first rock, the whole thing give way.

We stood there looking inside for a bit. Once the dust started to settle we seen it was a natural cave opening out from the entry. Matter of fact, it looked like someone narrowed the entry considerable so only one man could pass at a time.

After poking inside at the walls with a long stick , Keenan thought it was safe to go in, but I didn't want no part in it. "I'll stay outside in case it caves in again," I told him. "That way there's somebody to dig you out."

We was talking English but Mac translated what I said for Raven. When Raven answered, I known what he was saying even afore Mac translated for me. "Raven says you show uncommon good sense, lad."

"Someone has to," I answered back. "You got gold fever."

Keenan give me a startled look. Then he nodded and ducked into the cave. Raven looked at me and shaken his head. Neither of us followed and weren't but a minute or two afore Mac was back outside. "You've found the monks' crypt, Jack," he told me. "Toward the back there are skeletons laying on ledges cut in the rock, but I couldn't see much. I need a light."

When Raven learnt what it was we found, he didn't want no part of going into the cave. He was thinking we should leave the dead in peace. I agreed with him but Mac ain't done it. "It won't hurt to take a look," he said in Arapaho. "These are white men and their customs are different. Their spirits have already moved on to the spirit world."

Raven still didn't like it and neither did I, so we waited while Mac made him a torch from a pine knot and looked around inside. "This is strange," he told us. "There are four bodies laid out on ledges but it looks like five more were piled in later. Those must have been the ones the Captain tortured and killed."

Mac didn't say nothing more, but we could hear him moving around. Then he said, "Ah, clever." A minute later it sounded like he was digging. Then we heard him grunt, like he was straining, and the sound of something dragging. The next thing we known, there was a wood box being pushed out of the crypt.

"Grab hold, lad," I heard Mac tell me. "This box is heavy and there are two more."

Well, I drug the box out from behind the rocks and Mac went back to drag out the two others. I'd guess them boxes weighed fifty pound apiece and there weren't no question in my mind what was in them. I could of used a little help, but Raven just stood there watching. It was pretty clear he didn't want to touch nothing having to do with the dead monks. He was the only one of us with a lick of sense.

The boxes was all held together by wood pegs and they was shrunk with age. So it weren't too hard to pull off one of the top planks from a box. When we done so, it were full of small leather bags so old they was hard and brittle. So when Mac picked up one of the smallest ones and tried to open it, the thing busted apart like a dried gourd. What was left was chunks of gold that was still bright where they didn't touch the leather.

I taken a look at Mac and he had a funny look on his face. It was like he was holding a live rattlesnake but couldn't throw it down, and I known he wanted to keep it. "It ain't ours, Keenan!" I told him right sharp. I don't reckon I ever spoken to him that strong afore or since.

Mac blinked and dropped the gold back in the box. "You're right, lad, it's not," he told me. "Nor can I think of why I crave it so. It won't buy what I really want. I already have all I desire in this world." When he looked at me, I seen he meant it. I also seen the gold still had a grip on him.

Raven spoke up right then, saying something I didn't understand, and Mac told him back in Arapaho it was a good idea. "He thinks we need to go through a purification, lad. He thinks the gold does, too."

"You think that will break the curse?" I asked. "We can still just leave the gold where it lays. Or bury it again, either."

"We've already taken it, Jack," he told me. "At least, I have and you've helped me. If we bury it again, I'm afraid knowing where it is would haunt us."

"It wouldn't me," I told him. "I don't want no part of it."

"Then let the curse be on me," he said. "Would you at least help me bring it to Sister Carmelita?"

"We could scatter it in the river," I answered. "That way recovering it would be right near impossible."

"That wouldn't feed the orphans," he pointed out. "It wouldn't help keep them warm in the winter or buy them clothes."

We chewed it back and forth like that a while longer, but in the end I agreed. So Raven made a sweat lodge that night, and we taken the gold right into the lodge with us. I ain't never seen nothing like it and most of what Raven was chanting I couldn't make out. I guess Mac could of told me what he was saying, but he didn't and it didn't seem like asking was right. So I just listened and picked out the words I known, and I done just what Raven told me.

When it was over, I come out and plunged into a deep pool in the stream like Mac done, expecting to be half froze when I hit the water. Yet it felt cool, not cold, and when I come out, I felt as clean on the inside as I was outside. That night I slept like a log and I never felt so good when I got up.

We packed and headed out afore the sun struck the valley the next morning and we made good time headed downstream. So we was able to reach our fish camp that evening afore dark even though we was traveling on foot and leading our horses. We seen our cache of dried fish was till hanging safe in the tree, but the next morning there was scratch marks on the tree where a bear tried to get it. I guess we was lucky because it was a big bear and had moved on to easier pickings.

We was early heading out again that morning and we traveled late, camping without no fire and eating jerky. So it was early afternoon when we got back to the winter camp. I was grateful we got there without no trouble and me and I taken a long time showing Charlie just how much I missed her. I known she weren't too happy about us bringing out the gold like we done, but she was right glad to see me.

CHAPTER EIGHTEEN

The Abbot's Curse

Two days after we got back from the old monastery, the three of us headed east, me and Charlie and Mac, following the Arkansas downstream. It was sad leaving winter camp. Raven and Antelope and Hawk was all like kinfolk, and while we was there, we made a lot of friends amongst Raven's camp. I told Raven I hoped to see him for the next hunt and I give him and Hawk the horses we wasn't taking with us. We was planning to follow the Arkansas to Bent's Fort and to sell our horses for passage down river on a boat going east. So all we taken was a horse for each of us and two for pack animals.

We could of gotten by with just one packhorse but we taken the other in case one of our riding stock went lame. Mac figured there'd be a boat headed east from Bent's Fort, but if there weren't, we'd need good horses for the trip overland. Since we might have to make a run for it at some point, we was riding our fastest horses. Yet, we wasn't pushing them hard and it taken us almost four days to make it to the fort.

Since we was carrying so much gold, we kept off the main trail and stuck to higher ground where we could keep an eye on the country. There was a wagons moving up the trail by then, mostly freighters headed for Santa Fe by the looks of them, and the third night out we made camp with a large party of them. They was camped near good water and had butchered some winter kill they found froze in a snow bank, and we spent a good part of the night swapping tales. Mostly it was Keenan doing the talking and me and Charlie listening.

The freighters' talk was mostly about the war brewing betwixt Mexico and the US. We heard Congress had declared war on Mexico, but so far most of the fighting was several hundred miles south of us in Texas. Now the US Army was getting ready to invade from the north and word was that Bent's Fort was the jump-off point for that.

The next morning we was up early and in the saddle afore the sun come over the hills. We traveled steady and crossed the Arkansas, coming to Bent's Fort a couple of hours afore sunset. Since we was riding directly into the wind, I smelled the place long afore we got there. I noticed this when I first come to Taos, too, and when I asked Mac about it that evening we caught up there, he laughed.

"You've been out on the open prairies too long, Jack. Your nose has gotten used to fresh air, but didn't you smell the winter camp when we first got there?"

"Yeah, but it was mostly wood smoke and the smell went away in a couple of days."

"The smell didn't go away, lad. You simply got used to it and didn't notice. The same will happen here."

"I don't know as I want to get used to this," I told him. "This place stinks." Charlie nodded and Keenan grinned.

"Well, these folks would say the same about winter camp. Yet, I have to agree. This place seems to have a lot more aroma than most. I think it's the wetlands. Or maybe it's the smell of money. A lot of hides go east from here."

"It's worse than penned hogs," Charlie said.

Bad as it was at first, I stopped noticing the smell after a couple of nights. We made camp that night upwind of the fort, which helped, and we ended up sharing our supper with a couple of brothers from Missouri. They come to our camp asking if they could buy some of the biscuits they smelled baking and we spent a long time swapping tales that evening.

Turns out the brothers was both blacksmiths, which weren't no surprise. Both of them was almost as wide as they was tall and there weren't an ounce of fat on either one. Like a lot of folks, they was looking for a good place to settle and set up shop, but they was planning to spend the summer at the fort. With the war coming and the Army on the way, Bent's Fort looked good, even with a blacksmith already there. After that they didn't know where they was headed and I mentioned Sam Watrous. When I told them what he was planning to do they was interested and asked me where to find him.

As I said, we talked late and the next morning we taken our time getting up and walking over to the fort. It was built out of adobe, same as most of the houses in that country, and the walls was two to three feet thick. What struck me was how quiet it was inside the rooms, even with everything going on in the main courtyard square.

We looked around the store a good bit but the prices was pretty high. So I didn't buy nothing but some buttons and ribbon for Charlie, along with some needles and thread for us all. Mac bought himself some Virginia tobacco and Charlie fingered the women's dresses. Yet she wouldn't let me buy her a dress. So I got her a new pair of pants and a small man's shirt, along with a set of suspenders.

As I expected, the prices was high but I made out all right, too. The store keeper was glad to take most of the rifles off my hands and he give me a good price. I known he would sell them for twice what he give me but that was all right. They didn't cost me nothing but the price of powder and shot and I was glad to be shed of them.

We was sitting in the courtyard, sucking on some hard candy Mac bought us, when I overheard a couple of men talking. Charlie was startled when I got up and braced them, but when she heard what I had to say, she turned bright red. Mac, of course, thought it was funny.

"Beg your pardon," I said to the men. "Did I hear you say there was a reverend here?"

One of the men smiled. "No," he said. "My companion called me that." He glanced over at Charlie and Mac. "Is there something I can do for you?"

"We want to get married," I told him.

The reverend looked at Mac and Charlie again, but Charlie was wearing men's clothes and her hair was up under her hat. "I'd be happy to help you," he said, looking around. "Where's your bride?"

I grabbed Charlie by the hand and she taken off her hat. She was blushing bright red right then. "I see," preacher said, smiling. "What's your name, m'am?"

"Charlene," she answered. I don't know how she done it, but Charlie blushed even brighter. "They call me Charlie."

"I'm pleased to meet you. When would you like to get married?"

"Right now!" I answered but the preacher shook his head.

"You need to let your bride change her clothes," he answered. "How about this afternoon? Will that give you enough time, Charlie?"

We agreed to meet back there the middle of the afternoon and I taken Charlie back to the store and made her buy a nice dress and a pair of slippers. This time she didn't put up no fuss and even picked out a ribbon for her hair. Then she picked out a new shirt for me and some new trousers and a belt, but I drawn the line at new boots or shoes. By the time we was done, we'd put a good dent in money I made from the rifles, but I didn't care. There's some things a man just needs to do without counting dollars.

The wedding that afternoon was sweet and simple. A couple of the ladies at the fort caught wind of the wedding and insisted on helping Charlie get all gussied up. They taken her into one of the rooms above the courtyard and I didn't see her again until we all got back together for the vows. When I seen her, I hardly recognized her as the beautiful young woman walking toward me and the reverend on Mac's arm.

Since we was being married in the main courtyard, just about everyone at the fort shown up, including some Cheyenne who was there trading. And when Charlie come out of the room where she got dressed there was dead silence. Then someone started clapping as she was walking down the steps and pretty soon everybody was clapping soft like. Of course, when this happened, Charlie turned bright red but when she looked at me she smiled. Mac told me later my mouth was open so far it looked like my jaw was laying on the ground.

I must have been pretty stunned because I cain't recall much about the wedding. I do remember the reverend used our proper names, John for me and Charlene for Charlie. I also remember the conversation me and the reverend had after when I asked how much I owed him.

"Well, Jack," he said, smiling the way Keenan sometimes does, "how much is she worth?"

"There ain't that much money in the world," I told him.

"You're right, son," he said. "So just say a prayer for me from time to time. I'd be well paid with that."

"Let us at least feed you supper, reverend," Mac jumped in and Charlie nodded. "You and your companion, too."

So we ate supper that night in the fort dining room, and Mac insisted on paying for it all. There was a fiddler at the fort, too, and after supper he started playing in the courtyard. The first number was a sweet waltz and Charlie was surprised when I taken her hand and led her out. Like I told you, I don't dance, but it ain't for not knowing how. One thing my mama taught me early was how to dance, and I don't know if Mac or Charlie was more surprised. It didn't take much time for people to start dancing and the night was getting old by the time we got back to camp.

The next day we was late getting up. After breakfast we headed down to the landing to see if there was any boats headed downriver anytime soon. There was lots of boats at Bent's Fort, but none of them was heading east until they got enough cargo to make the trip worth while. Most of what they was loading was furs and hides, and the first boat out wouldn't be leaving for at least a couple of weeks.

We could of waited, I guess, but the stink of the boats was more than me and Charlie cared to put up with and some of the boatmen was downright surly. They taken me for Indian or half-breed and they wasn't shy about letting me know how they felt. One of them took offense at me asking and started to come at me with a knife, but I sent him flying flat on his face. Mr. Colt persuaded his friends it wouldn't be a good notion to jump us. Drunk as they was, they could still study that one out. It didn't hurt that Charlie was backing me up with a Colt's in each hand and that she was dressed like a man. They might of jumped us if they had recognized her as a woman, but that would of been a fatal mistake.

When we got back to camp and told Keenan what happened he agreed it might be best to break camp and head east overland. So we rode out that afternoon, keeping a close eye on our back trail. Far as we could tell, nobody come after us but we rode on through most of the night. First light was just showing when we found a good spot and stopped for a few hours, making camp without a fire and taking turns on watch.

We crossed over the river and followed the north bank for a couple of weeks until the river turned south and then swung back north. Mac thought it might be good to cross over again and head southeast until we hit it again further down. The way he figured, that would save us fifty miles of riding and maybe more, and we was all anxious to get shed of the gold. We didn't talk about it much, but it rode heavy on our minds and more than once I thought about just dumping it in the river. I don't know if it would have saved us any grief, but it might have. Or it might of made things worse. There's no telling.

Heading overland rather than following the river may of saved us a few days' riding, but we was in Pawnee and Kiowa country by then and we was traveling too fast to hide our tracks good. We was keeping to hard ground as much as we could and the high grass helped. It was mostly dead by then but the wind kept moving it, like waves on the sea Keenan said, and that covered our trail, too.

That overland short cut taken us ten full days to make, but we never run into a soul all that time. We didn't even cut nobody's trail, neither. So when we come to the river again, we found a good spot to camp and rest our horses for a couple of days. This given me and Charlie some time, too, and I was glad of it. Traveling hard and fast, all the time keeping watch, don't leave too much chance for being husband and wife, and it was good making up for lost time.

When we headed down river again but the land was beginning to change. The river never run straight nowhere, but where we was it begun to wind itself around like a snake. So the river might run two or three or even four miles inside a mile as the bee flies. Between this and the brush in the bottoms it got to be slow going and it taken us a good part of two weeks to make Ft. Gibson.

Back then Ft. Gibson weren't much, just an army post and a few stubborn settlers that traded up and down the river. There was a steamboat landing and we was able to get passage on a boat big enough to carry our horses, too. The captain was waiting for cargo to carry south, but he been there a week afore us and his prospects didn't look too good for getting a full cargo. There was at least four boats ahead of him and when Mac asked him about taking us, the captain was glad to get the trade. There was people backed up all the way to Little Rock waiting for passage west, and he weren't earning a dime sitting there by the river in Ft. Gibson.

After damn near two months of hard travel, I was glad to let the steamboat and the river do the work for a while. The captain offered us a cabin but neither Charlie or me cared for it much. It was small and cramped and weren't that good to smell, neither. Since we was less than a week from Ft. Smith, me and Charlie bunked out on the deck with Mac where there was always a fresh breeze coming over the bow.

That ride down the river was so pleasant I got lulled into forgetting about the curse. So when trouble come, it were the last thing on my mind and I never seen it coming.

We was about a day out of Ft. Smith when somebody flagged the boat and the captain pulled into shore. There was a beat up landing there and we could see a couple of people waiting, so when the captain turned in, me and Charlie went up front to watch. So did some other passengers that come on board with us at Ft. Gibson.

The last thing we expected right then was trouble, but it was sure waiting for us at that landing. Yet, I don't remember a whole lot of what happened when we come into shore. I'm told I taken a bad lick on the head and my memory's still fuzzy. I do remember seeing it was a man and a woman we was picking up but I weren't paying much attention to neither of them. Then I recognized the woman as the one from the badger game back in Washington. Last I'd seen of her was in Taos and it surprised the hell out of me to see her here.

I recall turning to Charlie to say something about it and then looking back. When I done so, I seen the ugly rat faced man she worked the game with talking to the woman and pointing at me. Then he looked back toward me and I seen a spark come out of his finger. I realized he was firing a pistol and something hit me hard in the chest and I felt myself falling. There wasn't much I could do about it, but afore I hit the deck I heard the boom of a Colt's pistol coming from behind me. Then I my head hit the deck and the light went out. In the darkness, it seemed to me I heard somebody screaming my name. Then there was some more shots that sounded like they come from somewhere a long ways off. After that there weren't nothing.

When I first come to, it taken me a long time to figure out where I was. I was laying on a soft bed in a room somewhere, but I couldn't remember how I come to be there. There was light coming in a window and I seen the walls was papered, but my head was aching like fury and I couldn't think straight.

"Jack?" Someone was spoke softly but when I looked around I didn't know Keenan at first. "Are you back in the land of the living, lad?"

I must of drifted off to sleep again because when I come awake it was dark out. My head weren't hurting so bad by then but when I tried to get up, I was weak as a baby. I must of made some noise because the next thing I heard was a rocking chair creaking as somebody stood up. When I turned my head to see who it was, I seen Keenan.

"Are you awake, Jack?" the old man asked me. He looked drawn and seemed to me the lines in his face was deeper than ever I seen them.

"Where's Charlie?" I asked him, but I seen the answer in his face.

"Charlie's gone, Jack," he told me and there was tears in his eyes. "She was killed back at the landing."

"I want to see her," I told him. "Help me up."

The old man pushed me back onto the mattress. "We never found her, Jack," he told me. "There was blood on the railing where she went overboard, but her body never came up. We spent all day searching down river, but we never found it."

"Where are we?" I asked him. Somehow what he was saying seemed all wrong and I wondered if I was having a bad dream. Yet I known I weren't sleeping.

"We're in Ft. Smith, lad," he told me. "We've been here for two days."

"I'm thirsty," I told him and he given me a drink. Then I asked him to tell me how it happened.

"Do you remember those people you saw in Taos? The woman and the rat faced man from Arkansas?" I nodded and he went on. "The man spotted you right away and started shooting. He hit you in the chest but you were damned lucky. The bullet hit your medicine pouch and that stopped it. I don't know why, but it did. You'd have been all right but for falling and hitting your head so hard on the deck."

"Tell me about Charlie." I said. I must of been in shock because my mind weren't able to get hold of her being gone.

"I didn't see it happen but there were others who did. They tell me Charlie cut the bastard down in his tracks. She fired four times and every one was a fatal shot. Then the woman threw down on Charlie with a pepperbox pistol and hit her, but Charlie got off two more shots afore she went over the railing. One caught the woman through the neck and the other straight through the heart. She was dead afore she hit the decking."

The old man sighed. "Some of the men were angry that Charlie had shot down a woman until they found out Charlie was a woman, too. Then a couple of them went into the river there at the dock but they never found a body, not even with a net, and the captain took a lot of time searching the river bank for five miles down river. The only thing I can figure is that a current pulled Charlie under and kept her there. I hired another boat to go up the river with a canon yesterday, but nothing ever came to the surface."

"I've got to get out of here and go look for her," I told him. I tried to get up again but couldn't get no further than sitting up. My head was swimming too bad to stand.

"It's been three days, lad. I don't think we're ever going to find her. Besides, it's night and we're in the dark of the moon."

I don't know how I made it through them next few days. For a while I felt dead inside, and when I stopped feeling dead, it felt like someone torn out my heart. It was a week afore we headed for Washington, and the day we left, Keenan and me stood down at the river. He read from my family bible, but tears was streaming down his face the whole time and I seen it was all he could do to keep from choking. There weren't no way I could say nothing. It felt like I'd been kicked in the gut by a mule.

It taken us most of two weeks to get over the mountains between Ft. Smith and Washington. We drifted along slow and spent a lot of time riding quiet and catching fish. I ain't thought to buy no whiskey afore we left Ft. Smith. Keenan ain't brung none neither but I don't think it was from forgetting. I think he was worried what I might do with a load of rotgut in me.

Thing is, I really didn't want no whiskey, even hurting like I done. I wanted to be clear headed remembering Charlie and I couldn't see how drinking would help. When I sobered up she'd still be gone and I'd be hurting even worse. So we rode mostly in silence, looking at the leaves turning bright.

I always liked that, watching the gum trees turn bright red and the others turn yellow, but seemed like there was a deep shadow between me and what I was seeing right then. I couldn't help wondering why Charlie had been taken and why I'd been spared. I'd of gladly died in her place and I said as much to Keenan. He just nodded his head and we rode on, but not afore I seen the tears in his eyes, too.

I guess under normal circumstances I might of been worried coming back to Washington after the way I had to leave the year afore. Seemed hard to believe it was less than a year and a half since I rode out like the Devil was on my tail. Yet there weren't nobody left to accuse me. Old rat face and his whore was in the ground and nobody else ever seen me face to face except Sister Carmelita. About all anyone could of said for sure is I had spent a lot of time that evening drinking and dancing with the woman.

Keenan must of been thinking of this, too, because he said it might be better if we headed straight for the orphanage. There weren't no other place I wanted to go so that's what we done. That's what we come here for and I was damn sure ready to get rid of the gold. Had I known what it was going to cost me, I'd never of gone along with bringing it out.

Of course, when we got there, Sister Carmelita was glad to see us. She remembered Keenan and I think she hugged him harder than she did me. She also known right off something real bad was wrong and had to hear the whole story. Keenan done most of the telling and it taken him all afternoon to hit just the main parts.

As I sat there listening, I seen how much the old man had aged in the last few weeks. Then, when it come to his telling how we found and lost Charlie, I had to get up and walk away. It felt like my heart was being tore out all over again and I could hardly breathe.

I sure wasn't wanting company and there weren't no other place to go, so I ended up wandering into the church house and sitting there a spell. I remember asking Whoever might be listening why it was Charlie who was taken, but there weren't no answer and I just set there quiet. Then I started thinking about the men I'd killed and wondered if that was why. Yet I didn't see how I had much choice at the time.

I guess I must of been there a long time because the light was gone when I heard someone come in. I looked around and it was Sister Carmelita, but when I got up to leave, she stopped me. She was as tall as me, and as broad across the shoulders, so there weren't no getting around her.

"Oh, Jackie," she said, opening her arms and taking me in like a little child. "Poor Jackie. How awful it must be." She held me close and I felt something come loose inside, like the cork out of a jug. I begun to cry like a baby. I ain't never cried like that afore or since, and when I was done, all I felt was empty. There weren't no hurt nor rage nor nothing else, just a hole in my soul so big I ain't never seen the other side.

Keenan and me stayed in Washington for a couple of months. We sold our two packhorses and found a good place we could stable our riding mounts. I couldn't bear to sell Charlie's horse, so we kept it for a packhorse for when we moved on. For a little more money the owner of the stable was willing to let us sleep in the hay loft, and we taken most of our meals at the orphanage with Jesus, the gardener.

During the days we done a lot of looking around the countryside and seeing what was there. Keenan found him a good fishing hole and we spent a lot of time there. Every once in a while we'd bag some game or a mess of fish and take it to the sister who done the cooking, and after a while I begun to feel like living again. The hurt come back again and again and I shed a river of tears, but there come a time I could laugh at some of the old man's stories, even if I heard them afore.

It was the first of October when we rode in from Ft. Smith and it weren't but a few weeks after Christmas I begun to feel restless. Sleeping on the hay was softer than sleeping on hard ground, and the barn roof turned most of the rain, but after spending all that time on the prairie, I was craving open spaces. There's something about sitting around a campfire eating camp biscuits and fresh game that fills me like nothing else can. The food tastes better and you don't have to live with the smell of yesterday's cooking. It's also easier to fall asleep at night, feeling the wind on your face and looking at stars so bright it seems like you can reach out your hand and gather a handful. Even when it rains, it don't last for days and days like happens in the woodlands sometimes, and when it does rain, things dry up fast. Mud turns to dust real quick and if you get soaked, it ain't long afore your clothes is dry again.

This may sound strange coming from me since I grown up in the Arkansas hills, but Arkansas weren't home no longer. The Great Plains was and it was like I was born for them. There's something about coming to the top of a rise and being able to see thirty miles and more. There's something about watching a twister wind its way over the prairie or thunderheads building a long way across the prairie. There's something about having a sky so big it makes even the prairie look small.

Then, too, I ain't never seen nothing in Arkansas like the sun going down over the prairie and setting the sky afire. But most of all, there's a sense of freedom out on the prairie I never felt nowhere else. As pretty as Arkansas can be, and as pretty as it was while we was there, I was longing to be back to rolling plains.

Of course, I known that season of year weren't no time to be heading out nowhere. Winter was on us like flies on stink and there weren't no getting around that. There weren't no place better we could winter than right where we was at and spring weren't that far off. So I kept my notions to myself and tried to keep busy by helping Jesus put in the garden for the orphanage and helping him fix the things that needed fixing. Word got out I was handy with a hammer and a saw, and I even made a little money helping the blacksmith build him a new barn and tending the stock he had stabled there. I guess I could of stayed there and made a place for myself, but I known I weren't long for that country.

Of course, I ought to known that Keenan seen my restlessness even afore I known it was there. I think he seen it because I'm so much like him. Even so, he bided his time, letting me get good and ripe afore he said nothing.

It was long about the end of February when we was eating supper one night that he brung it up. "So you think it's time to be heading west, Jack?" he asked.

I nodded. I ain't said a word about it, but I guess the signs was written all over me. "It ain't that long until the first buffalo hunt," I told him. "Raven's folk will be breaking camp and heading east soon."

Keenan nodded. "We'd have to ride pretty hard to make the first gathering, lad. Are you thinking we should try?"

I shaken my head. "I'd like to get there in time to make the last hunt and winter with Raven's band, but I'd like to see some new country first. I'd like to see Taos again, and Santa Fe. It should be safe to go there by now. Sounds like the Mexicans didn't put up much of a fight with Kearney."

"That's what the papers say," Keenan nodded. "Of course, I learned a long time ago that a war isn't over until it's over. Mexico is a big place. Still, I'd think it would be safe enough traveling with a salty soul like yourself."

"Well, I ain't looking for no fight," I told him. "If I was, I'd of rode off with the Army. A man might as well get paid for fighting if he likes it."

McAdams laughed. "Well, Jack, I never found the pay that good. I always found it easier to make a living off the land." He give me a look I known well and I seen he was just as restless as me. "There's a wonderful sight to see up the Red River if you don't mind a few Comanche," he went on. "And if you want to see some prairie, there's nothing quite like the staked plains. Remember me telling you about the Palo Duro?"

"The hard wood canyon?" I asked and he nodded.

"That's up the Red River," he told me. "I'd put it fifty or sixty miles south of the Canadian. Matter of fact, it might be better to head for that rather than attempt the staked plains west of Palo Duro."

"What's the staked plains?" I asked. "I cain't recall."

"It's a place where the prairie is so vast and the watering places are so few that even the Indians have to mark their way across with stakes. Otherwise a man could wander in circles until he ran out of water." He looked at me and grinned. "Or so they say. We've been across part of the Staked Plains following the Canadian. Remember when those buttes rose up three hundred feet from the plain? That's what Coronado called the Palisades and that's where the plains get their name. He called them *llano estacado*, or the palisades plains. I call it the Big Empty."

I remembered the buttes. I doubt I'll ever forget them but I weren't sure what a palisade was and asked him. "It's a wall, like a fort has, used for defense. That's what those buttes looked like to Coronado from the desert floor."

I told him it sounded good to me. "When you thinking we could head out?" I asked.

"Any time, lad," he told me. "We may run into a March blizzard, but it will take us a while before we get to high enough elevation it will matter. There are settlements where we can hole up all the way to Spanish Fort, and by the time we get there, I doubt we'll run into much cold weather."

"Unless it's like last year," I said. "I remember them teamsters that froze. On the other hand, I guess if we freeze, we freeze."

"That's the spirit, lad," he said, and for the first time in a long while, Keenan looked the way he done when first I met him, in good spirits and ready for whatever might come down the pike. I even felt my spirits picking up, too.

CHAPTER NINETEEN

Choctaw Country

We headed west three weeks later. We could of headed out sooner but I was in the middle of a job of helping Jesus fix the church roof and it taken most of both weeks to finish that. Then Sister Carmelita insisted on giving us a big send-off and that had to wait until the next Sunday afternoon since it was Lent. I never did figure out what that had to do with it but I never got around to asking Keenan, neither. So it weren't until late March that we was able to get away, and when we did, Sister Carmelita handed me a sack full of silver dollars and another one of food.

"I can't take this," I tried to tell her, offering back the money, but augering with Sister was like trying to corral a thunderstorm. So we ended up with more money than we needed for the trip and enough fresh bread to last four men a week. Strange thing is, the way it was baked didn't none of that bread go bad.

The trees was budded out when we left, but the leaves was still small and a man could see a good ways underneath the pines. We headed southwest toward Fulton, intending to take a boat up the Red River as far as we could, but when we got there, there weren't much boat space on hand. What there was cost more than we cared to pay, so Keenan and me headed west overland, following the Little River until we found a place to ford.

I was just as glad we done so. With Texas opening up to settlement, there was so much traffic along the military road a man could hardly keep from bumping into people looking for land. Traveling close to the river weren't that easy, neither. What roads there was, wagons chewed up, especially in the wet places, and there was stories of outlaws looking for easy pickings amongst travelers west. Having had a belly full of outlaws, I was glad to follow our noses and whatever game trails we come across.

Once we was out of the river bottom, there weren't so much undergrowth, and the trees was mostly pine. There was stands of them damn near a hundred feet high, and the way the light come filtering down through the needles was like a soft rain. As long as I lived in Arkansas, I'd never seen nothing quite like it, and for a while it made me forget my troubles.

Keenan felt it, too. "You know, Jack, I've seen fine cathedrals and grand temples," he told me. "Yet none of them measure up to what we're seeing right here. Seems to me that if God needed a place to live, this would be his house, right here."

After a while, of course, we left the pines behind and moved into the cross timbers. At first the oaks was big, but the closer we got to the prairie, the shorter they was and more there was of them. The way they clumped together, it was harder to find a way through, and we begun to run into some other plants that made the going tough. One of these was green briars with long thin vines covered with spines shaped like cats' claws. Another was thorn bushes that grown to the size of a small tree and was covered with sharp thorns ready to grab a man if he come too close. I only done so once.

The morning of our fourth day out of Fulton we was going through a patch of these when we heard some yelling from around a bend in the trail just ahead of us. Then there was a shot, followed by two more, and the sound of men laughing. When I heard the first shot I was off my horse with my Colt's out, and out of the side of my eye I seen Mac take a dive, too.

When I heard the laughing, the men was talking back and forth, too, but I weren't able to make out what they was saying. Then I heard one of them say something about a strange looking coon, and I began to move forward. Not knowing what I was getting myself into, I drawn the other Colt's and kept close to the brush. Keenan was right behind me, leading the horses.

I ain't gone more than fifty or sixty yards when I come around the bend in the trail and seen two rough looking riders staring up a tree. I seen one of them raise his pistol and take another shot, knocking loose a small branch, and when I glanced toward where he shot, I seen a young Indian trying to keep the trunk of tree between hisself and the riders. Didn't look to me like the kid was more than ten or twelve.

Then one of the riders told the other he was tired of messing around and wanted to get on to where they was headed. "Let's finish him off," he said. "You go left and I'll go right and whoever gets the first clean shot gets him."

"That ain't no sport," the other said. "You couldn't hit a bull in the ass twenty feet away with a shotgun."

"Maybe you'd like to put your money where your mouth is," the first man said. "I've got ten dollars that says I'll get him first. On the first shot, too!"

"You ain't got ten dollars to bet!" the second man sneered.

"Hell I don't," the first man told him and started digging in his pocket. When he done so the first man laughed and spurred his horse to the right, raising his pistol for a quick shot.

Well, I couldn't abide seeing the kid shot down like that. So I yelled and let off a shot in the air with my left hand while I covered the rider with my right. Tired as I might be of killing, I seen no shame in cutting the man down if he didn't stop.

That got their attention. The second man whipped his head around and started to draw down on me, but he seen I had him cold. "Drop it!" I hollered but the second man just laughed and the first man started drawing down on me.

That was a mistake and I never did figure why they done it. I had them covered but I guess they didn't think I was that good with a pistol. That was the last mistake either of them ever made because I put two balls in both of them afore either of them got off a shot. My first shot caught the first man in the chest and I put a ball through the gut of the second rider with my left hand. Then I put a ball through his head and another one in the first man as he was falling off his horse. I think that last shot was a waste of powder and shot, but it was better to make sure.

"My God!" Keenan said from behind me. I glanced his way and seen he was lowering his rifle. "I've never seen anyone shoot like that, Jack."

"Didn't have no other choice," I told him. I walked over to the outlaws, picking up their guns with my left hand and making sure they was dead. It was only then I holstered my weapons and taken a look up the tree.

I seen right off the kid was older than I thought. That's the way it is with Indians to me. They look older or younger than what I'd think and it turned out this youngster was fifteen. Amongst Indians, that's almost old enough to be called a man.

"You all right?" I called out but the kid didn't say nothing. He looked sort of familiar, the way second cousins does, so I asked him the same thing in Choctaw and he looked a lot less scared. He answered right back and told me he was all right. I invited him to come down and join us. "Unless you're busy being a bird," I added.

The youngster smiled when I said this and shinnied down the tree. Once he was on the ground I seen he was a lot taller than I thought. He looked older, too, now that he weren't looking so scared, and he helped Keenan round up the horses while I searched the bodies.

There wasn't much in the outlaws pockets but a few dollars and a pocket knife, not even no wanted posters. They was carrying the same Colt's I do and I seen their pistols wasn't taken care of the way I do mine. They was still good enough to shoot, but the barrels of both was dirty and pitted. They was pretty worn on the outside, too. One of them was fitted with horn handles and on the other I seen where somebody had cut four notches in the wood. This was the one the first man had been shooting and I guessed he cut the notches for men he'd killed. Some men do that, mostly to brag, I think, without ever saying a word, and to show how tough they are. I never could see no sense in it. Seems to me taking another man's life ain't nothing to be proud about.

The saddlebags was a different story. We found things in them that wasn't a good fit with the men I'd shot. One thing was a lady's mirror and a hairbrush and comb that looked like it went with it. There was a leather bound Bible, too, and a crucifix on a necklace of black beads. To me it looked like a smaller version of the one Sister Carmelita carried, and when I shown these to Keenan, he had the same thought as me.

"It looks like you sent a pair of bandits to meet their Maker," he said. He opened the bible and there was a name in it. "Adele Simpson Holder," he read. "Poor lady. I hope they killed her outright." After seeing what was done to the women in Charlie's party, I known exactly what he was saying. "I don't think it's likely the lady was the mother or wife of either of these scalawags."

There was one other strange thing I found in the second man's saddlebag. It was sort of like a cup and made out of silver, but I couldn't figure what it was. When I shown it to Mac, he chuckled. "Now that's worth a pretty penny, Jack. I haven't seen one of those in a long time."

"What is it?" I asked. "Some kind of female thing?"

"I suppose a lady could use one, but I don't think most would be caught dead with it," he laughed and fitted the thing over his ear. "This is an ear trumpet, Jack. It's for people who can't hear very well." He handed it to me and I tried it on, too. When I done it, I was amazed how good I could hear. I'd of sworn I could hear Keenan's heart beating.

The youngster spoke up just then, pointing at the ear cup. "He says he known somebody who had one of these," I told Keenan. "He seen him using it when the man come to his camp." The young Choctaw spoke again. "He lives at some kind of mission a day or two north of here and the man and his wife visited not long back. They was some kind of missionaries."

Keenan give this some thought. When he answered, his face was grave. "I guess we better head there, Jack. This lad needs to get back to his people and someone needs to know what happened to the missionary."

"What about these men?" I asked, nodding toward the dead bandits. "I'm thinking they're part of a gang."

"Right, you are," Mac answered. "We wouldn't want to be leading trouble to the mission. We better take them with us until we find a place to hide them. It's too bad we're so far from the river."

"That would probably poison the river five miles down," I pointed out. "Maybe we can find a hungry pack of 'gators." When I asked the Choctaw if there was any 'gators around, he told me he knew right were to find them.

When I passed this along to Mac, he give me a strange look. "I thought you were just talking, lad," he said. "Are you sure you want to do that?" I shrugged and he didn't say nothing else. Far as I was concerned, it weren't no different from feeding vermin to the hogs and I told him so.

"That's one way of looking at it," he agreed. "There's a certain justice in turning such people into pig shit. But keep in mind, Jack, that every one of them was a mother's child. They may have been a blessing or a curse, but they were all a mother's son. Despite what they may have done, we need to respect that."

Well, I thought he was dead wrong at the time, but since then I've changed my mind. We never can know for sure what turns a man one way or another. I've seen a lot of good men do some bad things, and I've seen some bad ones turn good and fly straight. So I've learned not to judge. I just ain't wise enough and there's too much I don't know. What I do know is sometimes a man has to make hard choices. I wasn't judging those men when I killed them. I was out to stop them from killing what I thought was a child and that was righteous. Yet I ain't so sure about getting rid of their bodies the way we done. Gators got to eat, too, but it ain't up to me to feed them.

On the other hand, I ain't able to see no difference between that and leaving bodies lie for the buzzards. Even burying people is feeding the worms. A man can get a headache trying to puzzle out such things.

Turns out, the youngster's name was Red Owl and it taken us the best part of three days to bring him home. We wasn't in any rush, but the way he taken us wound all over the countryside and without him to lead us, it would of taken me and Mac longer, if we ever got there. The trees was so tall it was hard to see where the sun was and the underbrush was so thick it was almost impossible to get through. Without knowing the trails, we could of wandered around a week without getting nowhere. Even with Owl leading us, there was times it looked to me like the trail was plumb run out. Yet whenever we got to what looked like a dead end, there was always a way to go if a man knew how to find it. Even Mac admitted he was lost half the time.

When we finally got where we was going, I was surprised to find such a large settlement. I would of expected Owl to head straight home but he led us straight to the small church house near the middle of the settlement. When he done so, I even more surprised when a Choctaw man dressed in white man's clothes come out of the church to meet us. Weren't no doubt in my mind this man was a preacher.

Owl explained to him in Choctaw who we was and how he come to meet us. When he was done, the man turned to us and offered his hand. "I'm Michael Oaks, Luke's father," he said in English better than mine.

Keenan and me introduced ourselves. "I'm glad to meet you," I told his father. "He said his name was Red Owl."

"That's because you spoke to me in Choctaw," Owl answered in English, grinning. "That's my name among the People."

"How come you didn't say nothing?" I asked him, but Owl only grinned.

"This is a wise young man," Mac said, giving Owl a knowing look. "He wanted to be sure of the lay of the land first. I suspected as much."

"So you speak the People's tongue?" Michael Oaks asked me in Choctaw. "How did you learn it?"

I told him it was from my uncle and we spent a few minutes talking about my Indian relatives. While we done so, Owl translated for Keenan. Come to find out later, Keenan was stringing Owl along and giving him a dose of his own medicine. Even with all that time we spent together, I never suspected Mac known almost as much Choctaw as me.

I was surprised to learn me and Oaks was distant cousins. He told me some things about my uncle's band I never known afore and it give me the strangest feeling. Afore then I ain't never realized how alone I felt in this world and how hungry I was for kin. This surprised me cause I considered myself a loner. Aside from Mac and Charlie, and a few others like Carson and Watrous, I shied away from other folks and preferred my own company to being with strangers.

When I mentioned this to Keenan that evening, he set me straight in a hurry. "What in the world are you talking about, Jack?" he asked. "What about Raven and his people? Or the others we hunted with last summer? Or even Hawk? The last thing you are is a loner, lad. You may not like to be around white folk much, but around Indians you fit right in. That shouldn't come as a surprise. You were raised among them and you know their ways. Everything else being equal, I think you would rather have stayed on with Raven's folk at the winter camp."

Of course, I known exactly what he was talking about when he said "everything else being equal." He was trying not to mention Charlie and the gold directly, but it didn't help none. Just thinking of winter camp right then made me think of Charlie and all I wanted to do was to dig a hole to crawl in and die.

Even so, I known Keenan was right. It was around Indians I felt at home and these people was my kinfolk. It give me cause to wonder what in the hell I was doing headed west. I said as much to Keenan, but he only nodded. "Maybe you need to give that some serious thought, Jack. Maybe you need to look inside yourself and find your heart's desire."

"My heart's desire died saving my life!" I told him.

"Aye, lad, and you're right to grieve," he said and the look in his eyes told me he known exactly what I was going through. "You've lost the one in this world you loved most. All I'm saying is maybe you need to be here among your kin for a while. They understand that kind of loss and

I think you might find some peace here."

"What about you?" I asked him. "What about going west? We're partners, ain't we?"

"Yes," he said. "Of course, we are and we always will be as far as I'm concerned. Right now I think it may be good for us to stay here a spell afore we move on. We can always make the fall hunt, and if we don't make it this year, then we can shoot for next year. We have all the time we need, lad, all the time in the world."

"This ain't what we planned." I tried auger, but even I could hear my heart weren't in it.

"No, but neither was wintering with Raven and Antelope while I convalesced," the old man replied. "That seemed to turn out pretty well, didn't it?"

Well, there weren't no way I could deny that. "Don't worry, Jack," the old man added. "I'll not be leaving soon. I think I'd like to get acquainted with these good folk, too. Who knows, I may find myself a lively widow and stay for good."

As close as I can figure, it must of been the first part of April when we arrived at the mission. Like all people, Choctaws don't care that much for strangers. Yet Michael Oak spread the story of how we saved Owl from the outlaws, and like all such stories, it grown with each telling. By the time it got all the way back to us, it was a whole gang of outlaws we taken out. It didn't help none that Owl fanned the fire.

Yet Michael Oak also done a whole lot more than spreading the word. He introduced us around and helped us feel welcome, and he found us a place to lodge near where he and his family lived. This was a good day's ride west of the mission and Oak told us it was a healthier place to live. Since coming west, the Choctaws was troubled by fevers and lung illness, and a lot of them died. Yet, from what Oak had seen, folk living further west wasn't afflicted as bad.

Of course, seeing this was one thing. Getting other folk to believe it and do something about it was something else. Try as he might, Oak could not get more than a few families to move west. Them as did found they wasn't sick so much, but wouldn't nobody believe them, neither. I guess this is nature's way of weeding out the stupid ones. What it tells me is that Choctaws ain't no different from nobody else when it comes to being pig headed. Later I learnt just how true that was.

The place Oak found for us to lodge was with a widow with a couple of young children. The widow's name was Meadowlark and I don't know exactly how old she was or how she come to be widowed. I heard her husband was killed when the Army forced the Choctaw out of Mississippi and Louisiana and moved them to Oklahoma, but it weren't clear exactly how or when he died. They was in the first bunch the Army moved and the Choctaw lost a quarter of their people along the way. Some of them starved and some died of sickness and fever, but some of them was killed by hostile white people.

Later on they called this first move the Trail of Tears, and it was. Didn't nobody get through in good shape but like always, it were the women and the children that suffered most.

Meadowlark's two sons wasn't that old, maybe six and eight years, and they was neither of them her natural children. Their mother died of fever not long after the younger boy was born and Meadowlark taken them to raise. She had some kin connection to their natural mother but I never figured out exactly what that was.

Later Meadowlark said she had an older son who survived the Trail of Tears. When she told me this I got the sense he was the only one of her children who survived. He was married and had a son the same age as her youngest. So she was more like a grandmother to the boys.

When I got to putting ages together I guessed she must have been at least thirty-five, but she weren't bad looking for an old woman. The Trail of Tears had left deep lines around her mouth and next to her eyes, but she had all her teeth and when she smiled, it like to broke my heart. She looked a dozen years younger and who she reminded me of was Charlie.

Meadowlark taken a like to Mac right away and I could see he was taken by her. Yet when I asked him why he didn't do nothing about it, he given me the strangest look. "Are you serious, lad?" I didn't know what to say to that and Mac just shaken his head. "I am not the man her heart is set on, Jack. Yes, she flatters this old man by flirting and teasing him, but there's another man she wants."

"There is?" I asked. "Who's that?"

Keenan just shaken his head. "Use your eyes, lad. Look closer and I think you'll see."

"I guess we'll have to find somewhere else to board if she marries him," I said and Mac caught a fit of laughing. "I don't think you need to worry for the foreseeable future," he told me. "Just keep your eyes open, Jack, and be patient. You'll see."

One of the things we done to pay for our lodging was keeping Meadowlark and her sons in fresh meat. So Keenan and me spent a lot of time hunting and fishing and more often than not, Red Owl come with us. I started taking the boys with us hunting, too. I taught them how to make a bow and how to make arrows, and then taught them how to shoot. Keenan showed them how to catch fish, and pretty soon they was almost as good as him. I also given them each a knife and shown them how to dress game. Then they wanted to know how throw it, so I shown them that. They was also curious about my Colt's but I told them they was going to have to be a lot older afore I taught them that.

Meadowlark also had a fair sized clearing where she grown some corn and squash, and when we wasn't hunting or fishing, I set the boys to helping me clear her some more. Sometimes Red Owl would give us a hand, but not often. He had to help out at home, too, since his dad was away so much.

Towards the end of summer, me and Keenan taken the boys west a good ways to see if we could find us a buffalo. I cain't remember why, but Red Owl didn't come with us that time. With as many people as the Army moved in, there was a lot of pressure on the game for fifty miles around, and Keenan figured a buffalo would put the family through the winter in good shape.

Sure enough, we found a small herd and taken a young bull. Then we spent the better part of three days butchering him and drying the meat into jerky. We must of eat twenty pounds of meat apiece, too, and when we headed back, there wasn't much left but guts and bones. Unlike us, Raven's folk would of even used the guts and bones but our pack animals was almost overloaded as it was.

It was then Keenan taken leave of us and headed west. Busy as I was with clearing and teaching the boys, I ain't noticed when he left that he'd packed all his stuff and brung it with us. I wondered why we was bringing the extra pack horse, but I never asked. I figured I'd find out soon enough, and I did.

"I'll be back in the spring, Jack," he told me. "Either that, or I'll be dead." Seen the look on my face, he said, "No, I'm not planning to meet my Maker on this trip, lad. Nor do I have a premonition. You needn't worry about that. I've just got a strong feeling I need to be out west for a while."

"Let me go back and get my stuff and I'll come with you," I told him. "I can be back here in a week, maybe less."

"I don't think that's your heart's desire, Jack," he answered and when I heard the words, I known he was right. "You're needed here right now," he added. "I think this is where you want to be and what you need to be doing. There's a lot yet you need to teach these boys." Then he said his goodbyes to the boys in Choctaw, and turned his pony west.

When we got back, of course, Meadowlark known Keenan wouldn't be with us. She seen him packing and known what it meant. She also known how much Keenan meant to me, and how I'd lost Charlie. So that night she come to my lodge for the first time. When she done it, I was amazed how soft and smooth her skin was. Her hands was tough and callused from the work of tending her crops, but her breasts and belly was soft as a baby's butt. It had been a long time for both of us, and didn't neither one of us much sleep that night.

After that, Meadowlark and me spent every night together. When the boys left for mission school in the fall, I moved out of the small lodge me and Mac used and into the main lodge and we lived like man a wife. I was worried how the boys might take this, but they seemed glad of it. I never come to love her the way I loved Charlie, but she was good for me. She was also good to me and after a while I come to care for her a whole different way.

There was a lot of sickness among the Choctaw that winter. Even the white missionary, Cyrus Byington, got sick and his family lost a child that year. Me and him was never that close and seen the world a whole different way, but I respected the man and admired his sticking tight. When I met him, he'd been with the Choctaw twenty-five years and come west after they was forced to move.

Even though there was so much sickness, we had a mild winter that year. The first really cold weather weren't until around Christmas and by the middle of February we was planting potatoes and onions. It were quite a while since I done this, not since I helped my mama afore she was killed, and it felt righteous.

Mission school let out around Easter, so me and the boys headed west to scare up a buffalo or some fresh venison, and Red Owl come with us. We was still all right for dried meat from the fall hunt but I was getting tired of jerky and wanted fresh game. I was also feeling need to stretch my legs and see different country for a bit, and after being cooped up at school all year, the boys was ready to ramble, too.

We was gone a good week afore we come home. When we got back, I seen Meadowlark was putting on weight but I didn't think nothing of it. Indian women does that when they get older and we had eat well that winter. I also seen she was eating more than she done when I first known her, and when I teased about it at supper one night, the boys given each other a strange look. When I asked them about it later they laughed and told me women do that when they're carrying a child.

Sure enough, when I said something about it to Meadowlark when we was alone, she smiled and looked right pleased with herself. She told me it was true and she expected the child in the summer. I must of looked downright stunned because she laughed and said she hoped she would give me a son. I still had enough wits about me to tell her a son would be all right, but little girls was real sweet, too.

That got me thinking that maybe me and Meadowlark should get married. I had no idea what the Choctaw customs was and asked Michael Oaks. He told me that they was changing. There was strong opinion against letting Choctaw women marry outside the tribe. He also said some included half-breeds as white.

That got me all stirred up. "That ain't right!" I declared. "I was raised by Choctaws the Indian way and I'm as Choctaw the way I think as anybody! I'm even raising two Choctaw sons I didn't sire!"

"Easy, Jack," Oaks told me. "I agree with you. You're a better Choctaw than a lot I could name. It's stupid, but that's the way some people are."

I taken a deep breath and calmed myself down. "What I'd suggest is that you wait a while," Michael said. "There is talk about you and Meadowlark, but people think highly of you, as do I. Once she has your child people will see the righteousness of it and things will change."

Well, this didn't set right with me but I seen the truth of what Michael was saying. I was up against something I ain't got no control over, and it wouldn't do no good pushing. A man might as well try to push a river as push someone into changing their mind. As Keenan told me once, there ain't no sense trying to teach a pig to whistle. Doing so will only get a man all worked up and annoy the pig.

CHAPTER TWENTY

Coming Home

couple of weeks after I talked to Michael Oaks I was working in the garden one day. I guess I must of heard something because I looked up to see Keenan riding up the trail. I give out a whoop that like to raised the dead and run to meet him, and we shaken hands so hard it like to wrenched my shoulder. Then he seen Meadowlark coming, too, and his smile changed. I could see something was troubling him and there weren't no doubt in my mind it was the sight of her carrying a child. She was getting pretty big by then and there weren't no doubt she was with child.

Yet nobody who ain't known MacAdams well could of told he was troubled. He give Meadowlark a big smile and greeted her warmly, and after the horses was put away, he given her a pair of beaded moccasins he brung her. He brung moccasins for the boys, too. These wasn't beaded, but they was well made with buffalo hide soles and buckskin tops.

"I have something for you, too, Jack," he said, handing me a knife I known was made in Washington, and I known right then he'd gone there first. "I have something else for you but I'll give that to you later." He said this in English and even though he was smiling, I seen something in his eyes that told me it weren't no present. I wondered if he was going to tell me Sister Carmelita died.

After supper, him and me taken a walk and when we got out of earshot of the lodges he stopped. "I've got some strange news for you, Jack," he said and handed me a letter. "I think this pretty well sums it up. It was waiting at Bent's Fort when I got there about a month ago. Another one apparently went to Taos."

I looked at the envelope and it was addressed to both of us. The handwriting was good and when I taken out the letter, I could read it real easy. When I seen the first line, I looked down at the signature.

When I done so it felt like I was kicked in the belly and I had to sit down to finish reading the letter. Keenan told me later my face turned white as a sheet.

Dear Jack and Keenan,

I am writing this to let you know I am alive. When I was shot I was pulled under the boat by the current but I didn't drown. I came up fifty yards from the boat and tried to call out, but I was choked by the water and couldn't call out loud enough to get anyone's attention. Then another current pulled me down again and I almost drowned afore I broke the surface again. I was over a hundred yards downstream by then and so weak from being shot I couldn't swim. I was able to grab a large branch floating back and hold on, but I wasn't able to get to shore until I was thirty miles down river. I don't know how I ever hung on so long. Some people on shore saw me and pulled me in or I surely would have drowned. I was so cold and weak by then I couldn't speak and that night I came down with an awful fever. It was four days before I was coherent enough to tell people who I was, and it took six weeks until I was strong enough to do more than hobble around.

The family who rescued me was very kind and let me stay with them until I was strong enough to travel. I wasn't carrying any money when I went overboard and they were very poor, so I had to get a job on a passenger boat to earn my way down river to Little Rock. Then I had to work for several weeks to earn enough to take the stage to Washington. When I arrived there, I did find Sister Carmelita, but I arrived a week after you left. I would have taken off after you, but I was still weak and couldn't afford a horse. Even if I could, I think Sister Carmelita would have locked me in my room until I came to my senses and understood there was little chance of me finding you. She told me I was welcome to stay there as long as I wanted and suggested that I write you in care of Kit Carson in Santa Fe and also at Bent's Fort on the Arkansas.

I love you both and will be waiting here at the orphanage in Washington until I see or hear from you, no matter how long it takes. I hope you are both well.

Love, Charlie

Keenan set down beside me and give me a while to get hold of this.

After a bit I read the letter again, but didn't seem possible it were true. "Have you seen her?" I asked.

The old man nodded. "Yes, lad, I have. I wanted to be sure this wasn't a hoax before I said anything about it to you. I told her I wasn't sure exactly where you were, which was close enough to the truth. I also said I'd bring you to her." He shaken his head. "Of course, she wanted to come with me. I had a devil of a time convincing her she needed to wait and it took Sister Carmelita helping me." He grinned. "I even circled back and waited a half day to see if she was following me. Twice."

"I guess you see my problem. Charlie's my wife and I need to be with her. I also have a child on the way-damned near here. A child needs a daddy, especially if it's a son. I need to have a hand in raising him. Or her. I can't just walk away."

Keenan didn't say nothing, just nodded. "Who else is going to feed Meadowlark and the boys, and the baby too?" I asked. I looked at Keenan. "I ain't just blowing wind here, Mac. I need a hand. My mind is running six ways to sunset."

"I think you need to talk to Charlie," he told me. "No one ever knows exactly how a woman will react, but I don't think Charlie will hold Meadowlark and the baby against you. She might at first, but I think she'll forgive you if she does. I also think she'll help you figure it out once she's accepted the situation."

That made a lot of sense to me. "I guess we better let Michael Oak know what's going on, too," I said.

Keenan give me a nod. "I think that's a good idea." Then he paused and I known he was going to say something else. "Jack, pretend for a moment that things were like they were before I brought you the letter. Are you with me, lad?" I nodded and he went on. "What would happen to Meadowlark and the children if you died or were killed? Do you think Michael Oaks or Red Owl would let them starve? Don't you think they might help raise the child?"

I give this some thought. Keenan was right. Red Owl would be old enough to take a wife by the time the child was two, and the boys looked at him like a big brother. Among the Choctaw, the children stayed with the mother if their daddy left, and as often as not, one of the mother's brothers stepped in to help raise sons.

"What am I going to tell Meadowlark?" I asked, but I known exactly what Keenan would tell me.

"Tell her the simple truth, lad," he advised.

When I let Meadowlark in on the news the next morning she didn't say nothing. She known something was wrong the night afore. She known I was married afore and, like me, she thought I was widowed.

Some women might of thought I'd been lying but Meadowlark known I weren't. She just nodded and went out to tend her garden. Yet I seen tears in her eyes afore she went.

Michael Oaks seemed to be relieved when I told him the news. He didn't say nothing but I known how he felt about the stir me and Meadowlark was making in the tribe. "You don't have to worry about the child, Jack," he told me. "I'll make sure he or she is looked after and is brought up right. I promise you that."

"You don't understand," I told him. "I want to be part of raising my child."

"Oh, I do understand that quite well," he answered. "I'd be surprised if you didn't. You're an honorable man. However, I think it might be best for all concerned if you let go and backed away. I'm thinking of the tribe, Jack."

"I'm part of this tribe!" I told him but I seen right away he ain't agreed.

"Are you?" he asked. "You know our ways but you weren't raised among these people and they don't accept you. That's not true of me. I'll always owe you a great debt for saving my son. Yet as a leader of the tribe, I have to think about the good of the tribe. first"

"How is the good of the tribe served by sacrificing the good of an honorable man who has done nothing but good among its people?" Keenan asked. I known how angry he was by how quiet he asked. "I seem to remember that a certain Nazarene was sacrificed for the good of his tribe. Are you making the same choice as Caiphas, Michael?"

Michael Oak turned deep red, but he didn't answer. Keenan got to his feet. "We need to be going, lad. These people are not like the Arapaho. They share your blood but they are apparently not your kin."

Red Owl was just coming into the mission as we was leaving. He seen something was wrong and followed us to our horses. He asked what was going on and I give it to him straight, including what Michael Oaks said. I seen right away he didn't like it none. "I'll never forget," he told me. I'll always be your brother and you will always be welcome in my lodge." He started to say something else but stopped. Then he said, "Some of us have become too much like frightened women!" Even though he didn't say it, I known he was talking about his father.

Well, it didn't take us near as long to get to back to Washington as it done when we was coming west. I was anxious to see Charlie, but I was worried, too. Then, when I first seen Charlie, I seen she was feeling as shy as I was. So I taken her hand and led her to a quiet spot where we could talk.

I didn't know what else to say, so I jumped right in and paddled like hell. "I cain't hardly believe what I'm seeing," I told her. "I thought you was dead. It was like my heart was tore out."

"I was afraid you were killed, too," Charlie said and there was tears in her eyes remembering. "I knew you were hit when I saw you go down but I didn't know. I didn't dare hope too much, but I had to find out. Then I got to Washington and Sister told me you were alive." She smiled. "That's the first time in my life I ever fainted."

"That must have been something," I told her, not knowing what else to say. Then I said, "You got to listen to me, Charlie. You need to hear what I'm telling you. Me and Keenan buried you in Ft. Smith. We said words for you at the river and every night after that I went to sleep hoping I'd never wake up."

Charlie pulled back and the way she looked at me like to broke my heart. "All right, Jack. Just tell me what you're trying to say."

"I was true to your memory," I said. "But I'm a young man and I've got the appetites of a man. It was a long time afore they come alive again, but after a year they done it."

I could see Charlie didn't like this, but she didn't fly off the handle the way I thought she might. It taken her a moment to answer, but when she did, her voice was quiet. "I understand, Jack. You thought I was dead and you resorted to sporting ladies. I can't hold that against you."

There weren't nothing to do but grab the nettle hard. "Charlie, it weren't sporting women. It was worse than that." Told her about rescuing Owl and deciding to remain with my kin in Oklahoma. "About a year after I thought you died, I taken up with a widow and she become my woman."

Charlie's face was chalk white. "I see. Did you get married, Jack?"

"No, nothing like that. We just taken up living together. You know how things is among the Indians."

"Do you love her, Jack?"

"Yes, but not like I love you, Charlie. I like her and she's a good woman, but I don't love her the same. I don't think I could ever love anyone the same as I do you."

"I don't understand," Charlie told me. "Why can't you just explain it to her?"

"I did and she accepted it. Thing is, she's carrying my child, I can't abandon my child, Charlie. I won't. That ain't right."

"I'm your wife, Jack. We belong together."

"I know and I won't abandon you, neither. I love you more than I love life and we need to be together. I just cain't study out what to do about my child." I told her about what Michael Oak said. "Child needs a daddy, especially if it's a son. I guess Oak and Owl could raise him all right, but it's my child. That's what grieves me."

"Would the woman let us take it to raise as our own?"

"I don't know. I ain't asked her. Would you if you was in her place?"

"No, I don't think so," Charlie said. Then she taken mad. "Hell, no, I wouldn't! Does she have other children? "

"Three," I told her. "The youngest one's seven. I've been helping raise him and his brother." I had to explain about the boys and their older brother.

Charlie nodded. "Well, it sounds like they have people to provide for them, Jack," she told me. "They have men folk to help bring them up. I understand your being concerned but it sounds like it isn't your business any longer."

"It's my child!" I said.

Charlie didn't answer that. She taken my face in her hands and said, "You're a good man, Jack Bear. Thank you for marrying me."

Then she come into my arms and I felt her shoulders shaking. I thought she was crying, but when she pulled back her head she was grinning. "You know, I can give you a child, Jack. I will need a little help, but if you're willing, I'll show you how."

Down the Years

ell, that's the story of our first western adventure, me and Charlie and Keenan. We had more but that telling will have to wait. Setting this down helped fill the hours of a long winter but spring is come and there's more living to do.

One thing I did want to tell is that our bringing the gold out seems to of broke the abbot's curse. Sister Carmelita is still going strong and the gold helped her to start two more orphanages. One of them was among the Choctaw and Cherokee, and despite the fact Sister Carmelita is Catholic, Cyrus Byington, the missionary out there, was glad to have the help. As he said to Sister, God is probably more concerned about taking care of orphans than differences in religion. When I heard this, my respect for the man, which was already high, doubled. It takes sand in his craw for a man to fly in the face of what most folks believe. Even when that's what the Good Book tells him to do.

I seen Red Owl quite a few times over the years. His dad, Michael Oaks, went on to become a famous preacher, though I never seen him again except at a distance. Owl and Meadowlark done a fine job of raising my son by her, and she named him Little Bear after me. When the boy was twelve, me and Owl taken him and my other two sons west to hunt with Raven and his band, and we seen a white buffalo again. Raven told me this was really good medicine, seeing the white buffalo twice in my life, and I guess it was. With all I been through, I should of been dead ten times over.

As things turned out, Charlie didn't give me no baby. She given me twins, a boy and a girl, and I'm glad it wasn't two boys. Not that it made no difference. My daughter is just like her mama, the sweetest little hellion a man could ask and headstrong as a mule. Some ways it was a lot harder raising her than her twin or their brother. I do pity the man she marries if he ain't got the sand to stand up to her. On the other hand, if he can, he's in for a life as good as mine.

Charlie didn't go west with me and Keenan again, even when the kids was grown, and it weren't quite the same without her. Owl taken her place and it was good having him along, but I missed Charlie something awful when I was away. Yet, I known how much her helping Sister Carmelita meant to her and to the orphans. They was like her children, too, and I never said nothing. She was happy with that and I was happy to be roaming the plains, and the homecomings was always sweet.

Keenan didn't make that last trip with me and Owl, neither. He was in his eighties by then and said his eyes and ears was giving way. You couldn't of proved it by me. The truth is, Sister Carmelita roped him into helping with the orphans, too, and he was like their grandfather. Not having grandchildren of his own, he taken to it like a duck to water, and over the years the stories he told them grown with the telling. I know cause I was there for a lot of them, both the living of them and the telling, too.

Thinking about this as I been writing it down, I'm grateful of two things. One is the fact I never had to do no more killing after I shot the outlaws that was after Owl. The other is that none of my kids has never been forced to take another's life. I guess part of this was because every time it come up in one of Keenan's stories, I made damn sure they known how awful it was to be forced to do it. I also made damn sure they known how to do it if they was forced into a corner and had to fight their way out. I never done no fighting for sport and I never allowed as that were ever right.

Having said this, it struck me that the treasure I come away with on that first trip with Keenan was some things more precious than the gold we brung out. Part of it, of course, was Charlie and Keenan. Life without them would of been a lot poorer, like it would of been not knowing the folk we met like Raven and Owl and Meadowlark and Carson and Watrous. We was part of history and I find knowing that brings a good feeling.

Another thing more precious than gold was seeing that part of the country afore it was settled. The mountains is still there and so is the rivers and plains, but it ain't the same. Fences and homesteads and even towns has broken up the land and a man has to go a long way to find wild country these days. It's still beautiful but it ain't the same.

Yet it was talking to Keenan about all this that made me understand the greatest gold I brung out from that first trip was the man I become. I didn't believe him when he first told me this. Then he called to mind what I was like when he first met me. "You were always a good man, Jack," was the way he put it. "Yet when I met you, it was an angry and frightened young man I encountered, and bitter, too. After that I saw you make some hard choices, but it was almost always for the right reason, and when you made mistakes, you owned up to them. You also seem to understand quite clearly what's important and what is not, and somewhere along the way you lost the bitterness you had. I admire the man you've become."

I shrugged. "That weren't nothing, Keenan," I said. "That's how I was brung up. All you're saying is my folks done good."

The old man just grinned and shaken his head when I said that. "I rest my case, lad. You also seem to have acquired a remarkable measure of humility along the way, too. That's rare in a man so young."

Charlie was busy with something else but she was listening, too. I seen her nod smile when the old man told me that last and I didn't know what to say. Then I had a flash of pure inspiration. When I answered, Charlie had to work so hard to keep from laughing I thought she was going to choke when she seen the look on McAdam's face.

"Well, Keenan, you may be right. On the other hand, I reckon it takes one to know one and I had a damn good teacher." I never seen the old man so lost for words.

About the Author

Very little is known about Joe Pete Blackwolf. This book comes to us as a twenty-first century version of the over-the-transom manuscript of an earlier publishing era. Sent as a simple text document attached to personal e-mail from an unknown sender, it ended up in the spam bin and was scheduled to be routinely deleted. By an odd set of circumstances, the attachment survived while the original e-mail was lost.

That Blackwolf is American Indian seems apparent, though nothing is known about what tribe Blackwolf might claim or might claim him. It also seems reasonable to believe that Joe Pete is a middle aged male of mixed European and indigenous ancestry. Other than that, very little can be said of the author of this remarkable odyssey. The only clues lie within the text itself and how it is written.

Anyone with knowledge of the author is encouraged to get in touch with the publisher.

www.ingramcontent.com/pod-product-compliance
Lightning Source LLC
Chambersburg PA
CBHW071314250626
47159CB00004B/1426